Sacred Dark

By Meg Castro

ISBN: 978-0-9986518-3-5

Published by: Bohlander House Press Dover, NJ USA

Www.bohlanderhousepress.com

To My Husband For Still Putting Up With Me And My Ideas

Chapter 1

Danika Joseph was forced into another family dinner. A dinner that had been mandated since she was adopted by Marcus and Helena Joseph almost fifteen years ago. Now that her brothers and her were all adults they had hoped Marcus would do away with the decree. He didn't and when Marcus Joseph summoned his children to his home in New Rochelle, one listened. Marcus wasn't just any father, he was the head of the Centurion Line which was one of the oldest Vampires lines around. His word was law even if you were family. So once a week he would summon his five children to have dinner with him and Helena, his wife and their mother. For Dani, if they all survived each weekly dinner then it was a success.

"Danika," Marcus stated, pulling Dani out of her thoughts, "How are things at the archives?"

"Slow, which is giving us time to get ready for the summer audit," Dani informed her father.

Much to the dismay of her father and her oldest brother Alexius, Dani worked as an Archivist for the Accords. While she was working for the ruling body that oversaw paranormal creatures through out the world it also meant she working outside of the line, in other words Marcus couldn't keep a close eye on his only daughter. For Dani, she loved it, she loved history, her degrees were in history. Her role also wasn't trivial, Dani was the head archivist for the Nightwalker Branch of the Accords. She got to explore a world of history, a world of blood lines that were a delicate balance between the seven main houses of the Vampire world. Jihns were also part of the Nightwalker Branch, and anytime she was able to delve into them was always exciting for they were the rarest of the supernatural creatures.

"Any interesting research?" Sayad asked. He was the

third oldest of the four brothers, he taught ancient history at Harvard, and was often excused from Family dinners because of this.

"Yes, Gregoir was going to reach out to you," Dani told him. Gregoir was a Necromancer and was the archivist for the Spellcaster branch of the Accord. The Spellcasters were witches, necromancers, and seers. "He is going to be presenting a paper at the Supernatural Summit in the fall regarding his findings on the witches that were killed in Salem. He is focusing on whether they were born witches or scapegoats."

"Will you be presenting?" Alexius asked with a sneer. He did not agree with his father allowing Dani to not only work outside of the line but live outside of the house.

"No, I presented last year," Dani replied. "There are six of us, so we alternate between us as to who is presenting."

Sayad looked interested, he was good friends with Necormancer. "Do you think Gregoir would let me look at his notes?"

"He was going to let you see the whole study," Dani replied, she noted the excitement in her brother's eyes. Sayad and she could often lose themselves in discussions of history.

"We should change the topic now," Nicholi warned as he noted the look between Dani and Sayad. Nicholi was the second oldest, he was only a few years younger then Alexius. "Or Sayad and Danika will lose us on their research methods."

Both Dani and Sayad rolled their eyes at their older brother. "How is my grandson?" Helena asked Dani.

"Grunt is good," Dani told her mother. Grunt was her dog, a mutt that she rescued a few years ago. Grunt never came with her to her parent's house because Marcus hated indoor pets.

"I had Marcella put together a treat bag for him," Helena told her.

"You spoil the mutt more than us," Bertram informed their mother. He was the youngest of the four brother's. He currently was lounging in the dining room chair as he turned the wine glass in his hand.

"Well, since he is my only semblance of a grandchild I have, he get's to be spoiled," Helena stated as she sipped from her wine glass.

"I take it he hangs out with Claire while you are here," Nicholi assumed.

"It's Aunt Claire time, as she calls it," Dani confirmed.

"The fact that father lets you live with a witch…" Alexius began.

Helena shot him a warning look. "Claire and Tabitha are family, Claire and Danika were raised along side each other, and Tabitha has always been welcomed in this home."

"It reflects poorly on our image," Alexius countered his mother.

"Alexi," Nicholi sighed. Tabitha Jensen was a renowned healer and the current High Priestess of the local coven. She was also a close friend to Helena.

"She's not even oathed to our line," Alexius continued as if he did not hear Nicholi's warning.

"ENOUGH!" Marcus yelled slamming his fist on the table almost causing the glass table to crack under the force. "Helena, tell the servants we will be taking a break in the course. Alexius, my office now!"

No one said a word as the matriarch of their family stormed out of the dining room. "You've really done it now, dear brother," Bartram smirked.

Alexius growled at him before following their father. Dani pulled back from the table. "I'm getting some fresh air," Dani said.

Grabbing her wine glass, Dani headed to the kitchen through the patio doors. She flopped down on a chair in front of the outdoor fire place. Dani sipped her wine as she stared off into space. Ever since Alexius and Bartram had returned from their holdings in the Middle East and Mediterranean, Alexius had been insistent on her taking the Oath of House. It would be last ceremony she would take before she became a vampire. Four of the five branches of the Accord held ceremonies for the different points of one coming into their own power.

For the Nightwalkers, the Oathing Ceremony happened at Thirty years of Age. It was when a born Vampire officially declared their oath to the Line that would help them prepare for the 'Last Kiss' as they called it. Dani turned thirty next year, the only way an Oath Ceremony would be moved up was if the person began to show signs of the Vampire gene becoming stronger.

A whiff of spice mixed with wine alerted Dani that Nicholi had come outside. He sat down next to her, refilling her wine glass as he did.

"Alexi and Bertram messed up during their six months overseas," Nicholi informed her. "I haven't found out the extent, but mom is fuming with some of their mistakes, and Marcus is refusing to let her know more."

"Despite it being her line that he married into," Dani pointed out. "Is that why Alexi is after me taking the oath?"

House Joseph, or House Centurion was an ancient line dating back well before some of the others. Their origin was Jerusalem and then present day Turkey. Helena was the only surviving child of the last head, Caius Catigernus who had been one of the longest heads of houses to rule. It had only been in the last several decades that the house began to be known as House Jospeh.

"I think his hope is that the House and the Accords would be focused on you taking the Oath and would forget about his mistakes," Nicholi theorized. "Sayad has been getting the most information out of Marcus, since you know he's in Cambridge teaching and not involved in any of the business, Marcus tends to be more loose with his tongue around him."

"Where with me, he's worried I'm writing down his every word to be immortalized in the archives," Dani laughed.

"And why aren't you?" Nicholi teased his sister.

Raised voices could be heard from the back of the house. To a mortal, they would barely be able to hear words, but for Nicholi and even Dani, they could make out words.

"They switched too Arabic so that the staff won't understand what they are saying," Nicholi noted.

"Like when mom and I speak in Greek to keep Marcus out of my business," Dani replied.

Nicholi nodded. He rested his elbows on his knees then looked at her. "It is hard to think that Alexi is only four years older than me, that we were raised during the same time period, that I was able to move forward, embrace the changing times, but he still misses what he thinks of as our glory days. It always mystifies me," Nick admitted.

"Look at Mom and Marcus," Dani replied. "Mom was born during the renaissance, she has always been the voice behind change, behind embracing technology. And Marcus is right there with Alexi and Bertram. But only in private, never in public when someone could hear that the great Marcus Joseph turned his nose up at races intermingling."

"I almost wished you and Claire would date just to piss him off," Nicholi informed her. "I don't know what he would be more pissed about: you dating a woman or you dating a witch."

Dani almost snorted on her wine. "We've tried."

Nicholi raised an eyebrow and looked at her. "What?"

"We figured since we live together and are always each other's plus one, let's see if we can work romantically," Dani told him.

"How did it turn out?"

"It was like kissing a relative," Dani said. "We drank a bottle of wine each afterwards realizing that we still have to find a partner."

"Promise me if you ever settle down, you still will bring Claire around," Nicholi asked.

"I promise, it's not a good time if Claire isn't here."

Nicholi went to say something but they both heard Dani's work phone go off. This phone wasn't for the archives, but for the Special Task Force. The STF were the police force for the paranormal community, working to ensure that the laws of the Accord, and of their country and state were followed. They worked within the State Police force and Federal agencies. Dani worked as an outside consultant for them.

"Joseph," Dani answered.

"I'm ten minutes from your house," Claire informed her on the other end. "Grunt has been dropped off at Nick's, his house keeper took him. We're meeting the rest of the A-team."

"Where?" Dani asked as she handed her brother her glass of wine.

"The Algonquin Hotel," Claire stated.

"That's impossible, that's a Neutral place," Dani replied. Neutral places were rarely a crime scene for they neutralized any paranormal or supernatural ability.

"Hence why Team A is being called in," Claire said.

Dani stared at her phone when Claire hung up. Nick looked at her and knew something was wrong. "What is it?" He asked.

"Claire will be here in less than ten minutes," Dani said. "Our team is being brought in, something happened at the Algonquin."

"Shit," Nicholi said understanding the seriousness of the situation.

"No swearing," Helena's voice called out as she walked outside. She saw Dani's face and knew immediately that something was wrong. "Is everything all right?"

"Claire is coming to get me, we've been called in on a case," Dani told her mother.

"Then I will have Marcella pack up food for you," Helena replied. "Is it just the two of you this time?"

"The whole team," Dani replied.

"Then I will have her send enough for everyone including blood for Dom and Michael," Helena said. She squeezed Dani's hand before heading back into the house.

"I'll handle Marcus," Nicholi promised her. "Go get your to-go bag and change."

Dani nodded. She headed back into the house, she had left her black to-go bag in the foyer to the house. Her father and Alexius hated that she brought it with her, but she never knew when she was getting called into a case. Alexius despised that she used her 'witch' talents for the world to see. Dani stepped into one of the hallway bathrooms and slipped out of the black dress and heals she had been wearing. She pulled on well worn Jeans, a t-shirt, and sneakers.

Once dressed, Dani braided her black hair so that it would be out of her way. Her moss green eyes stood out against her light skin tone. Only when she tanned did one realize she had middle eastern blood in her. Her brothers and Marcus all looked like Roman statues with bronze skin color, sandy color hair and blue or green eyes. Her mother had black hair, the same green eyes, but caramel colored skin. Dani, she was told, was the perfect blend of her biological parents: her mother was from from what was now Turkey and her father had been born and raised in New York.

Shaking her head out of her wandering, Dani stuffed her dress and heels into her back pack. She would leave her makeup on, she never really had a lot on to begin with. Dani headed out of the bathroom as her mother came down the hallway.

"Marcella is just finishing up with your food," Helena told her. "I let Claire through the gates."

"And Marcus?" Dani asked.

"I will handle him," Helena assured her daughter. "Honestly, I think I might just have Nicholi and Sayad join me in my parlor and eat there."

"Madam," their butler interrupted. "The red-headed witch is requesting entry."

"And she entered anyway," Claire stated following the older vampire. "Hi, Helena."

"Hello, my dear," Helena said kissing Claire on the cheek. She noted the change in hair do. "I like the tiny braids."

"I went to see my Dad's family yesterday and his sister did them," Claire said as she touched the tiny braids the now covered her head and hung down past her shoulders.

"Horace," Helena said before the butler turned to leave. "If you don't introduce Claire or any non-vampire properly next time, I will have Nicholi deal with you."

The butler froze before nodding. Helena waited until he was well out of ear shot. "I want to get rid of that man so bad," Helena replied. "But enough. Marcella has food for the mortals, and is packing extra blood for Dom and Michael."

"Helena," Claire began. Though she knew it was pointless to even argue.

Marcella appeared with a large cooler in one hand and a large bag in the other. Nicholi took the larger cooler, both Dani and Claire took one after thanking her.

"Now go," Helena said. "Text me when you both are home."

"Can you text my Aunt, let her know I got here and that we are on our way to the scene," Claire asked Helena. Her aunt was also the head of the coven Claire was a part of as well as part of the Spellcaster's for the New York area. "She is on call at the Jensen Clinic."

"I'll text her now," Helena promised as she hugged them. "Now be safe, both of you."

Dani kissed her mother good bye then followed Claire out the door to her beat up Jeep. Nicholi helped load the food and Dani's book bag into the back seat before Claire climbed into the driver seat and Dani into the passenger seat. They didn't speak until they were past the gates of Marcus' estate. Too many ears on the property that could hear things they weren't supposed too.

"What did Marcus think of you changing into civilian clothes?" Claire asked noting that Dani was already changed. Usually if this happened on a family dinner night, Dani would be in the back changing.

"He was screaming at Alexi in the back of the house when you called," Dani told her. "So I could actually change in the foyer bathroom. Mom is going to fill him in on why I left."

Claire raised an eyebrow as she looked at Dani after flashing her lights to get around some cars. "What did Alexi do that interrupted the order of Family Night?"

"Rumor is that he and Bertram screwed up when they were away and Marcus is not happy about it," Dani told her.

"Well shit, it has to be bad," Claire replied. She had been to more than her fare share of family dinner at Dani's to know Marcus did not break protocol unless it was serious.

"So what are we walking into?" Dani asked Claire as she kept the lights on so they could get into the city faster.

"All I know is that when Alistair called he sounded freaked out," Claire replied.

"Yea, well, Neutral Places don't stop being neutral," Dani

pointed out.

"It's not just that but the wards are off as well," Claire informed her. Dani stared at her. "Trent called to give us a heads up. He is already at the scene with Michael."

"How bad?"

"Vampires are having a hard time retracting their fangs, Alistair feels like his skin is crawling, and the non-supes are complaining of headaches and nausea."

"Do we know what happened?" Dani asked. This was serious if the natural wards of the place were thrown off. There were a few places throughout the world that contained what was thought of natural wards, where the somehow the area contained wards that protected the area. This usual meant that it prevented supernaturals from using their power on each other or on mortals. They became known as Neutral Places.

"From what the doorman could put together for Trent is this: Somewhere about an hour ago it was as if for a brief moment the world inside of the Algonquin froze. Most concur that there was this haunting scream for a split second, then nothing. When it was over no one felt like they could stay in their rooms.

The farthest anyone has been able to re-enter is the lobby, even the cat won't go near the front doors."

"Is Dom there yet?" Dani asked. Dominic Talon was Claire's partner.

"He is going to meet us there, he was training with the Talon guards," Claire told her. "I'm sure you already know, but Lucas comes back tomorrow, so he wants them extra sharp with the Three Talon's being back in the city."

The Talon's were another Vampire house and one of the Five oldest. Lucas was Heir to the line, his parent's -Harold and Josephine- were the heads of the house. Like Alexius and Bertram, Lucas spent six months every year over seeing their people and properties which for House Talon was mainland Europe, Greenland, and Iceland.

"He had told me last week he was coming home tomorrow," Dani confirmed.

"Still saying nothing is going on between you two?" Claire teased. Claire had noticed a shift in Dani and Lucas shortly before he had left for Europe. She had spent the last six month's trying to get it out of Dani.

Dani rolled her eyes as they drove toward the city at break-neck speeds. The longer the wards were screwed up, the longer the Neutral Place was unbalanced, the larger the area would be.

"Alistair put out a bulletin to all cops in the area that if they saw my jeep to let us go through," Claire told her.

"He doesn't do that often," Dani replied.

"I know."

Neither of them spoke about how they feared what they were going to find.

Castro - Sacred Dark

Chapter 2

Claire pulled up by the Police Barricade outside of the Algonquin Hotel, one of the NYPD recognized her jeep and lifted the tape for her and Dani as they piled out of the jeep. Dani smiled at the officer, they had worked with him before. Trent Donavan was one of the good one's, he was well liked not just in the NYPD but also at STF.

"Trent," Dani said as she hugged him. "Tell everyone working there is food in the blue cooler and bag in the back and there is blood in the red cooler."

"Your mom is a saint," Trent Donavan said as he shook hands with Claire. Helena had won over many hearts and calmed many fears with ensuring that anyone working on a crime scene her daughter attended had food and water. "Alistair and your team is over by the main entrance. You are going to start feeling the effects when you hit the middle of the street."

"Has it moved?" Claire asked as she unlocked the back of her jeep so that the food could be accessed.

"No, but we already have a plan in place if it starts to spread outward," Trent informed them.

Dani and Claire looked at each other and nodded. They nodded to some of the other NYPD cops that had roped off the area as well as SPD officers that Alistair called in as added protection. Trent was right, the moment they hit the yellow line they felt the first wave that something was wrong. They each took another step and it was like a wall shot up preventing them from getting further.

"The ley lines are vibrating," Claire whispered, referring to lines of energy that ran through the earth.

In the paranormal world, Ley lines were lines of magnetic

pull, energy that paranormals could use. To non-paranormal, they were straight lines that seemed to connect important sites across the globe.

"The wards, something un-natural did this," Dani said as her head began to pound. "We have to fix it."

"Are you ready?"Claire asked Dani.

Claire placed a hand on Dani, letting her power center Dani. No one had yet to be able to explain what Dani and Claire could do, they were able to use each other's energy to amplify their own natural abilities. It was a trait that was often seen in twins or sometimes in victims who shared the same trauma. For it to appear in two individuals with no blood relation or shared trauma was unique.

When it had been noticed in their early teens, Helena and Tabby made sure they learned to control and harness it, and how not to let it loose control. Marcus had hated it, hated that Dani was linked to a witch. He had hoped that Dani had inherited nothing from her biological father, who was witch. That she would be all vampire like her biological mother. And while she was in deed a living vampire, she also had witch abilities, which wasn't completely uncommon.

"You okay?" Claire asked Dani as she watched the raven haired female take a deep calming breath.

"It's wrong," Dani replied.

"Well that is why they called us," Claire reminded her.

Dani flipped her off before continuing. "The magick is wrong," Dani explained. "The wards reacted, the neutral magick shut down, as if it was a way to defend itself."

"You're right, whatever did this isn't from nature," Claire told her. "Let's talk to Alistair," Claire suggested.

Taking another deep breath, Dani headed toward the Captain of STF and the rest of their team. Michael Cooper, Grant Torres, and Dom Talon all stood there with Alistair Clarence, talking in hushed tones. Dom looked up when he felt Dani and Claire approach, he could already see the effects this was having on Dani, as well as, Claire.

"Hey," Dom said as he walked over to Dani. A quick shake of her head let him know not to touch.

Alistair grabbed his walkie when he noticed the exchange. "No one is to touch, brush up against, or anything involving physical contact with Danika," Alistair stated. "Claire and, if need be, Dom are the only two with permission."

Dani let out a breath as she approached Alistair and the team. The fact that the STF never once made her feel like a freak, and not only did they embrace her gifts but her as well, always made her feel at home amongst them. If they were told to give Dani a wide berth to prevent them from touching, they understood there was a reason behind it.

Michael, who was part of Dani's house, looked at her. "So what do you have?"

"Whatever did this, it's like it goes against nature. It disrupted the ley lines which set off the natural wards that lay here," Claire replied.

"Explain the neutrality thing again to me," Michael asked Claire. While he might be a vampire, magick and witches, and magickal theory confused him.

"There are places throughout the planet that are naturally Neutral," Claire explained. "It dampens any paranormal or supernatural's abilities. For example, Alistair wouldn't be amble to transform, a vampire couldn't glamour or use mind tricks, and a witch couldn't summon. Most of the time they tend to be where old temples were located, but it can happen in Cathedrals, sometimes museums, or a battlefield. In this case, the Algonquin happens to be one of those spots."

"And someone fried it," Grant summed up from Claire's explanation and his own feelings as a witch. "Which is impossible. The thing about a Neutral Place is that no one's power can interfere with it, no one can control it, use it against another."

"Ok but if Dani is right saying it acted as a defense, then in theory it would allow us to use our abilities," Dom replied.

"Allowing us to defend ourselves if need be," Alistair realized.

Dani nodded. She moved away from Claire and walked toward the main doors to the luxury and historic hotel. Dani laid a hand against the metal and waited. It took a second for images and noises to come slamming into her mind and then there was silence and a sense of confusion. There was an unknown power somewhere mixed in with it all, tainted, it didn't belong there, it wasn't natural.

"Dark magick," Dani gasped. "They used a blood ritual

of some kind. I can't tell, too much static."

"Which would explain how they were able to use any power at all," Dom noted. Dark magick wasn't natural at all, it was forbidden under the Accords.

"Claire," Dani said.

"Right here," Claire told her.

"I need to go in and straighten out the pathways, once I do that most of the issues will be gone," Dani told her.

"How deep?" Claire asked. Over the years they had developed their on levels of how deep Dani had to connect with the astral world.

"Not nose-bleed deep," Dani said. Nose Bleed level was equivalent to Code Red.

"Alright, I'll ground you," Claire said.

"And Claire can use me to ground if she needs it," Grant said stepping next to Claire so that if need be she just had to grab his hand.

Placing her hands on both of Dani's shoulders, they both took deep breaths until their breathing was the same. Dani focused on their heart beats until those too were in line with each other. From there she closed her eyes and entered her version of the astral plane where she could see all the pathways of magick and energy. She tuned out all the supernaturals that were in the area, focusing instead on the natural wards that had been set here millennia ago. Instead of an intricate spider web, the lines were all jagged and wrong. None were broken, which would make things easier. Once she found the first that could be untangled it was easy to undo the mess. Dani didn't even have to put them back together, as soon as they were untangled they positioned themselves back to where they should be.

Dani heard the collective sigh of relief before she even opened her eyes. A steaming mug of tea was handed to her as she opened her eyes.

"Well step one is done," Dani replied as she sipped the tea. It was a special blend for her to use after such a session.

"Now we go in and find out what the hell happened," Michael answered.

"The touch rule?" Alistair asked her.

Dani thought for a moment. "Keep it in place, I have no clue what we are going to find when we enter the hotel."

The Touch Rule was simple: when active, no one was allowed to touch Dani. If they did, then Dani was not responsible for whatever memories, emotions she received, or how she might react to being touched when she had to go deep into the astral plane.

Alistair radioed that they would be entering the building, as they secured each section he would call in with more instructions. For now everyone was to stay out.

Dom went first, opening the doors and entering the deserted lobby. The hotel, that had been bustling and filled with people two hours ago, was quiet and deserted. He motioned for them to follow, with Michael taking the lead and Alistair in the middle. With two vampires on the team, it made sense that one would take the lead and one would take the back, they could take the most damage.

Dani paused as they moved toward the center of the lobby. "What's up?" Grant asked her when he almost bumped into her.

"It's all centered around something on one of the upper levels," Dani said.

"Then let's go hunting," Dom said.

****

Dom noted that as they got closer to the tenth floor the more agitated Claire and Dani were getting. As they searched the tenth floor, Alistair switched his spot, putting Claire and Dani behind Dom. Dani had a death grip on Claire's arm and much of her color had faded. Even Claire, who despite her bright red hair and green eyes had tan skin, was looking pale. Dom looked at Grant and saw that he was sweating from strain. Even Alistair was having an issue keeping the Were-panther in him in check. Alistiar caught Dom's eye and they both knew that whatever they were going to see was going to be bad. As they went to the elevator, Dani leaned against the cool metal.

"The twelfth floor," Dani said as the coolness of the metal seemed to calm her. Dom studied her, he had worked with her enough, seen what she could do, to know better than to question. "Twelfth floor it is."

They climbed into the elevator and skipped the eleventh floor. This time when the door opened, Dom let Dani take the lead. But he was right behind her, Lucas would cut off his head if anything happened to Dani on his watch.

Dani walked down the hallway, her fingers brushing against the walls. She froze before one of the doors that led into a suite. Alistair took the master key that the Hotel Manager had given him and slid it in the reader. When the door swung open the smell of death greeted them.

Dom grabbed Dani from walking into the room as Alistair called in for a crime scene team. Grant was handing out gloves from his pack, they all took a pair except for Dani. Dani's prints were on file for when she had no choice but to touch parts of a crime scene in order to understand what was going on. Claire followed Dani as she moved through the suite, it was obvious that Dani was being pulled by something as the raven haired female slowly weaved around the living room area toward one of the doors that led to a bedroom.

"This would be the master bedroom," Dom informed them as she readied himself for whatever might be on the other side of the door.

Dani laid a hand on the closed door and immediately regretted that decision as it felt like her hand was being burned. Dom went to reach for the door handle but Dani grabbed his wrist before it could make contact.

"Did you not see me hiss in pain," Dani asked him. "This door has been warded to keep us out."

"So un-ward it," Dom suggested, noting the blisters that were forming on Dani's hand.

"I can't," Dani admitted. "It has to be Claire and Grant."

"Why us?" Grant asked. He could undue a ward but with Dani and Claire it was easier and quicker to have them do it.

"Because this ward was created with a spell, and I can't undo spells," Dani replied as she held up her hand. "And there is something on the door that is not good for vampires."

"I'll deal with your hand when we're done with the door," Claire told Dani.

Claire looked at Grant and they both took a deep breath. Michael and Dom both stood to the side by Dani, allowing the two witches room to work. Dani could feel the power the two were summoning from world around them. It was what made natural witches different from those who joined the craft. Natural witches didn't need to invoke a spirit to make a spell or charm work, they could use the five elements to do that.

"Do you see their glow yet?" Dom asked Dani.

Dani was a born vampire, which meant that as she got older her senses slowly developed until they were almost that of a fully turned Vampire. When she finallay did do the oath ceremony she was told that there would be a huge jump with her senses.

"No, but I can feel them pull from the energy around us," Dani told him.

"For most vampires, they just see the same glow," Micheal explained. "Dom here is one of the few that can see an individual aura's around them when they use power."

Dani turned to the giant vampire standing next to her. "You're an empath?" Dani asked.

While she had known Dom pretty much for most her life, he was very private, she wasn't even sure if Lucas knew everything about his body guard.

"Supposedly," Dom answered narrowing his eyes at Micheal.

The lankier of the two Vampires just grinned as he watched the door to the hallway for anyone entering. Alistair was on the phone again out in the hallway so Micheal wanted to make sure that there was no surprises. While he might not be an empath, or whatever the hell Dani was, his senses were on edge because of whatever happened here.

"Done," Claire said. "We're going to have to talk to Aunt Tabby because there were parts that were created with blood."

"And that is a HUGE no no without permission," Grant added as he took the bottle that Dom handed him.

Alistair walked in with two energy drinks and a fresh tea for Dani. Which answered why he had been on the phone. "Why is it a huge deal? And what do we have?"

"Blood rite mixed with traditional charm," Grant informed him.

"And a unique poison that I can't make sense of," Claire stated as she studied Dani's hand.

They all looked at Claire. Claire could have been an extraordinary healer because she could detect poisons and the cure for them. She was one of the few that had been granted access in her training as a witch to see the sacred black tomes. If Claire could see how the poison was created she could better under-stand how to make a cure for it. Of course there had been some who said it was Tabitha Jensen showing favoritism with her great niece but most knew what Claire could do was beneficial to everyone.

"I'll have Nessa take samples," Alistair said as he fired off the text to their pathologist and head of the Paranormal Forensic department.

"And it's huge deal because using any blood in a ritual or spell requires permission from the heads of the Coven," Grant explained. "Because most rituals involving blood are in the Black Tomes and they are strictly restricted because of every-thing that is in them."

"So this person is using magick that is forbidden in away," Alistair replied.

"Pretty much," Claire agreed as she finished with Dani.

"We're all good to go in?" Dom asked Claire.

"Yeah, just don't touch the door," Claire suggested to the two vampires on their team.

With that, Dani entered first and gasped at the carnage in front of her. Two bodies were sitting on the edge of the bed completely entwined with the other. But not in the act of love, more as if their bodies had been melded together some how. The facial skin had been burned to prevent identification. What made it even more chilling was there was no blood, no body fluids, nothing to show that a crime had even been committed.

"I think Nessa has her job cut out for her," Dom mumbled under his breath as he began to look around the room. Vynessa, or Nessa, was the medical examiner for STF and the city of New York.

They all nodded their agreement. Claire went with Dani toward the bed while the rest pulled on new gloves and began to look around the room for any type of clues.

Dani ignored the noise around her, instead focusing on the two people in front of her. There was a familiarity to them, as if she should know but couldn't figure out why. The air around them seemed tainted as if someone did something to make it hard to detect what had been done.

"This is bad," Claire said as she picked up on the taint.

Dani nodded. Without saying a word, she reached out and just barely touched the female before being slammed with images and feelings. She barely felt the hands that steadied her, instead it felt like she was falling down a dark hole.

It was all swirling around Dani's mind, there was laughter, flashes of images that were just a bit blurry to make it hard to focus, this overwhelming pain, then manic laughter, and a sense of triumph. There was so much and Dani needed to weed through it all to figure out anything. She focused on the laughter and the happiness, the sense of a strong love and bond.

Images of Lucas, of Dani, of others she knew and didn't know, appeared before her. The scent of vanilla and green tea could be detected, a long with a hint of expensive whiskey. Dani knew who they were and the grief brought her to her knees.

Then her head was filled with this wild laughter, she was holding her ears so she didn't hear it. It brought her back to when her parents had been murdered when she was five. When she heard the same laughter as a red mist began to circle around her as if trying to suffocate her.

Dani had no idea she had been crying, that she had been

mumbling "Get him out," that Dom had lifted her up and carried her out of the room. It was all still swirling around in her head, almost overloading her sense. She didn't hear someone yell for Claire to grab her medic bag. There was nothing but immense pain and grief.

Then a wave of calm from so far away began to float into the chaos. It was warm, familiar, and it helped her calm her mind down as she slipped into blackness.

****

"And she is back, somewhat," Dom said with a slight smile as he was bent over Dani. Dani went to sit up but his large hands kept her down. "Nope. You are staying put."

"Explain to her what is going on," a disembodied voice said.

Dom nodded. "We're at Tabby's clinic," Dom said brushing a strand of her hair out of her face. "You're fine, this is just a precaution. That poison on the door, it got more potent when you did your thing. The easiest way to talk to you is through a kind of dream world experience."

She went to talk, but Dom shook his head making her see

a few too many of him and a faint golden glow. "Just rest, and let Tabby and Claire get you back."

Dani mouthed Lucas' name. "He is getting an earlier flight back. That thing that started with you two before he left, it appears to have gotten stronger."

Dani went to tell him to be careful with what he was saying. "We're in your head kid," Dom told her. "No one can hear us."

Dani arched up to lay her hand against his head. 'If we are in my head why won't you let me move or talk'

"Because I need your body calm and still," Dom said. "Talking and moving take up energy. Energy you depleted back at the hotel."

'Dom, I know who they are.'

"You told us," Dom told her, his voice trying to hide his own grief. "Thankfully while still in the hotel room so right now we have kept it sealed because of who the victims are."

'Lucas...I think he knows...I think he helped me...'

"Kid, I need you to stop talking to me through our heads," Dom said. "Tabitha just smacked me upside the head

because you are using energy."

"She really did," a familiar voice said filtering into her head.

"Claire is pretty excited that you have given her a new poison to experiment with," Dom informed Dani. "They have two of the black tomes out and both are practically drooling at being able to work with them."

Dani could only imagine how excited both women would be to open the rare tomes. The tomes were usually under lock and key, as well as, wards in Tabby's office at the clinic. In order to access them one need permission from the hierarchs of the Coven for the area. For Tabby to be able to use them it meant whatever occurred back in the hotel room was deemed dangerous enough to overrule the stipulations. As the High Priestess for the not just the local Coven, but for the mid-Atlantic states as well, she would have authority to do so.

"You are going to be fine," Dom assured her as he sensed her anxiety rise. "Helena and Nick are both here, they are in Tabby's office. Sayad is with Grunt. So focus on yourself."

Dani nodded. That was always her problem though, she

rarely focused on herself, always too worried about everyone around her. Tabby had always told her that her empathy toward others, while a strength, also drained her faster than most. It was easier though to ignore her needs and thoughts. When she did, she would dwell on mistakes from the past, focused on what she could be doing now. Her mind was never quiet.

Taking a deep calming breathe like Tabby taught her and Claire, she focused on things that calmed her. She couldn't help but smile at the thought of Grunt and how he was the biggest mush ball in the world. Going through the it all she found herself more centered. Images of the crime scene filtered toward the edge of her mind but she kept focusing on being calm. The crime scene could wait, it all could wait.

****

"Well hello, Sleeping Beauty," a soft familiar voice said.

Dani opened her eyes and saw her mom sitting next to the bed. Looking around, Dani didn't recognize where she was.

"You are in one of the healer suites at the clinic," Helena assured her daughter. "Claire is asleep in the living area of this suite with Grant. Michael and Nick are standing guard and Dom went to confirm the identities of the victims."

Dani closed her eyes as grief slammed into her. She wasn't sure how she would tell her mother that Josie was dead.

"It's alright, Darling, I know," Helena whispered. "Dom and Alistair told me in confidence, they did not want you to have to be kept from telling me."

"What time is it?" Dani asked surprised at how harsh her voice sounded.

"It is close to six in the morning," Helena told her. "Whatever Dom told you to do worked and around three this morning you stabilized to the point that Tabby felt it would be better for you to recover here than in one of the patient rooms. How do you feel?"

"Honestly?" Dani asked. Helena nodded. "Better than I have in a while. Which is weird given what happened."

Before Helena could reply, both her and Dani heard the outer door to the suite open, and voices were heard talking. Tabby had come to check on her niece and her patient. Helena noted that Dani had picked up on the sounds as well.

"Your senses are getting more heightened," Helena observed.

"I can't hear heartbeats from a room away yet," Dani assured her mother.

"And if they are in the same room as you?"

"Only if I know them well," Dani answered.

Helena nodded concern flashing in her eyes. "Dani, Marcus can't know this. If he learns of this he will agree with Alexius about rushing the oath ceremony."

"I know, only Claire and Dom know," Dani replied.

The door to the bedroom opened and Tabby walked in. Her silver hair was pulled back in a messy bun, she wore a white doctor's coat over a gray blouse and black dress pants.

"I see my patient is up," Tabby said as she approached the bed. She rested the back of her hand against Dani's forehead. "No fever. Is she coherent?"

"Yes," Helena answered.

"How do you feel?" Tabby asked Dani.

"Oddly better than I have in a while," Dani replied.

"From what Dom said, you finally learned to focus on

yourself," Tabby said. "This allowed your body to recharge on its own without having to use energy from something else."

Tabby smiled at Helena. "Could you wake both Claire and Grant, tell them breakfast is in my office, I already told Michael and Nick there is food for the three of you as well."

"Of course," Helena replied. She understood that Tabby was also asking for privacy with Dani.

Tabby waited for Helena and the other two to leave then she watched Dani. "Let me know when you hear my office door open and close."

Dani nodded. After a few moment's she nodded. "They are all in your office."

"So you're hearing has improved greatly," Tabby noted. Dani went to say something before realizing the older woman had been testing her. "You turn thirty next spring."

"And then it's the official Oath ceremony," Dani said. Something she was terrified of happening.

"Yet your senses are increasing at a rabid pace," Tabby warned.

"I know," Dani agreed.

"So are your abilities, they are becoming more powerful, intense, you are seeing and remembering more," Tabby went on.

"My dreams, I can smell things now, the colors seem almost too intense at times," Dani admitted. "Even in my office at the archives I can hear the others, like whispers being carried by the wind. Sometimes even walking Grunt, I sometimes stop because it's like the world is rushing all around me and I'm standing still."

Tabby nodded as she sat down in the chair that Helena had vacated. "Dani, I believe you are what some would call a Dream Walker," Tabby told her. "I have had my suspicion for a few years now but when we were in your mind earlier it confirmed it."

"I haven't heard of a Dream Walker," Dani said.

"Because I think there are only ten in the world at this moment," Tabby informed her. "Witches can walk the Astral plane, we have to ward ourselves, cast charms and spells, to ensure we are safe, and bring no unwanted guest back with us, but we can do it. It is draining to do so, for you are essentially separating your soul from your physical body."

"I remember the training you did when Claire and I were sixteen," Dani replied.

"To walk the Astral Plane is always filled with thoughts of excitement and adventure that I like to put the fear of it in earlier than some other covens," Tabby confided. "Now how does this play into you? A Dream Walker does not need the ceremony and rituals to enter the realm of dreams. They do not need wards, or charms to protect them. For their blood is the protection, it is what wards you to the physical realm while your soul or spirit goes elsewhere. Dream-walkers can see magick flow in the everyday world, they can see lay-lines, see entrances into this world from other realms. Some can see past events when they walk into the room."

"Me being able to see a crime scene," Dani realized.

"Yes," Tabby replied. She rested her hand on Dani. "The reason that there are so few Dream Walkers is it is easy for one to lose themselves, to separate themselves from the mortal realm. Some can be driven mad, some choose solitude as the only way to handle it."

"But others?"

"There have been a few that have been able to handle their gifts and live a normal life surrounded by people, some have married and had children, which it doesn't mean you would pass this on to your off-spring."

"Is there training?" Dani asked.

"Your training should have started when you were thirteen, but I believe because you are Vampire more than you are witch, it has allowed this ability to slowly mature, and now as your senses improve your ability is coming out more and more."

"So what do we do?" Dani asked.

"I will give Claire some meditation and yoga routines to work on with you," Tabby told her. "You will also need to learn to focus on your own energy, as well as, those around, you will have to learn signs of when you are pushing too hard, when to back off. Meanwhile, I will look for a teacher that could come and help us."

"Thank you, Aunt Tabby," Dani replied.

"Now go back to sleep," Tabby told her as she stood up. "You need to rest more."

Chapter 3

Dom waited outside an office at JFK. Dom had felt his phone vibrate, glancing down he saw a message from Claire that Dani was up, eating, and looked good. That eased some of the tension that Dom had been carrying. But nothing was going to have to help with bringing his best-friend, a man he saw as a brother, to identify his parents. He had lied when he told Tabby he was going to do the identifying, because for security reasons he didn't want anyone knowing just how early Lucas was coming home.

The doors opened and the lawyers for House Talon, came out followed by an exhausted looking Lucas. Lucas had pulled his black hair back into a messy bun, sunglasses covered his light blue eyes. He wore a black dress shirt and gray dress pants. Both tailored to meet his tall and lanky frame.

Lucas walked over and hugged Dom tightly. They said nothing as they touched foreheads, an old ritual they had started when training against each other.

"I have the car waiting," Dom said.

Before they headed through the security doors, Dom tapped his ear piece three times, letting the security team know he was coming out with Lucas Talon. They were going to have to change that code now. The three taps signified that the Heir was on the move. The heir, though, was now the head.

Keeping the sunglasses on, Lucas followed Dom through the doors, and soon was surrounded by his security team. Because it wasn't even eight o'clock in the morning, the airport was relatively quieter then it was later in the day. Most didn't pay attention to the group, a few glanced wondering what famous person was walking through at this early hour. There was no media, no flashing lightbulbs, no inquires about why Lucas arrived almost twelve hours earlier than originally planned. Dom got Lucas into the middle car then slid in after him. The media tended to treat the Heads of Houses, Packs and Covens like celebrities. He told the driver they were good. It was all routine, with a few changes here and there so that it would throw off anyone looking for a pattern.

"Dani?" Lucas said as they pulled out first.

"She is up, eating, and looks healthy," Dom told him. "Claire texted me while I was waiting for your sorry ass to charm immigration."

"Shit, I'm surprised they didn't ask me to produce my fangs for proof," Lucas said as he rested his head against the headrest. He then looked at Dom. "And my parents?"

"Nessa is with them," Dom told him. "Do you want me to text the girls?"

Lucas shook his head. He needed time with his parents, they were his only blood relatives. Lucas was now the last of the Talon Line.

Dom nodded and sent a quick message to Vynessa with

the number of people who would be coming. No names were mentioned. The ride to the STF headquarters was quiet, the car turned into the underground parking lot. Alistair was waiting already at one of the secured doors that led into the building. He was the only other person that knew who Dom was bringing with him.

Alistair said something into his radio then nodded to Dom letting him know all was secure.

Dom slid out first, then let Lucas out next. He held a hand up to the rest to stay put. Alistair walked over to Lucas, and breaking protocol, hugged the grieving son. Lucas returned the hug, noting the strength that Alistair was trying to give him.

"I will be there with you every step," Alistair whispered so that only the vampire could heard.

"I..." Lucas began but he couldn't form words.

"You owe no one any comments or words," Alistair told him. He placed a hand on Lucas' back and guided him to the door.

Dom followed. No one was going to write Alistair up on breaching protocol when interacting with a member of a different accord branch in the time of mourning. Weres are emotional and touchy, what Alistair showed as a leader of a Were pack was that to him Lucas was an honorary part of the pack.

The three men headed down the narrow hallway. It was used to bring either extremely dangerous individuals to lock up, or to bring easily recognizable people to various parts of the building without being seen. They stopped at an elevator, Alistair swiped his card, then scanned his palm before the doors opened. When they all entered, he hit the button for sub-basement.

This time when the door opened, they stepped off into the forensic and morgue level. They turned toward the morgue where Dr. Vynessa Johnson worked. She was their coroner, medical examiner, and Forensic Anthropologist. Unlike many other times when Alistair or Dom would bring family members to view a body, Nessa was waiting for them outside of her lab. She wore her lab coat over her blouse and pants.

"Lucas, may they find eternal peace as they slumber, may they be reunited with those they have lost during their long journey of life, and may your grief remember all the moments you had with each other," Nessa said as she took his hands in hers. She had recited a blessing that was custom to be said at a Vampire's memorial.

He nodded, not being able to form the words. Dom hugged her instead, kissing the top of her head as he did. "Thank you," Dom whispered in her ears.

"They are ready for you," Nessa told him. "Let me know if you want time with them."

Lucas nodded once again as he motioned for someone to open the door. Vynessa held open the door to the large area of the morgue. Two medical tables were waiting in the center of the room, both draped in black cloth instead of the common white. It was a sign of respect for who Josephine and Harold were to already be draped in black.

Vynessa moved to the head of the two tables and waited for Lucas to let her know he was ready. "I... had my assistant make burial masks for them," Nessa told him. "I thought it would be easier for you."

Lucas again nodded his appreciation and she pulled the sheets back. The masks were beautiful for having been quickly made. They covered the damage that had been done to the faces so that Lucas would not have to bear witness to the trauma. But he could see the burns on their throats.

He saw his mother's hand and he reached out to touch it, no one stopped him. His thumb traced the gold bracelet that was now imbedded in the skin. A gemstone for each of his siblings and he were woven into the branch pattern of gold. She never took it off.

"It's her," Lucas said in a rough voice filled with heart-breaking emotion.

He moved to the next gurney and asked Vynessa if he could see his father's shoulder. She warned him of some of the damage he would see and he nodded that he understood. Vynessa moved the sheet farther down so Lucas could see it. He saw the scar from spear. It was just above the heart, a reminder to his father that while they were stronger than mortals, they could be killed.

"It's him," Lucas said.

"Right now the official cause of death is poison," Vynessa informed him. "What kind we don't know but it was able to weaken them so that the person could kill them."

No one spoke after that. Lucas looked at Vynessa. "Could I have a few moment's?"

"Just come to the door when you are done and take as long as you want," Nessa replied.

She then ushered the other two men out of the room. Lucas stared at his parent's not sure what to say or think. Vampires could live past one thousand years of age, though it was rare. Five hundred years of age was considered your prime, when you were at your strongest, most powerful. True bonded mates were known to live longer than most, for they share a life force and power, making them stronger. His parents were close to seven hundred and fifty years old, he had been their last child to be born. They had already lost two children before he was born.

"I will be fine," he whispered touching what there was of his mother's hair. "You will be reunited with those you haven't seen since before I was born. I know you think I'm alone, and I'll hide away in my grief. I never got to tell you this, we wanted to wait until we were more comfortable with the idea of it, but Dani is my mate. We felt the pull before I left this last time. I will get through this, we will find who did this, and Dani, Dom,

and Claire will make sure they pay."

Chapter 4

Dani walked toward the main branch of the New York City Public Library. The building had been made famous by a movie in the 1980's involving a ghost and a green slime ball. Which was ironic because in the sub-basement of the building was the Archives for the Accord. As she walked, Dani heard her phone ring from one of the side pockets of her book bag. Grabbing it she saw it was her mom.

"Hey mom," Dani answered. They had talked late last night when Lucas called all the heads of Houses, local Covens and Packs to inform them about his parents. Today at noon, his man of affairs would be holding a press conference with Alistair with an official statement.

"How is he?" Helena asked from her office at the Metropolitan Museum of Art.

"He was still asleep when I left," Dani told her. Very few people knew that Lucas had crashed at her and Claire's apartment, and most likely would be there for the next few days. Most would think he was holding up in one of the apartments that his parent's owned for visiting dignitaries.

Their apartment was warded against anyone meaning harm, only those allowed through the wards could enter, making it the best place for Lucas to hide away from the press. This was the first time a Head of House had died in the modern era of social media and instant news. The fact that it was a bonded pair and they were murdered, was going to make it even crazier. Dom was almost at his breaking point last night when Michael had to step in and call Dom's second in command to take over security while Dom worked the case. Alana promised that everything would be past on to their team and Dom before being implemented.

"I told him that I would meet him this evening at his parents' apartment to help with some of the legal things," Helena told Dani.

"I have his phone set to go off in plenty of time and Alana or Dom will bring him," Dani told her. "Mom, he really appreciates what you are doing."

"And how are you doing?" Helena asked.

"Claire put fresh ointment on my hand this morning and wrapped it, she gave me a packet of the herbal remedy to make at lunch time," Dani told her. "Is Sayad at the house?"

"No, after the fight he had with your father and two brothers, he will be staying at Nick's for the summer," Helena informed her. "Honestly, I might be joining him if something doesn't change. Marcus' paranoia is reaching new levels."

"Lovely," Dani sighed. The last thing she needed was Marcus to become even more demanding. Soon he'll be agreeing with Alexi to rush her Oath ceremony.

"Don't worry, between myself, Nick and Sayad, we will keep you safe," Helena assured her.

"I'm almost to the archives, have Sayad contact the Accords, see if they can put him on as my assistant, but only call after the news conference."

"I will tell him," Helena promised.

Dani greeted the two Lion statues that flanked the entrance to the historical library. Tourists were already lining up to have their pictures taken with Patience and Fortitude. Smiling at the groups, Dani headed up the steps and into the main foyer. She nodded to the concierge desk before heading toward the elevators. Taking the one down to the basement she stepped out and headed toward the back of the room.

Harold, the day time security guard for the Archives, smiled at her when he spotted her. He set his paperback down when he stood up.

"Well hello there, Miss Dani, how are you today?" Harold asked as he took her back pack and put it through the scanner. "I heard your team was called out last night."

"It was a late night," Dani answered as she stepped through the body scan. "Is everyone here already?"

"The main ones are," Harold answered. Referring to her

five co-workers.

"Sayad might be coming in later," Dani told him.

"Is he up for summer now?" Harold asked as he handed her the back pack.

"He is," Dani confirmed. "Have a good day, Harold."

He saluted her as she stepped into the temperature controlled elevator that would bring her to the main sub level. Sandy, the receptionist for the archives, looked up when Dani stepped off the elevator.

"We're closing the archives," Dani told her.

"I just got off the phone with Alistair," Sandy told her. "I sent out the mass text stating that all appointments and meetings have been postponed. We will contact them to reschedule at a later time."

"And the response?" Dani asked her.

"I muted all the lines but my personal one," Sandy answered.

"You are the best," Dani replied.

Sandy chuckled as she waved Dani through the glass doors that lead into a massive room. For the fact it was all underground, the main floor of the archives was bright. The walls were done in pale tones, with lights hanging from the high arched ceilings. Tables and reading areas made up the central area while book shelves and cabinets lined most of the walls. This was where the generic information could be found on the Accords, and the five different branches. To access the information on this floor required a signature from a head or an academic institution.

Towards the back of the room were six offices and three conference rooms, a small kitchen, and several bathrooms.

There were five main archivists, one for each of the five branches of the accords. There was a sixth archivist who mainly dealt with general inquires and information. He also helped if one of the other archivist needed it. Then there were two apprentices and sometimes officials from the Accord building.

Dani gave a whistles to signal them all to meet her at one of the long tables next to the back. She set her bag down on a chair and waited for them to arrive. Gregoir and his apprentice were the two first to arrive. The tall necromancer walked over and gave Dani a huge hug, a rare thing for a necromancer to do.

He was the archivist for the spell-casters and a close friend of her brother Sayad.

"We all felt it," Gregoir whispered in her ear as he hugged her. "Our thoughts are with Lucas and the house. Whatever we can do, tell us."

"Can you have your clan write up what they felt?" Dani asked.

Gregoir took for his satchel a stack of parchment. "I already did," Gregoir told her. "I sent it to Alistair this morning."

"You are amazing," Dani said as she hugged him this time.

The rest had joined them by then. Dani nodded and they all sat. "This does not leave this room until after noon today," Dani began. "All cellphones, tablets, anything not work sanctioned on the center of the table."

There were some grumbling but everyone, including Dani put their devices in the center of the table. This was the protocol when highly sensitive information was going to be discussed.

"Saturday night at around 5pm Josephine and Harold Talon were..." Dani hesitated because she still couldn't say it.

"Murdered," Gregoir finished for her.

The shock was written on all the faces of her co-workers. Gregoir quickly summoned tissues from nearby to the table. "It happened at the Algonquin," Dani went on. "Not only were they murdered but the neutrality of the place was thrown off. There were wards placed in the suite they were found in to prevent entry. There was also a poison that even Claire Jensen had difficulty identifying. We have been asked by STF to help with research on several questions."

"Of course, whatever you need, Dani," Sylvia answered. She was in charge of the Fae archives, being one of the few fairies that could live in the mortal realm full time.

"I am going to split us into teams, we will each focus on one of the areas," Dani went on. "Gregoir, I want you and Gloria to work on specifically how the wards were placed on the door. Claire and Grant wrote up everything for you guys."

"We can do that," Gloria promised. She might be a werewolf but she had the unique ability of being able to sniff out wards.

"Alistair is getting you access to the crime scene, Gloria,"

Dani told her. She then looked at Tobias, who was Gloria's apprentice. "Toby, you and Luci are going to work on the potion. Tabby said you both are excellent with herbal research, she should have the analysis of what was in it later today or tomorrow. You can work with my medical report and examine my hand if you want."

"Is that why your hand is bandaged?" Justin asked. He was their general archivist.

"And why your blood smells off?" Gloria added.

"Yes to both questions," Dani said. "Lars, you and I are looking into how the neutrality of a neutral place can be altered."

"Sounds good."

"Justin, you are going to be bouncing between the four groups, helping with overflow, you can also help Toby and Luci since you are quite good with potions."

"Whatever you need," Justin told her.

"Dani," Sylvia inquired. "Lucas?"

"Is releasing a statement through Angan this afternoon," Dani answered. Angan was the public relations person for House Talon. "Today will officially start the five days of mourning for

Lucas and House Talon. Everything will be directed through Angan."

"I can't even begin to imagine what he is going through," Sylvia whispered. "When you see him, please tell him the Fae will be lighting the fire in their memories. They were devoted allies to us, and treasured by all of us."

"I will," Dani promised. She then looked grimly at them. "Alright. I'll hand out all the notes we have, there are reports from Vynessa as well in regards to the poison, and the effects on the body. There also is some unusual magick that was used in their killing. If Gregoir and Gloria could look into it, that would be beneficial too. Right now I'll be running as liaison for us but we are trying to get Sayad in as well, since he is off for the summer."

With that, Dani pulled out the heavy files that had already been sorted into the four groups. She handed them out and answered any questions she could. With that everyone took a different table and began to go over the files. Not much was going to be solved today, today was going over the information.

They worked until Sandy came with bags of food for

them, ushering them into the small kitchen knowing if they were left on their own they would eat and work. She then turned on the television for the press conference. It was being held outside of the STF headquarters in Harlem. Alistair came on in his Captain's uniform and silently held up his hands to quiet the press down.

"We have called this press conference to go over information about the events that occurred at the historic Algonquin Hotel," Alistair began. Usually they would all be commenting on him being in uniform and looking official, but not today. "Saturday night at 7pm the STF were notified by local NYPD about a situation at the hotel. It was explained that the natural wards seems to have changed causing the entire hotel to be emptied out. There was also a rumor of a crime that had been committed. When the initial STF officers responded they realized the severity of the disturbance and requested that Team Alpha be called in."

He paused to give people time to jot down notes or questions. "Myself, and Team Alpha arrived on the scene close to 8 pm. There, two of the team members were able to restore the location back to its neutral warding. From there, we and a team from the NYPD entered the hotel. After canvasing each floor we found the crime scene on one of the upper floors. It was there, after entering the suite, that we learned that whoever this criminal is, what he did was monstrous. The room had been warded to keep specific types of people from opening the door to the bedroom. A member of the team was injured in the process. Once we gained entry into the bedroom, we only then learned that the crime that had been committed was a murder."

Hands and questions began to raised and yelled. "Until that moment there had been no evidence that anything had occurred," Alistair said answering several of the questions that had been thrown at him. "Despite what was done to the bodies there was no blood around them. Whoever did this cleaned up after the crime."

"Do you know who the victims are?" A reporter yelled.

"We had to wait until we contacted their next of kin before their names could be released," Alistair answered. He closed his eyes for a moment as he knew what he was about to do, their entire world was about to be upended once he spoke the names. "The victims of the heinous crime were Josephine and Harold Talons, bond-mates and heads of House Talon."

There was silence as the news sunk in. "I will turn the podium over to Mr. Liefson," Alistair informed them.

Angan Liefson nodded to Alistair as he came to stand behind the podium. "Their only surviving child, Lucas, was made aware early yesterday morning," Angan began. "He was the person that identified their bodies. At this time Mr. Talon asks that you allow his house to grieve in privacy. I will provide Captain Clarence with how to get in touch with me for any questions."

"Mr. Liefson, what happens now?" a reporter asked.

"As is customary with those protected under the Accord, we will enter five days of morning which beings today," Angan explained. "This is a private affair for the house to mourn. On the sixth day a service will be held for the community to gather and give their support."

"Does any of it change because it involves two Heads of a House?"

"For Lucas, it will allow him to spend the next days to grieve with his house, he will be out of the public eye for the duration," Angan answered. "The memorial ceremony will be a bit more of an important affair, think of it as the death of a world leader or former leader. And for Lucas, on the seventh day he will officially be named Lord Talon."

"Can you tell us how he is doing? Is he at his parent's place?"

"He is grieving," Angan answered simply. "He is in a secure place away from prying eyes. This was a shock to everyone. Lady and Lord Talon were heavily involved in not just the communities under the accords, but of the human world as well. They were some of the most sincere people you could ever meet. They suffered through the deaths of six of their seven children. They were bonded to each other, something that is rare among us. No one would ever conceive that they would die in such a horrific way."

"What are bond mates?"

"There is a legend that explains once we were all joined physically with our mate," Angan explained. "In a fit of rage, the gods were angered by mortals, and split the pairs apart sending them to opposite ends of the world. In the case of Vampires, there is a true mate, one that completes us, compliments our abilities, strengthens us, as we do the same for them. It is rare when two mates meet, for the bond can happen at first glance or decades after knowing the person. For House Talon, they were blessed by their leaders being a bonded pair."

* * * *

He watched from his private office, the one not many people knew about. Since Saturday, he had been waiting for this moment. For the police to admit there had been a murder, that the wards had been disrupted, that they were at a lost. He watched, sipping his brandy, as Captain Clarence gave his statement.

At the mention that a top team had been brought in, he was conflicted with emotion. Part was anger, because it would take the fun away if answers were found too quickly. But the other part in him felt honored that the top had been called in because of the chaos he had created in their world. Their precious rules and laws, oh how he was going to enjoy watching them crumble.

When the good captain announced a representative from

House Talon was here to make a statement, he stood straighter. It was impossible for them to have already identified dear old Josie and Harold. He had made sure to make it difficult for them to be identified. There was a time table he had plotted.

The glass shattered in his hands as the captain said the names of the victims. The glass cutting into his hand, the brandy burning the cuts from the slithers. He didn't feel the pain for anger pulsated through his entire body as he yelled at the the television. They brought the bitch. There is no other way they could have figured it out.

ChApter 5

It was almost midnight when Claire stumbled through the door to their apartment. She hung her bag on the hook by the door, smelled something warming in the oven, and heard a video game on in the living area. Heading into the kitchen section she saw a note on a plate that said "Eat Me." It was in Lucas' hand-writing. Smiling, she poked her head in the oven and saw lasagna and garlic bread. After she served herself a portion, she grabbed a beer from the fridge that had "Drink Me" on it. Then the bottle of water that had Dani's name on it.

Claire headed into the living area where Dani was curled on the couch playing a space role playing game from which she had gotten Grunt's name from. Claire sat next to her and noticed that said dog was missing.

"He's on the roof with Lucas, Dom, and Alana," Dani said, as if she had read Claire's mind. "He hasn't left Lucas' side all day. He even went with him to House Talon."

"And Lucas cooked," Claire noted. She loved when he cooked.

"It keeps his mind off things," Dani told her. She took the water that Claire brought and took a sip. "How was the precinct?"

"It got crazy after the Press Conference," Claire told her. "Thankfully, Mike, Grant, and me were already at the hotel working with Forensics so we missed most of the chaos."

"Dom didn't say a word when he arrived, he just told Lucas that they would be up on the roof," Dani replied. "Alana is going to take over security so Dom can focus on the case."

"She has done that before when we have a huge case and Lucas is in town," Claire agreed. "I like her, she doesn't put up with Dom's crap, but still respects the role he has."

They were silent for a few minutes while Dani moved her character through the enemies on the screen. "How's your mom?" Claire asked.

"A wreck, trying to be strong for Lucas and me but her and Josie have been friends for centuries. Add in that they were murdered and she's numb."

"They all are," Claire agreed. "Kira stopped by the precinct to drop off food for all of us."

Kira, or Kamaria, was the heir for House Impuldulu. Their House was a block away from the STF headquarters and had a strong relationship with the precinct. Often during long and tough cases, they would bring food to precinct so that no one had to worry about eating or forgetting to eat.

"How is she?"

"Her mom is working on getting back here by tomorrow," Claire answered. "Kira already has reached out to those of their house that live nearby to grieve with those of House Talon."

"Nick wanted to do that as well, but apparently Marcus wants to wait," Dani admitted. Claire looked at her in shock.

"Yea, Mom is living with Nick now. She told me when she dropped off Lucas earlier. Marcus feels this is the time to see how Lucas leads, any interference in how he will move forward will undermine tradition."

"Screw tradition, his parents were slaughtered!" Claire yelled.

"Relax, Claire, the other's agree with you," Dani assured her. "This whole situation just sucks on so many levels."

Claire looked at Dani. "How are you doing?"

"It's a case, there are things that need to be done," Dani stated. "I can mourn after. "

"Dani," Claire sighed.

Dani looked at her. "Tell me that my attitude is any different from yours or Dom's or Mike's or Al's?"

"Okay," Claire replied. Because Dani was right, the only way any of them were getting through this was thinking as it as a case and nothing else. "But what about what ever you have going on with Lucas, it makes it different"

Dani eyed her carefully. "Marcus doesn't know that there is anything but friendship between Lucas and I."

Before Claire could respond, the door to the apartment opened and Lucas entered looking exhausted. There were dark circles under his eyes, only making his blue eyes look more bloodshot than they were. Grunt followed in after him, he spotted Claire and Dani and ran to them with his nails clicking on the floor as he made his way to the couch. Lucas headed to the fridge where he grabbed a bottle of blood. He drained it where he stood before coming into the living area.

"Claire, you are sure this is okay?" Lucas asked her. He felt that he was intruding on their private world.

"I sent my aunt over to make sure you were blended into the wards, that should tell you that I am okay with this," Claire informed him as she ate the lasagna. "Besides if you cook like this while you are here then all the better."

Lucas just smiled slightly as he sat down in the chair. He had noted earlier that none of the furniture matched. It was all eclectic, some pieces being repainted in bright colors, but nothing matching perfectly. It fit the two females perfectly, brining in their vibrant personalities but at the same time it also felt homey, allowing anyone to just relax by being here. There were no formalities here, no expectations for perfect behavior. Instead there were arguments over who got the game controller, who drank the last beer, or who left only a sip in the white wine bottle. All while Grunt went from lap to lap begging for pets or belly rubs. It was worlds away from the formal expectations of Talon House and Lucas loved it for that reason.

Chapter 6

Morning came too soon. Lucas had come to bed around 3, Dani had felt the bed dip when he laid down next to her. Grunt only left the bed when Dani got up so he could be fed and go on his quick walk around the roof top garden. Once he was done he wanted back downstairs and immediately went back into Dani's bedroom to lay with Lucas.

"I feel like he has left us," Claire sighed stepping out of the kitchen area with two travel mugs. "Like I've been forgotten."

Dani just rolled her eyes as she wrote a quick note for Lucas. They both grabbed their bags and headed out of the apartment locking the door. Dani spotted their neighbor, Martin, coming out of their apartment across the hallway.

"Do you need me or Tim to walk Grunt?" Martin asked.

"Actually Lucas is here," Dani told him.

"Hence why Tabby was here expanding the wards yesterday," Martin said understanding. "Give him our cell so if he needs anything he can text us. I have the night shift but Tim is off today."

"I will," Dani replied.

Claire felt her phone vibrate, after checking her message she groaned. "Dom is getting impatient."

"Go, we'll make sure he's taken care of and not found," Martin promised them.

Dani and Claire took the elevator to the main floor. Dom was leaning against the door frame with sunglasses on. He pointed to his watch as they exited the building.

"Alistair and Michael aren't even here yet," Claire pointed out.

"And you don't think he hasn't been annoying them," Grant inquired from his car. "Dani did they tell you the plan?"

"Michael, Alistair, and I are going to handle Marcus," Dani said. "While you guys get to deal with the rest. Then after lunch Claire and I will got talk to Brianna the Wise. Claire filled me in last night."

"How's Lucas?" Dom asked Dani.

"Asleep," Dani told him.

"He really needs to think about how long he can keep up without a death sleep," Dom sighed. "At this rate he's going to be consuming more blood."

"Who says he hasn't?" Dani inquired. Three sets of eyes turned to her.

A death sleep was a form of sleep a Vampire needed to keep their abilities strong. It was a sleep as deep as death that allowed their bodies to store up needed energy. Younger vampires needed it more frequently, by Lucas' age a few times a month was all he needed. Yet in situations like this, the need would increase. It was rare for a vampire to enter a sleep of death someplace that wasn't their own place.

"Dani, he's not going to enter that type of sleep sleeping on your couch," Dom pointed out.

"Wait," Claire said as she almost choked on her coffee. "You think Lucas is sleeping on our couch?"

"Well unless you got a guest room that I don't know about," Dom answered.

"He is sleeping in my bed with Grunt guarding him," Dani informed Dom. Grant was trying hard not to laugh at Dom's reaction. "And when I checked his pulse before I left the bed it was at two beats per minute."

Dom was still staring at Dani when Alistair pulled up with Michael in his car. "Why does Dom look broken?" Michael asked as he climbed out of Alistair jeep.

"Because Dani just broke him," Grant answered trying so hard to control his laughter.

"I don't want to know," Alistair said. He looked at all of them. "We all ready?"

Everyone nodded. "I got a warrant from the Accords Court in case Marcus argues," Alistair explained. "That's what held Michael and I up."

"Good idea," Dani agreed. "I am going to warn you all. Mom and Sayad have moved in with Nick because things have gotten worst, so I don't know what version of Marcus we are going to see."

"Nick called to tell me," Alistair replied. "It's why I wanted the warrant."

"Kira confirmed that the Asian Ambassador will be at the Impuldulu House," Claire told Alistair.

"I'm meeting with Sam while you guys meet with Brianna, and Maria is going to call into it," Alistair said. "Alright, let's get going."

Dani and Michael climbed into Alastair's jeep while Claire argued with Grant that she could drive. Once they were headed out of Harlem, Alistair looked at Dani through the rear view mirror.

"Grey wants you to call or text him," Alistair told her. "I told him what happened, he's trying to see if he can get back in time for the memorial."

"Alistair, Lucas understands," Dani said. Though it

didn't surprise her that Grey would try to do something like that.

Greyson Clarence was part of Special Forces unit that was solely comprised of Supernatural beings. They did more than just locate bad guys, often they ran rescue missions getting people out of danger zones that were too risky for other units.

"I know, Todd and Drake both assured him that they would help Parker with stepping in as my second," Alistair replied.

"I'll tell Lucas, it will mean a lot," Dani replied.

"Speaking of Lucas," Michael coughed. "What's going on with you two?"

"This won't leave the car?" Dani asked. The two men nodded. "It started a few months before he left. We started noticing signs that we might be bonding."

There was silence as her words sunk in. Alistair cursed and Michael just was shocked. "We both researched while he was gone on what it means when one part of the pair isn't a full blooded vampire and well there really isn't anything on bonding and nothing on our situation."

"Shit," Micheal said. "Dani, Marcus will kill over this."

"Who else knows?" Alistair asked.

"Claire hasn't said it but she knows, Tabby and my mother both know," Dani replied.

"I'll talk with Helena and Tabby about keeping you safe and your oath ceremony," Alistair told her. "Because that is also going to send Marcus into hysterics."

"You mean when the elders and ancients relieve my memories of the night my parents were killed?" Dani asked.

"You realize we're bringing her right into the lion's den," Michael pointed out to Alistair.

"I've been living in a lion's den the moment my parents were killed," Dani reminded him. "Mom had to take me, she was my next of kin. But it also kept me safe because Marcus couldn't touch me."

"You still think he's apart of the reason your parent's were killed?" Michael asked.

"He might not be the reason but he knows more than he is letting on and he is worried about what my memory would show," Dani said. "So yeah, even without this murder, a shit storm was already brewing.'

They were all silent for most of the ride after that. Dani watched as they approached the gates to House Joseph. Alistair explained to the gate why they were there, then Dani spoke into the speaker giving them permission to open the gates. They drove down the long driveway, Alistair parked in front of the entrance. As they got out of the car, the door opened.

"Ah, Igor how lovely to see you," Micheal said to the butler.

"My name is not Igor," Horace reasoned. "Lady Joseph, your father wishes to understand your arrival?"

"I will explain to him when we enter," Dani answered. "Is he in his office?"

"The formal sitting room," Horace said.

Dani and Michael both looked at each other. It looked like Marcus wanted to remind them all of who he was. Dani motioned for Michael and Alistair to join her.

"Is the cat trained?" Horace asked as they walked past him.

It was Dani that reacted first, surprising everyone. "You heard what my mother said, she might not be under this roof, but don't think for a moment she doesn't know exactly what is happening here."

She turned and headed into the modern foyer. The formal sitting room was to the left of the foyer. It had been done in whites and blacks with splashes of gray. To everyone who saw it, and never in front of Marcus, it was joked that it looked like a throne room. And Marcus had the biggest chair of them all. His and Helena's each had the house crest stitched in them as if to remind everyone who entered who sat in those chairs. If one looked closely at Marcus' chair, they would see in thread, a shade lighter than the black leather, a crown stitched just above the crest.

Marcus was already seated in his 'throne' wearing a dark gray suit and red dress shirt under it. His hair was slicked back as his green eyes watched them enter the room. "I was quite shocked when the front gate called to tell me who was arriving," Marcus said as he motioned for them to take seats.

"I assure you, that we are going to all the houses today," Alistair informed Marcus. "As we speak Ms. Jensen, Mr. Torres, and Dom Talon are at House Impuldulu."

"And you are questioning us at to what per se?" Marcus inquired. "Do you believe one of us would kill one of our own?"

"If you would let us speak before you throw out accusations, father, then you would know why we are here," Dani said staring down her father. Of the three of them she was the only one that could talk to him in such away, though it was still dangerous for her.

Marcus was caught off guard by Dani talking like him in such away. "As you know," Michael began, taking Marcus silence as the pathway to start. "Josephine and Harold of House Talon were found in a private suite at the Algonquin hotel on May Eighteenth."

"It is still quite the shock, they were in their prime and a bonded pair, the thought that someone could over-power the pair is unthinkable," Marcus answered.

"Which is why we are here," Michael said. "Josephine and Harold, as you said were Bond-mates as well as being Prime Vampires. Can you think of anyway killing them could be possible?"

"Michael how old are you?" Marcus asked.

"I'll be 300 this December," Michael answered. He wasn't sure why Marcus wanted to know.

"As you know we get stronger as we age," Marcus answered. "I think a recent geneticist figured that we age a year for every decade. But when we hit 500, unlike humans at 50 or 60, we are hitting our prime when we are at our strongest. We can move faster than the human eye can see. Many of our legends stem from Prime Vampires. To catch one of us by surprise is thought impossible..."

"But is there a way?" Dani asked cutting her dad off.

"Now I'm saying "if," but the only way is by another Prime," Marcus said. "But if that was the case, the suite would have been destroyed."

"Then what about another supernatural," Alistair suggested.

Marcus laughed. "Maybe if they tricked them but with heightened sense of smell and taste they would have detected it."

"Which we know would not be easy," Alistair replied.

"Dad, any reason that Harold and Josephine would be at

the Algonquin?"

"With it being a Neutral spot many of us have done business there," Marcus answered. "But being there on a Saturday without it being a dinner or private gala is unlike them."

"And there were no meetings that you are aware of?" Michael asked.

"Weekends are usually free of meetings," Marcus replied. "An emergency will pop up from time to time but most of us leave the weekends open."

"One last question," Alistair promised. "Any thoughts as too who would do this?"

"None," Marcus said. "Josephine and Harold were loved by all, they were the best of us, they truly embraced what the Accords were after and on building our relationship with mortals. If they had enemies, they were unknown to me."

"Why father, you didn't tell me we were having a gathering," A voice said from the archway.

Dani inwardly groaned as she realized that it was Bartram. Things were going to get bad quick.

"They were just leaving," Marcus informed his youngest

son.

"Please don't rush off on my behalf," Bartram said as he moved through the room.

"We have more people to interview," Alistair admitted to Bartram. "We are starting with the Heads."

"And then working down until you are left with the little people," Bartram suggested. "I take it Micheal is near the bottom?"

"Bartram!" Marcus snarled.

"Thank you," Alistair said to Marcus as he stood up. "You know how to get a hold of me if you think or hear anything that might help us."

"Of course," Marcus replied as he stood with them. "Danika, before you leave, a word alone."

"Yes dear sister, we don't often see you these days, always running about," Bartram drawled as he draped himself over a chair.

Danika nodded to Alistair and Micheal who followed the butler out of the sitting room. Danika looked at the man who had raised her since she was five. Marcs waited until he heard the front door close before he said a word.

Knowing there was no getting rid of Bartram, Marcus took Dani by the arm and brought her to the kitchen. A room that Bartram would never set foot in.

"Is that where you were when you left dinner?" Marcus asked as if she had snuck out of the house to go to a wild party.

"It was," Dani answered.

"I see," Marcus replied as he paced in front of his chair. "I don't like this, Danika. These cases that you are being assigned to, they are not fitting of a person in your station."

"If you are worried about safety, I assure you that I am well protected."

"I don't care about that," Marcus stated as he turned to face her. "I have put up with this act of rebellion long enough. I want you to resign from being a consultant."

Dani stared at him for a moment to let the words form their meaning. She bit back the laugh that wanted to escape. "I'm twenty-nine, I live on my own, you do not have a say in where I work."

"You underestimate my reach," he warned.

"And you underestimate my importance," Dani retorted.

She turned and left leaving her father speechless in the sitting room. Dani opened the front door for herself, storming outside and toward the SUV where Alistair and Micheal waited. Both recognizing the face she wore and entered the car silently. No one spoke as they exited the estate.

"He's scared," Dani said breaking the silence.

"Why?" Alistair asked.

"He wants me not just off the case but to resign from STF."

Micheal turned from the front seat. "That had to be a fun conversation."

"I might have challenged him, so I figure he'll call your fearless leader within a day or two demanding my resignation," Dani warned Alistair.

The commissioner of the Special Task Force worked side by side with the Commissioner of the NY State Police. James Holtzen, or GQ as they called him behind his back, had been appointed twenty years ago as the first captain of a small precinct that was a new division of law enforcement. He rose quickly for he knew the right people and how to play politics. STF, for the most part, tolerated him. As long as he didn't interfere too much in how Alistair ran their department as Chief, then they tended to ignore his existence.

"I'll handle James," Alistair promised her. He was not bowing to politics, they needed Dani on this case. "What else did you pick up?"

"Harold and Josephine knew their killer," Dani theorized. "It's the only way they would have ended up where they were."

"I agree," Michael replied. "They were known to not have security if they were meeting with friend or colleagues. Especially if it was an informal meeting."

"We'll have to get copies of their date books," Alistair noted.

"Call my mother," Dani suggested. "She's been helping Lucas go through their offices."

"I will," Alistair agreed. "Let's head back to headquarters, Claire can meet you there."

****

Claire, Dom, and Grant had returned to the precinct just

after 11:30. The general consensus was that Josephine and Harold knew their killer and were not threatened enough by them to bring security. Alistair had put in a call to Helena already to ask Lucas for the date books. Once they had lunch, Dani and Claire headed to get Grunt and then to Central Park for they had a meeting with a Fairy Queen.

It wasn't just any spot they were heading to, they were heading toward the Imagine Mosaic in the Strawberry Fields section of the park. There a large World Tree stood, connecting the world of man to the world of the Fae. Claire had showed it to her when they were freshman in college.

Claire had been learning about summoning the fae and was explaining all the intricacies that went into summoning them. Dani had commented that instead of tricks and spells why not a simple and meaningful display of respect? Within a few second they watched a stunning woman walked up to them with a smile then replied to Dani questions about how witches liked to put on a show. And that began Dani's friendship with the fae.

One that had been further built on respect and trust.

After they parked, they got out of the car. Claire grabbed her bag in case they needed to summon Brianna. Grunt was already dancing about in excitement. He knew where they were going and who they would be meeting. Nodding to a few tour guides as they made their way to the iconic spot they stepped around the tourist and headed to the tree nestled in a grove of bushes and flowers. Grunt laid down in his favorite spot by the tree and watched Dani and Claire get out what they needed. Honey wine was poured onto the roots of the tree then laid out a piece of bread onto the ground.

It was simple and it worked. No invocation, no casting, a simple sign of respect could sometime get you more than the other two. Dani and Claire sat next to Grunt and watched everyone else who was visiting the park. The fae came when they wanted to. Dani found that if you showed them you were patient enough to wait they tended to respect you more.

"And what brings Danika of the Night and Claire of Fire to my tree," a familiar voice inquired after only a few minutes of waiting. "And I see the mighty Grunt has also come."

Grunt was already on his back waiting for the Fairy to pet him. Smiling, Brianna bent down and rubbed the dog's belly before standing straight up to look at Dani and Claire. "We are hearing dark rumors."

Dani closed her eyes for a moment as the weight of what she was about to do hit her. Claire laid a gentle hand on Dani's shoulder as they both stood.

"We are here to discuss what has occurred," Claire stated measuring every word that was spoken.

"Josephine and Harold of House Talon are dead," Dani said her voice raw with emotion. "They were murdered."

Brianna the Wise stared at her as the words slowly sunk in. Her dress that had been emerald green now slowly changed to a pale gray. The flowers that had been woven through her blood red hair closed as grief washed over the Fairy.

"Not them," she whispered. Opening her eyes she looked sadly at Dani and then at Claire. "We had hoped that the young sprite who came to tell us had mixed up the information."

"I wish it was all a mistake as well," Dani answered; she looked out at the park. "There are so many questions with very little answers. I still can't wrap my head around any of it, Brianna."

"Then let us walk," Brianna suggested.

Dani and Claire nodded. They would not have to fear about being overheard by others. Brianna was a fae, where the fae met and gathered meant that those places were deemed politically neutral. In the world of man that meant that parks and bridges were deemed politically neutral for they were governed by the fae. Whatever was spoken at these spots would not leave the spot.

Claire grabbed her messenger bag as Dani took Grunt's

leash. They walked with Grunt trotting alongside them as they took one of the lesser walked path. "Tell me of the scene," Brianna said finally.

"It was at the Algonquin," Claire answered.

"Then it was done by mortal means?" Brianna asked shocked that such a method would kill such a bonded pair.

"Brianna," Dani said. "Whoever is behind this they broke the neutral barrier of the place."

Brianna stopped walking and looked at Dani. Grabbing her arm she pulled her toward one of the trees. "What did you just say?"

Grunt let out a warning bark as Claire went into a fighting stance, Brianna smiled softly at the dog as she let go of Dani's arm. "I am sorry Lord Grunt and too you as well Claire, she is unharmed," Brianna assured him. She then looked at Dani. "I am sorry to you as well, but Danika and Claire, you both must tell me everything. Your thoughts, impressions, and feelings."

Dani nodded. She would not be able to hold back from a Fairy of the Royal Court, not like she could with Claire, Dom and Alastair. "Chaos. Voices from its entire history all slamming together," Dani recalled. "I couldn't find a thread to follow for they were all frayed as if ripped violently apart."

"What of where you found ...them?"

"Coldness, unnatural silence, a sense of being watched."

"How was someone able to break the neutrality of the Algonquin?" Brianna asked no one in particular.

"Nothing about it make sense," Dani sighed.

"And the Wards," Brianna asked Claire.

"Utter chaos as if whatever was used to kill Harold and Josephine ripped through that wards," Claire explained. "It was unlike anything I had seen, even in my studies."

"And you both were able to set them right?"

"Yes," Claire answered. "Dani and I were able to reset

the natural wards. But, Grant and I encountered a charm that was twisted with dark magickk."

"I fear this is only the beginning," Brianna warned. "I fear that you will be in more danger than the others."

Brianna kissed Dani on the forehead and then did the same with Claire. "Be safe my children. I will alert my people and will let you know if we hear anything."

"Thank you," Dani replied.

"Now go home and get some rest before you are needed again," Brianna advised them both. She then bent down and scratched Grunt's ears. "You take care of your mistresses, Lord Grunt."

Chapter 7

They all met up on Wednesday at SPF headquarters in Harlem. Alistair had them in one of the conference rooms away from the main section of the building. Unless another murder happened or the building was on fire, they were not be disturbed. The whiteboards were cleaned, and markers were ready for ideas, notes, and theories.

"Kira had us on speaker phone with Sonja," Claire began.

"Sonja is beside herself, she had talked to Josephine earlier in the day."

"Really?" Alistair said as they all sat up straighter.

"It surprised Kira as well," Grant told them.

"Once she has landed and recovered from Jet lag she will call you Alistair," Claire informed him. "But she told us what occurred."

"According to Sonja, Josephine seemed annoyed when they talked," Dom reported. "Both her and Harold were receiving emails from different email accounts. They were both being told that there was information that the sender had that they would not want to get out."

"We are going to need those emails," Alistair commented.

"Forensics has brought them in according to their intake form," Grant replied as he read over the forensic file. "Two desktops, two laptops, and two cell phones."

"Can you call your buddy?" Alistair asked. He wasn't trusting this case to just anyone.

"He has security clearance so I can if you want," Grant replied.

"Call him," Alistair repeated.

Grant nodded and headed out of the room. "Keep going, Dom," Alistair instructed.

"They ignored them, tried to think of what it could be that they had done that would cause a shit storm," Dom summed up. "They know about scams, especially against our own kind, and using our long life-span against us. And that's what they thought at first."

"So what changed?" Dani asked, "They aren't gullible people. We know they didn't bring their security detail which means they knew who they were meeting with a didn't think security was needed."

"That Sonja didn't know," Dom answered. "All she knows is that they were thinking of legal action but they would make that decision after a casual meeting they were going to that night."

"Okay so we have a possible motive," Alistair said as he wrote it on the board. "And a possible electronic trail to follow."

"And if Grant can convince Tony to help us, he'll find the trail," Mike said knowing who it was that they were talking about.

"What about Jin and Charles?" Alistair asked, referring to the head of the Great Britain and Australia house and the ambassador for the Asian House.

"Charles hasn't spoken to them in a few weeks," Claire answered. "He had been dealing with Lucas because he was in Europe. He reached out to his ambassador and is waiting to hear back. Jin had met with Harold on Friday, so he is a bit shaken up as well. He is sending us the meeting notes to us so we can see what might be in there."

"I spoke to Sam and Maria while Claire and Dani went to talk to Brianna," Alistair stated, referring to the heads for North and South America. "Sam had spoked to Josephine on Friday, he thought she sounded a bit off but would explain it to him after the weekend. Now he wishes that he pushed Josephine for the information."

"And Maria?" Dom asked.

The door to the room opened and Grant came it. "He is doing maintenance on the wards at Never and Dust, he will be done tomorrow and then he can be ours."

"I'll notify the Accord Council to give him access," Alistair replied. Grant nodded and sat back down. "Alright, Maria said that Harold mentioned something to her about someone trying to blackmail them with information from their past. He couldn't think of anything that he or Josie had done that would warrant blackmail. He asked Maria if she could think of anything."

"Could she?" Dom asked.

"All she could think of was that during the Civil War they got into trouble for being part of the Underground Railroad and the council at the time worried it would expose the community."

"But that makes the council look bad for wanting to them to stop," Claire countered.

"The council didn't like there was a risk of exposure," Dom pointed out. "You, Grant, and Dani have only known us as being out. The council came down hard on anyone if there was a hint of exposure. There was fear that another Spanish Inquisition or Witch Hunt could occur if we were outed."

"So what if the black mail isn't about Josie and Harold specifically but about the Council?" Dani asked. They all looked at her. "I'm sure they were constantly driving the council nuts because they have never been able to ignore injustices."

"Then of all the Heads, why contact them?" Mike asked.

It was Claire that spoke. "Harold is a judge on the Court. He's the only head that is."

"And Josie is part of the charity end of the Council," Dom replied.

"So is my mom," Dani answered. "But they are the only heads that are truly joint heads and both have active roles on the Council."

They were all quiet for a moment. "If Dani's theory is accurate than this could be a larger issue than just blackmail that ends in murder," Alistair warned them.

Dani looked at Claire. "It fits with the warning from Brianna."

"And why she kissed both our foreheads," Claire replied.

"You both got kissed by a Fairy Queen?" Dom asked. "That explains the hint of nature to you both."

Alistair looked at them all. "What's the deal?"

"A kiss on the forehead from any fae is away of giving

protection, a predator will smell the scent and know that they know a fae. And in this case, not just a regular fae, but Brianna the Wise," Grant explained. "But Brianna is royalty so they don't just kiss foreheads for minor situations. If she placed a kiss on both of them then it's because she is fearful of severe harm may come to them."

"So what did Brianna the Wise say," Dom inquired.

"That she fears something big is coming, that Josie and Harold's death's are just the beginning," Dani replied. "And, her gown changed to gray when we told her. Grunt could smell when the fear overcame her."

"I could feel the change in her magick," Claire commented.

"She was going to alert her people and will pass on any information to us," Dani added.

"What does the Forensic report say?" Alistair asked. He was hoping that the Fae would have more information but it seemed like the rest of their community, everyone was in shock.

"They are still waiting on an official report of the poison but as of right now it doesn't match anything they have ever seen," Grant answered. "Which matches what Claire and Tabby have both said. Nessa makes note that both magick, and dark magick, was used on the bodies. She also noted that the magick used has not been taught in a few generations."

"So we're talking the Black Grimoires," Dani replied. "And those are in our most secure vault at the archives. Access is extremely restricted to those."

"How restricted?" Michael asked. He never really needed to access the archives, if the team needed something then they went through Dani.

"You need the Pantheon to sign off on it," Claire and Grant answered at the same time. Claire then took over. "Aunt Tabby had to write an official statement about my unique ability to allow me access to the tome on poisons. I also had to demonstrate my talents to the Pantheon High Council to show that what she said was true. It's not easy."

"Then once we get the approval we take a week to assure it's authentic," Dani took over. "Once it's authenticated, an appointment is set up, the archives is closed for the appointment and all the head Archivists are there and the tomes don't leave the restricted level. We take fingerprints, they sign a log, and then do an electronic signature."

"So it's not easy," Alistair surmised.

"Most requests don't even make it to the Pantheon because of all the steps," Claire confided.

"Has Vynessa identified the dark magick that has been used?" Alistair asked.

"Her notes state that it was rushed it seams and the user was new to the spell," Grant read over what had been written. "She believes he was trying some type of soul spell or a magick stealing spell but she's not sure which."

"Both of those are a life sentence in prison," Claire whistled. "Just toying with them is enough to be put away for ever."

"Which means someone has nothing to loose," Grant replied.

"Now, can only a witch use dark magick?" Mike asked.

"That's why it's dark, because anyone could use it," Grant answered. "For a non-witch all it will take is blood."

"What about a witch?" Alistair asked.

"Their power will be marked," Claire said. "Which

means their coven, their mentor, their community will know."

"This is all insane," Michael said. "What the hell is going on?"

"We are going to find out," Alistair said. "But I fear what is it."

* * * *

Dani was laying next to Lucas on the bed, she was going over what they had talked about at the precinct earlier. Alistair had told her it would be okay, hoping that Lucas might know something that could help them unlock something. Lucas lay on his back with an arm draped over his eyes. Grunt lay between the two of them.

"They never mentioned anything about emails to me or that someone might be trying to blackmail me," Lucas finally said as he sat up so he was leaning against the wall. He scratched Grunt's ears.

"Would they have told you?" Dani asked as she watched him. Like many vampires, he was so still when he was laying down. The rise of the chest was not constant, they didn't just move for the sake of moving. There was a calmness to it, Dani found.

"I don't know," Lucas admitted. He smiled sadly at her as he brushed one of her curls. "I want to say that if it was a serious threat then dad would have told me because he would have wanted to warn me. But I could see them not saying anything because they wouldn't want to worry me."

"She never mentioned a word to mom," Dani told Lucas.

Lucas turned so that he could look at Dani better. "That's odd."

"I thought so too," Dani agreed.

They were both quiet for a moment. Lucas was the first to speak. "That makes me think she was worried," Lucas stated. "Mom would know that if she told Helena or me about what was going one of us would have demanded to go or to take Nick if neither of us could go."

"So you don't think they met with someone they trusted?"

"No, I really don't. If they trusted the person they would have told me or Helena. I think they told the other Heads just in the event something happened. But Helena and I were kept out of the loop to protect us or something like that."

"Al said the same thing," Dani replied. Lucas arched an eyebrow. "He said that if it was nothing then either no one would know or Helena would have known every detail. And you would have flown in early if you were aware of what was happening."

"His insight has always been amazing," Lucas said.

Dani traced part of a scar on his wrist that his watch didn't hide. She was the only person that he ever let touch his scars, or had even seen most of them. "Dom said something to me when we were heading out," Dani began.

Lucas groaned. "Why am I worried about what he said to you. I swear the number of people I have been with is not as large as he told you."

Dani couldn't help but laugh at that. "No, it was nothing like that," she assured him. "He pulled me aside because he wanted to tell me that at first he was furious with me that I told you about your parents before he did. But that telling you before you landed had been smart because when he picked you up you were prepared for it."

"Prepared isn't the word I would use," Lucas commented.

"Lucas, I didn't tell you."

Lucas let out a long sigh this time as he pulled Dani closer to him. He kissed the top of her head before he said a word. "The night you found them, it was after four in the morning in Norway. I had only just gone to bed after a farewell gala thrown in my behalf. I first thought it was a dream as I slipped into my death sleep. It was chaotic, just impressions, flashes of color, and voices overlapping each other. Then I felt this utter anguish at whatever was being seen. It felt so real, so intense, then I felt you all around me. I realized I was feeling whatever you were, that you were at a crime scene, that it filled you with such intense grief and horror. I smelled the hint of lavender and my father's aftershave. I knew when you knew. When I felt you begin to panic, your emotions begin to loose control, I felt like I had to be calm."

"Lucas..."

He leaned forward and kissed her. "Don't apologize," he whispered resting his forehead against hers. "This link between us, it's a gift. Yes, it let me know before I was told, but it also lets me see what you see, let me help you when you feel ready to splinter into a million pieces."

"If Marcus learns about it before we're ready, you'll be a target," Dani warned him.

"Which is why we won't let him know until we are ready for him."

"That might be sooner than we planned," Dani admitted.

"What do you mean?"

"My senses are getting stronger, which means my ability is getting more intense," Dani explained. "Tabby doesn't think it would be wise to wait until I'm 30 to do the Oath."

"Honestly the sooner we have you Oathed to any house that isn't Marcus, the easier I'll sleep."

"I know the house I want to Oath too," Dani told him, biting her lip nervously.

"Dan," Lucas said cautiously as he realized what she was going to say. He wanted her to feel no pressure. "I want you to be sure. Oathing to another house is a huge deal."

"And they are all going to go nuts when they learn about our Bond anyway," Dani pointed out. She smiled at him, laying a hand against his cool cheek. "Besides, your's has always been a second home for me. Might as well make it official."

Lucas pulled her close to him so he could just hold her. There was a knock on the door, then it slowly opened to Claire with her hand covering her eyes.

"I'm coming in, so whatever is going on here just stop and make sure you are clothed," Claire said loudly.

Dani rolled her eyes at Claire then threw a sock at her. "We're decent," Dani informed her.

"Thank the gods," Claire said as she uncovered her eyes. She then joined them on the bed. "Dom called. He's got re-porters stationed at his building thinking that Lucas is there. He did some bristling at them, but is happy they were there and not here."

"That is good news," Lucas agreed as they made room for Claire. "You guys only have to put up with me a few more days. Once the Memorial service is over, I can stay at one of the rentals we have."

"Or you could just stay here," Claire pointed out. She and Dani had talked about it, Claire had been the one to bring it up first. "I mean I know it's not fitting for a Vampire of your stature and you know we can offer you our specialty breakfast of Cockroach cereal."

"Cockroach cereal?" Lucas inquired raising an eyebrow.

"It's what I tell Alexi we eat when we run low on money," Dani told him.

Lucas had to laugh at the face Alexius must make whenever Dani says that. He then looked at the two women. "You know it means a lot of security, an extra body, me intruding on Dani and Claire time. Or trying not to intrude because we all know that is sacred."

"See this is why I like him the best of all the others," Claire said.

"Ignore her," Dani told Lucas, rolling her eyes. "And we've talked about and we know what it means having a Head live here. But it makes sense. Tabby has let you into the wards, Grunt as accepted you into our little pack. Just think about it."

"I will."

The three of them laid there with Grunt snoring. "You realize how weird this is," Claire stated. "I'm willing sharing a bed with a dude."

"It's my bed, first off, and second you just climbed on here," Dani pointed out. "Which means you have to deal with whoever is in the bed with me."

"Grunt," Lucas said to the dog. "Are they always like this?"

Grunt just licked his hand then laid his head on Lucas' knee. "And this is the first person that Grunt has ever allowed in bed with you that wasn't me," Claire realized.

"You didn't realize that on the first night?" Dani inquired.

"Why what does he do normally?" Lucas asked.

"He will lay directly between us with his legs stretched out so there is no touching what so ever," Dani informed him. "Then if the other person tries to get close to me, he will growl at them."

"The rare times she allows someone to come back here, he usually sleeps with me or whines pathetically outside her door until she either lets him in or kicks the persons out," Claire added. Dani flipped her off, causing Lucas to laugh.

"Grunt, I'm glad you approve," Lucas said as he scratched the dog's ears. He was rewarded with a lick.

Chapter 8

Alistair sat at his desk while the Commissioner of Strate-
gic Task Force walked around his office touching his pictures
and things. James wore a tailored suit of light summer material.
As usually he looked like he stepped off the cover of GQ and not
like a police official. The times that he did visit the precinct, he
rarely talked with the men and women that made up STF. Instead he did what he had to do then left as quickly as he could.
Which is why pop-in's were rare and often politically motivated.

"Where are you with the case?" James asked as he studied a picture of the Clarence Pack, the pack that Alistair was in charge of.

"The Algonquin is back to normal, we released the room back to them yesterday after one final sweep by my team and forensics," Alistair informed him. "We have a few theories as to why the victims would be there at the time."

"And the method of killing?"

"Poison," Alistair commented leaving out the magick part. "We are waiting on the report on what the poison contains."

"I thought Jensen was supposed to be able to detect poison and its anti-dote?"

"She is, but this one is so rare that it's not even in the Coven's records," Alistair explained. "We are waiting on a sign-off from the Accords to access the black tomes, but until that and the report is in we are still clueless into how the poison works and how it kills."

"Motives?"

"It looks like a blackmail scheme," Alistair replied. "Along the lines of: I have information on something you did that you have probably forgotten, give me money, or I'll expose you."

"I don't see Harold or Josephine falling for such a scheme," James admitted.

"Which is why we're thinking they learned who it was and perhaps confronted them," Alistair suggested. "Lucas has given permission for us to go over all of his parent's tech devices to see if we can find out more."

"Do you think there will be more or is this isolated?"

"I think we are dealing with a meticulous mind that loves ceremony and tricks," Alistair answered. "I want to hope this was a one time deal but the amount of work that went into luring them there, I think we'll see more."

James nodded as he sat in one of the chairs for guests. "Danika Jospeh," James said. "How does she fit into the case?"

And that was why he was here, Marcus made the call he had threatened. "Vital," Alistair answered. "If she was not with us, we might still not know who the victims were, that gave us two days to gather info before we went to the press. Allowing us vital time we might not have had."

"Would Claire and Grant have been able to close the

Wards without her?" James inquired.

"No," Alistair answered. "The Algonquin would be still closed if Dani was not part of balancing the wards again."

"I see," James said with a sigh. "If she was to be removed from the case?"

"It would weaken a solid team and take longer to solve," Alistair replied. "I'm guessing Marcus made a phone call."

"Nothing get's past you," James commented. "He is concerned for the welfare of his youngest child working this violent crime."

"And where was his concern when she was off chasing down a Changeling a few years back?"

James held up a hand to let Alistair know he understood. "All I promised was that I would talk to you about her importance," James assured him. "I did warn him that removing her from this case was not realistic due to her how vital she is to the team and because she would see it through no matter if she was on or off the team."

"If you have to tell him anything, tell him that if there is another crime scene, I will ensure she is well protected, that her time at the scene will be minimum," Alistair suggested.

"Thank you for understanding, I know you hate when I have to come in here and ask these stupid questions for politician reasons," James said as he got up.

"Better you dealing with it than me," Alistair admitted. "I hate politics."

"Yet you lead a pack," James said as they walked to the door.

"And ask any of them and they will tell you that I hate politics and get cranky when they force it on me," Alistair replied.

James chuckled. "Copies of lab reports when you get them?"

"Vynessa already has you on the list of who gets copy," Alistair promised him.

"Good, now I will leave you to run the pack," James replied. He went to leave then stopped turning to look at Alistair. "I hope you're wrong though about there being more. I don't think you are, but I do hope that you are."

"So do I, James," Alistair said.

Saluting each other, James headed out towards the lobby. Dom came out of the team office and raised an eyebrow. "Dani?"

"Marcus made good on his threat," Alistair answered. "It didn't work. If you believe James, he already warned Marcus of that."

"And if you don't believe him?"

"Then he is going to be spinning a very good tale on why Dani is still part of Team A," Alistair replied. "What's up?"

"Tech thinks they might have the emails that Harold and Josephine received," Dom said. "They're sending them to us as we speak."

"Tony should be arriving tomorrow," Alistair said. "I'm going to have us all meet up there so we can go over everything with the archivist so they know what we are looking for."

"I'll pass the information on."

"Dom, how is Lucas doing?"

"I don't think it's hit him yet, I don't think it will until after the memorial," Dom confessed. "He was never supposed to be the Heir, he always figured he'd be an advisor or the ambassador living in their place in Norway or Germany. And now having it so brutally thrown at him, I don't know."

"Tell him that there is no time limit on grieving," Alistair replied.

"I will," Dom promised. "You know, people assume vampires are chill with death because we live 'forever', because we've seen it happen so many times. But it never gets easier, it never isn't numbing."

"I think that anyone who is immune to death is the true monster," Alistair agreed.

Dom felt his phone vibrate. He took it out of his pocket, when he glanced at the message that had come in he just stared at it.

"What's wrong?" Alistair asked knowing that look.

"Nick just sent a text to me, Claire, Micheal, Grant, and Dani," Dom answered. "He wants us to meet him at *Never and Dust*."

"Why?"

"I think we might have stirred a hornet's nest by going to the heads," Dom replied.

"Good," Alistair answered.

* * * *

Never and Dust was a bar situated at the foot of the Brooklyn Bridge. The bar was run by a goblin, a leprechaun, and a banshee and was one of the few places that was only open to the supernatural. Because it was run by the Fae, it meant whatever secrets were discussed here could not be overheard by others. If Nicholi wanted to meet there it meant he had something big to tell them. Something he didn't want anyone else to overhear.

It was close to one o'clock by the time they made it to the popular bar. It was always open and no matter the hour people were always inside. Being one of the only places in the city that only catered to the Supernatural world it was the one spot they could all be themselves. Dom opened the door, they all felt the pull of magick as they entered the place. If they had been uninvited mortals they would have been shoved back outside by the spell. Claire and Grant were already at a booth in the back cor-

ner. Nicholi was with them, he spotted Dani and waved them

over.

Gloria, the Banshee and part owner, came over to take

their order. They all placed orders of hamburgers and fries.

Nicholi and Dom ordered synthetic blood instead of burgers.

Dani knew that her brother would steal some of her fries and ask

for a bite from a burger. While vampires didn't need to eat to

survive they would eat food from time to time. Nicholi once ex-

plained that it did benefit them to a degree, allowing them to go

longer between blood but they had to be careful with how much

of a food they ate.

"Bartram was really there?" Nicholi asked as soon as

Gloria left the table.

"Marcus wasn't happy about it," Dani stated.

Michael and Nicholi looked at each other for a moment.

It was Dom who spoke. "Alright what the hell is going on?"

Dom demanded.

"It's not an easy explanation," Nicholi stated.

"Look, we know whatever it is that you need to tell us is bad," Dani assured him. "Otherwise you wouldn't request to meet us here."

Michael nodded at Nicholi. "Alright," Nicholi began. "Don't yell at Michael until you hear all of this. This started about twenty four years ago."

Dani sat up straight thinking she heard it wrong. "If this has to deal with my parents then that's impossible, their killer was caught," Dani stated.

"Just let me explain then you can all ask questions and yell when I'm done," Nicholi pleaded. "I need to explain some things that you might not know. Prior to your parent's murder, things were a bit different for House Joseph. Mom and Marcus pretty much co-ruled like Josephine and Harold. Marcus dealt with the financial and business end of it while mom dealt with our people."

"I remember that," Dom recalled. "I wasn't here often, spending most of my time in Norway, but I recall Helena being more prominent."

"She was," Niccholi agreed. He took a sip of his drink before beginning. "Shit I need stronger stuff."

"That bad," Dom inquired.

"This could bring down our world," Nicholi replied.

"Well, shit," Dom answered. He waved Gloria over. "Blood laced whiskey and beers for the rest."

"I'll seal you off as well," Gloria replied.

They felt the magick she erected around them. All memory of them being there would be erased, the booth would look empty with a reserved sign on the table. Only Gloria would be able to enter the bubble she erected.

"Dani's parents were the start," Nicholi explained. He held up a hand before Dani could interrupt him. "I know it was a burglary gone wrong. They caught the guy two days later strung out on drugs. You were given to Helena and Marcus because your mother was mom's niece. She was next of kin."

"It wasn't a burglary gone wrong," Dani said. They all looked at her. "This doesn't leave the table right?"

They all nodded. "Mom, Aunt Tabby, and Lucas knows," Dani began. "I've been having dreams. The memories from that night are more vivid. Mom had always told me not to tell anyone about the figure I saw in the kitchen, she feared it would put me in danger."

"Well shit, that makes this easier," Nicholi stated. "Because Alistair was never happy with the theory either."

"Alistair began digging into it more," Michael took over. "Something about the case didn't sit well with him. But he couldn't do it publicly because everyone thought it was over. And at the time GQ was his captain."

"He found something," Claire realized.

"A pattern," Michael answered. "Minor vampires were killed in home invasions and two or three days later an addict would appear with the information only a killer would know. No one caught on because they were spread out over the east coast. And the killer was always caught."

"But Alistair saw a pattern," Dom replied.

"So how does this tie into what's going on?" Dani asked, wanting to keep things on track.

"This is where it get's tricky," Nicholi admitted. "Like I said, it starts with the deaths of Dani's parents. No one knows what Dani saw that night, if she saw the murders, or if she saw nothing. Mom took her to our place in Istanbul for a few months, to get her away from the media attention, allow her to heal, and be seen by specialists. When she came back Marcus had called us all back to the City. He thought it would be best for Dani to have a strong family support. Sayad made the deal that during the school year he would live in Cambridge but come home on breaks. We all thought it was temporary."

"But it wasn't," Grant stated.

"It was a slow take-over," Nicholi admitted. "Alexius became in charge of our Middle Eastern holding, I became in charge of our East Coast holdings, Bartram was to be Alexius and mine's assistant, and Sayad taught. It was all what you would expect of a dynasty, but it came with strings. Mom focused so much of her time on Dani that Marcus conveniently picked up her duties taking over more and more control."

"A slow take over," Dom repeated. "One that is well-planned so that no one suspects a thing."

"One that went under the radar until Dani graduated high school and went to college," Nick answered.

"What happened then?" Claire asked.

"Murmurs, rumors, cautious warnings," Nicholi stated. Gloria came through with their drinks and food. "We all figured that slowly things would go back to how they were, instead Marcus became more strict with not just us but the House in general. You had to talk to him if you wanted to move, he began running it like we were in feudal system. So a year ago Michael and I were approached by the other Heads as well as the council and asked to look into what was going on."

"So what is going on?" Dani asked confused.

"On paper, nothing," Nicholi replied. "There is nothing but conspiracy theories about Dad and Alexius trying to take over the Houses or that they are embezzling House funds into Ponzi schemes."

"I've heard those rumors," Dom admitted.

"And didn't share?" Claire noted folding her arms across her chest.

"I didn't think I needed to."

"Anyway," Nicholi continued. "Michael approached Alistair who gave him the file of the murders."

"Only it's grown over the last two decades," Michael

added. "Someone is covering up these murders."

"It's not just the murders," Nicholi went on. "Shortly after Dani went through the rite to see if she was Vampire or Witch, Marcus starts making some 'odd' decisions. Bartram gets a larger share in our holdings, instead of assisting us, he now has a say in what goes on. Mom now has an allowance and is under constant watch. He installs surveillance cameras in all the public rooms. We have armed guards for the grounds, drivers to take us places."

"Alright so he becomes paranoid," Claire admitted. "Why?"

"Because when I go through the Blood Oath ritual the elders will see my memories," Dani realized. "Even the one's I don't recall."

"Marcus is worried about something that these memories might reveal," Nicholi theorized. "That it might shatter the cover up, place you in danger."

"And Bartram?" Dom asked.

"We think he's blackmailing Marcus," Nicholi admitted. "That he might have figured out the murders and is using that to be more prominent in our affairs."

"That's a lot of what if's," Dani stated.

"The night Harold and Josephine were killed Dad, Alexius, and Bartram all had meetings," Nicholi replied.

"That's family dinner night," Dani argued.

"Yes, but think carefully of that night," Nicholi told her.

Dani nodded and carefully brought back to the night. Vampires learned over the years how to recall even the smallest of memories for centuries ago. It took decades to master.

"I was the last to arrive," Dani replied. "Dad and Alexius were already arguing when I arrived.

"Yes because the Greek Pantheon contacted dad about how badly Alexius and Bartram screwed up overseas," Nicholi answered. "I arrived as Marcus hung up the phone. His eyes were red. And Bartram thought it was all hysterical."

"So how does this tie into Josephine and Harold?" Dom asked. "Look, the three are complete assholes, but I don't see them killing those two."

"I think whatever they are hiding killed Josephine and Harold," Nick explained. "I think this is only the beginning. I think that Marcus is fearful of whatever it is that Dani might re-member, I think Bartram is going to use his distraction for his own depravity, and Alexius is going to try to hide all the dirty laundry."

"You said that Bartram is blackmailing Marcus," Grant recalled. "How do you know?"

"Marcus never puts up with Bartram's antics, I can't tell you how many times he has been cut out of the estate, lost his al-lowance, or kicked out of all our properties," Nicholi began. "But over the last decade, he's turned his back to everything that Bartram has done."

"Nick," Dani sighed.

"I know it's all circumstantial," Nicholi said. "I get it. Hearing me talk about, I know how it all sounds. But something is going on. The closer we get to Dani being of age to take her Oath the edgier Marcus becomes. He dragged Alexius from the dinner table Saturday over him mentioning Dani taking the oath now."

"We need evidence," Dom said.

"Then we have Tony look for it while he's helping us out," Michael suggested. They all looked at him. "Look, the killings that are similar to Dani's parent's, they line up with times that Bartram were in that area. We know that Harold and Josephine got an email about blackmail."

"No one would be able to know we are doing this," Dani warned. "If Marcus got wind, we will all be dead."

"And that has been part of the problem," Nicholi admitted. "But you guys will have the resources that we didn't."

"This could create a whole separate shit storm," Dom stated. "With your House at the center of it."

"But if we're right, then it could get us closer to a killer," Nicholi replied.

Chapter 9

Several hours later, Lucas pulled his motorcycle into a spot near the entrance to the Strawberry Fields section of Central Park. It was near where he was so when Dom called saying no one could get a hold of Dani, Lucas had a feeling he knew where she was. Instead of rushing to where she would be, knowing she needed time, he finished what he needed to do for his parent's memorial. He knew she wasn't in danger and that she also need-ed some time to herself. Heading through the gates, Lucas walked past the tourists snapping pictures of the Imagine mosaic. He headed for the large oak tree set off from the memorial.

Grunt noticed him first, stretching before clamoring over to Lucas for an ear scratch. Lucas smiled as he crouched down to give him a good rub down. When he stood up he headed over to the tree then sat down next to Dani. She had changed into jeans and a Volbeat t-shirt. Neither said anything, instead they just sat there and watched people.

"I had this recurring nightmare when I was younger," Dani began not even looking at Lucas. "My child therapists and Helena told me I was mixing things up in my head. That with everything that had happened my brain squished things together."

"The brain has a way of protecting us from things we don't know," Lucas replied.

Dani looked over at him. "Even if it means protecting a killer?"

Lucas didn't know what to say, he looked at her and saw so much pain and confusion in her eyes. "Everyone thought I was afraid of Marcus because he was a large man, and well, a bit intimidating," Dani recalled.

"You're wondering if it's more than that," Lucas realized. Dani didn't talk much about the night her parent's were killed.

She had been five at the time, and it shattered her world.

"In my nightmare he is standing in the kitchen of the farmhouse I lived in," Dani replied. "He was talking to my parents about something. Then he looks at the door where I'm standing and smiles. It's not a friendly smile but one that can chill you to the bones. He says 'what a pretty little girl, what a shame'. Then a red cloud fills the room and I don't remember anything else."

"Shit, Dani," Lucas whispered.

"Three people knew about the dream: Helena, my therapist, and Josie."

"You didn't kill my mother," Lucas informed her as he turned so she could look him in the eyes. "What happened to my parents, that wasn't you. That wasn't because of a memory that you were told to forget. A monster chose to do that, they chose to kill them."

"But…"

"No," Lucas said softly. He laid a hand on her cheek staring into her eyes. "We will figure this shit out. We will figure out what the hell Marcus is up to and who did that to my parents, and if you want we will figure out how to unlock your memories. But you need to understand that you are not responsible for any of this."

Dani let out a sigh as she leaned against him, she felt his sincerity, his grief, and his urge to protect her. "I wanted to come straight to you," Dani admitted. "After the lunch meeting. I was on the way to your parent's office then I realized how '90's rom-com that was. So I went home, grabbed Grunt, and we came here."

"Dom filled me in," Lucas told her. "With Nick's help. You should text both of them, they are freaking out that you won't answer either of them."

Dani rolled her eyes as she leaned against the tree. "Lucas, what are we going to do?"

"That's up to you," Lucas answered. "How do you want to do this?"

"We need to focus on the now," Dani realized. "Which is your parent's killing. But at the same time we do need to look into these other killings that have occurred. See if there's a connection or if it's nothing at all."

"Maybe you can split up, have two team members work on cold cases and two work on the current," Lucas suggested.

"We'll have to if we don't want people knowing what we're doing," Dani admitted. She let out a long sigh. "I need to talk to Tabby, find out how we can unlock my memory."

"Then you have a plan," Lucas told her.

"First we need to get through tomorrow," Dani sighed.

Lucas closed against the wave of grief that came over him. He felt Dani lean against him, felt her head lay against his chest as she ran a hand up his arm. Her strength overwhelmed him at times, it helped keep him from drowning in his grief.

"Stand with me," Lucas asked as he kissed her forehead. "Tomorrow, stand with me."

"We won't be hiding anymore," Dani warned him. Though part of her was thrilled at the idea of the world knowing that Lucas was hers.

"I think I want the world to know right now that if they think of messing with you it means dealing with me," Lucas answered.

"So it's to protect me," Dani replied trying not to sound

upset.

"You can protect yourself," Lucas said as he kissed her lightly. "I need you there, I'm not going to be able to do this on my own. You are this beacon, I need that right now."

"Alright." Dani saw the surprise in his eyes when she agreed. "You realize hiding the bond is going to be a lot harder after tomorrow."

"Right now the bond is the only thing that does not terrify me," Lucas admitted. "You focus on the case and I'll try and find more information on our situation."

Chapter 10

The Haupt Conservatory at the New York Botanical Garden was closed for a private event. Lucas stood at the entrance of the stunning victorian styled structure with Dani at his side. He wore a black suit, with a white shirt, and deep blue tie. On his tie was a tie pin with his House's seal on it. On his right ring finger he wore the House signet ring, the same one his father wore for special events. Only Dani knew that around his neck he wore a chain with his parent's wedding bands on them. Vynessa had given them to her last night, Dani had Tabby bless a chain with them on it before she had given them to Lucas.

Dani wore a deep navy blue A-line dress that fell to her knees, a short black cardigan covered her shoulders. Her dark hair was swept up in a french twist where she wore her pearl earrings her mother had gotten her for when she graduated college. She also wore the double strand of pearls that Josephine had given her as a twenty first birthday present. Most of House Talon had already arrived for they held a private memorial for just their House. Dani was sure most would not want her there but they had welcomed her with warm hugs and thanking her for being there for Lucas.

Dani felt herself tense when she recognized the limo that rolled up to the front. Lucas took her hand in his as the doors of the car opened. Marcus was the first to be let out followed by Helena. They were followed by Nick, Sayad, and Bartram. Another limo was pulling up, Alexius got out with his wife Antonia. Together they approached the doors where Lucas and Dani stood.

"Our condolences," Marcus stated as he took Lucas' hand in his.

"The support from your wife and daughter have been a true help through this time," Lucas replied.

"It is their duty to aid when there is need," Marcus answered as he narrowed his eyes at Dani.

Helena stepped up giving Lucas a tight hug. "Remember, today is for your grief. Do not play to the crowd."

"Thank you," Lucas said kissing her on the cheek. "Dom is inside and will escort you to your row."

Marcus took Helena's arm leading her inside. Bartram followed without looking at Dani while Nick and Sayad both gave their respect. Alexius approached them taking a long look at Dani's dress.

"Wearing their colors I see," Alexius commented.

"We're all wearing their colors," Dani stated.

"Ignore him," Antonia suggested as she hugged Dani. "Be careful," Antonia whispered in her ear.

"Thank you," Dani replied.

"We will talk about this," Alexius informed Lucas before he was pulled inside.

Dani ignored her brother as another limo pulled up. It took thirty minutes before the heads or representatives were greeted and presented inside. Once the last guest arrived Lucas took Dani's hand and they headed into the conservatory. Both ignored the murmurs as they walked up the aisle that had been created by chairs to where Tabby stood with a minister.

"I ask all to rise for a blessing," Tabby instructed. She rested a hand on the urn that sat on the altar. "May the air carry your spirit gently. May the fire release your soul.

"May the water of life wash you clean of pain, sorrow, and suffering. May the earth receive you. May the wheel turn again and bring you to rebirth."

The audience recited the simple prayer. When they were done, Tabby smiled softly on the crowd. "I usually enjoy moments when our community shows up to support each other," Tabby began. "The ties we have shared over the centuries. Joy and sorrow. And here we are gathered to celebrate two lives that have touched all of us. Lucas asked if myself and my brother Ralph would speak today. He knew his father would want a Christian send off and Ralph was the only Christian minister that Harold trusted."

Ralph took his sister's spot. "I met Harold when I was eighteen years old," Ralph began. "My ability with magick was weak, yet I came from a long line of powerful one's. Harold often counseled with Tab's and my parents. He was always kind, always willing to get to know people. But this day was when I truly saw who he was as a person. He was the reason I became a minister."

There was a few murmurs. "When you are raised around witches you learn that all faiths are represented: Christians, Jews, Muslims, Hindu. We cover all walks of life. I was conflicted because of my beliefs. Harold sat down next to me on our front stoop, he told me about watching the Christians burn his people, of Jews being forced into hiding. I thought he was going to tell me to find a different path. Instead he told me to be better than the past. To embrace the good and the bad, to teach wisdom, spirituality, to comfort those who are lost. Harold had seen so much hate but he did not hate."

Ralph then took out his worn bible and recited the Lord Prayers. He then closed his eyes laying a hand on the urn. "For as much as it has pleased Almighty God to remove from the world the soul of our brother, we lay his body here to rest awhile, then to be buried in the ground, then shall the dust return to dust as it was, but the spirit returns to God who gave it."

When he finished Tabby took to the podium again. "Lucas provided something to say," Tabby stated. "At first I was going to read it but instead he has decided to read it himself."

She stepped back for Lucas to take the podium. Tabby hugged him quickly before sitting next to her brother.

Lucas took a deep breath. "To answer the question that you are asking yourself, there is a reason for the one urn," he began. "My parent's came into this world as two separate people. They lived many years without the other. It wasn't until they were both one hundred did they meet each other. My mother was a healer who aiding the injured on a battlefield. She found my father near death, she knew what he was, risking revealing herself, she hid him so that she could heal him. From that moment she would say they become one."

Lucas paused to take a breath. He looked back at Dani who gave him a reassuring smile. "Their love was enduring, it never wavered. They buried six children and seven grandchildren, yet they never faltered. When I would feel the burden that fell on me of being their only surviving heir, my mother would lay a hand on my shoulder and tell me that there is a reason for everything. We might not agree with the reason, not see its purpose, but someday we will find why this horrible thing happened. Then she would make me tea and everything would be alright.

"I hope she's right. I hope I can look back one day and see what she meant. But right now I can't. Right now I am burying my parents, my only family. They are the last of my bloodline, my last connection to those who came before me. As creatures of the night, we walk a path filled with the past yet focus on the now, on what will be. I see the past clearly, I see my childhood filled with love. The present is filled with pain and grief. It is the future that scares. Not because I will walk it alone. I fear the future because of what was done to my parents, of what we have all ignored. There is a threat in this community, it didn't just arrive with the death of my parents. It has been here, lurking in the corners."

People shifted in their chairs, looking uneasy. Lucas noted that Marcus looked ready to explode. So he continued. "You are now looking at me as if the grief has driven me crazy. But let me explain the one urn now. You want me to say there is one urn because like their love they were one being, that I had their ashes mixed together. But I can't say that. Their bodies were contaminated by a poison so strong and unknown that they had to be disposed in a way that would prevent a hazardous situation. So this one urn that should share the ashes of my parents is empty."

Shock went through the room as gasps filled the silence. Lucas said nothing as he went back to his seat. After that Tabby and Frank finished the memorial services. When it was over the guests were ushered into a different hall for food and drinks.

Dom walked over to where Lucas stood with Dani. The cocktail hour was somber, the words that he had spoken were sitting heavy on many. Dom wanted to punch Lucas not just for having Dani up there with him but also because of his speech. Yet at the same time he was proud of Lucas

"Warning would have been nice," Dom stated. He took the champagne flute that was offered to him.

"You would have told me no," Lucas replied. He looked around the conservatory as guests mingled. "I had to be the one to do this."

Dom hated that Lucas was right. "You just put a target on

yourself and on Dani."

"I've had a target on me for twenty four years," Dani reminded him.

"So you knew about this?" Dom asked her.

"I did," Dani answered.

"And you agreed?"

"I did," Dani repeated.

Dom ran a hand over his bald head. "Next time let me know, I can't protect either of you if I don't know what you are planning."

Lucas watched him storm away. "That went better," Lucas admitted.

"It did," Dani agreed. "Go talk to Maria and Jonathan. I'll go talk to my mom."

"Alright," Lucas answered. Maria and Jonathan the dual heads for North and Central America. "Dani, thanks."

She rolled her eyes at him as she headed to where her mom was talking. A cold hand grabbed her arm and pulled her toward one of the more private corners. She looked up at Bartram who was smiling down at her in a creepy way.

"And they always say I'm the problem child," Bartram drawled as he studied Dani closely. "But here you are. Standing beside the Heir to House Talon, standing beside him after his daring speech."

"Bartram, what do you want?" Dani asked trying to conceal her annoyance.

"Just to see how my dear little mouse is doing," Bartram said using the old nickname he had for her when she was small. "Who would have thought that the little thing dad brought home would actually turn into a classic beauty."

"Bartram, I want to talk to mom, can I go now?" Dani asked.

"For now," Bartram answered.

Dani didn't even look back at him as she headed to where Helena stood, she could feel Bartram watching her though. Helena laid a hand gently on Dani's arm.

"Are you alright?" Helena asked quietly.

"No," Dani answered.

Helena smiled politely as someone walked past them. "I was told the rose garden is stunning, shall we take a look darling," Helena inquired.

"That would be wonderful," Dani agreed.

They headed toward the doors that led to the rose garden, a guard opened the door for them. The garden was said to have every type of rose known to man. Due to the bright lights and the glass enclosure there wasn't as many people out here. Helena led Dani to a more quiet corner.

"What is it?" Helena asked.

"When I have been a the scenes for this case, I felt this feeling of being watched," Dani tried to explain. "I knew the person wasn't really there but it felt like their presence was. Like he left a part of himself at the scene."

"Perhaps he did," Helena suggested. "What the killer did, it broke every law and rule we have. It would make sense that it cost him something in return."

"I felt it here," Dani stated.

Helena stared at her as comprehension dawned on her. "You're sure?"

"It's never happened before."

Helena took Dani's hands in hers, she felt her daughter's

fears. For she had been an empath before turning, making her powers stronger what she became a vampire. Then she felt a calmness wash over Dani as the door to the garden opened. Lucas walked out with Dom behind him. Helena smiled softly at her daughter then stood up when Lucas joined them.

"Are you alright?" Helena asked Lucas. "And that is a stupid question."

"It's fine, Helena," Lucas assured her. "I just needed room to breathe."

"Then take all the time you need," Helena informed him.

"Helena, was I right in my speech?"

"Yes," Helena told him. "It was a shock to many, something that most would not do. You broke protocol at such functions. So that is going to ruffle feathers."

Lucas went to talk but Helena went on. "You are not your parents, you are not Marcus, or any of the other leaders. You are Lucas Talon, so be yourself. Don't try to be what they want you to be. Be the leader you think you can be. Also, take time to mourn. You lost your parents in a horrific way. Ignore those who tell you to move on, to not dwell on it. Mourn, grieve, process it."

Lucas nodded as Helena left the garden almost pulling Dom with her. He had to smile at Dom looking confused as to why Helena was dragging him out of the garden. Lucas then looked at Dani, she stepped toward him wrapping her arms around him. He pulled her closer so he could rest his chin on top of her head.

"I don't want it to be real," Lucas whispered.

"Neither do I," Dani replied. The grief was rolling off of him in waves, she just held on.

"I can't go back to the house," Lucas went on. "I tried, but the minute I walked through the door it was just too hard."

"Then don't go there," Dani suggested. She looked up at him before she took his hand and led him to the bench. "Do what my mom said. Mourn, grieve. Don't rush it. This case, their death, it's not over. Returning to their home, it doesn't need to be done today or even next week. You can run the Talon line from anywhere. Just because they ruled from there doesn't mean that you have to. And these are all decisions you don't have to make right this moment. Claire and I were serious in our offer, you are welcome to stay as long as you like."

"Dani, if I'm cold one minute then begging for your help the next…"

Dani smiled softly as she shook her head. "Don't even apologize, I get it," Dani assured him.

Chapter 11

The task force met at the Archives, this way they were away from the prying eyes of the rest of the force. At the moment they didn't want anyone to know about what Nick had told them about Dani's family. If Alistair thought something was up he didn't say anything when Dom told him their plans to meet there. Dani gave Sandy all the paperwork from the Accords, approving the task force to work in the Archives for the duration of the case.

"Ah, Miss Claire," Gregoir replied smiling as he hugged her. "You brighten any room you walk into."

"Hi Greg," Claire said smiling. Despite him being a necromancer, he was one of the warmest people she had ever met. "How are you doing?"

"We are all still reeling, but starting to process what happened," Gregoir admitted.

"I read the report," Claire stated with sympathy. "I can't imagine, Greg, what it was like to feel all that."

"I have been working with my group," Gregoir assured her. "Your Aunt has also been amazing. We are working on it, it will be a slow process."

"This has hit all of us hard," Claire agreed.

"How is Lucas? I spoke to him at the ceremony but that doesn't say much."

"He is taking it one day at a time," Claire replied.

"That is all we can do at such times," Gregoir commented. "Those who say otherwise are fools. Now what are you here for?"

"Can we have your log book?"

"Of course," Gregoir said as he went to his desk. Grabbing his keys from his belt chain he unlocked a file cabinet.

Pulling out a large leather tome he closed the drawer then locked it. "I just need you to sign off that you have it, it can not leave the premise nor can it be photocopied."

"Understood," Claire declared. She signed off on a form that he gave her then into the login book. This is also required for her to give her finger print. Gregoir provided her with the ink pad to do so.

Leaving Gregoir, she took the tome to the conference room they would be using. Dani came in behind her with another large tome. Setting them both down on the table, Claire and Dani took a seat.

"Well I was not expecting all the security measures that one must go through in order to get a book," Claire stated to Dani.

Grant looked at the dark brown tome that Claire had brought in. "What are they for?" He asked.

"Most of the library is digitized," Dani explained. "As long as you are in our system you can take out something, with the exception of the vault. For the vault you need approval, there is a digital sign-in but we also need a written sign-in as well as what you are looking at."

"Which means we would have handwriting samples," Grant realized.

"You can just hand them over like this?" Michael inquired.

"No, but because it could help with the case we need to have access to them without jumping through the usual hoops," Dani answered.

"Are they all kept in locked drawers?" Claire wandered out loud.

"Yes and they have to be signed-out with a fingerprint," Dani replied.

Grant looked over everything they had. "This is going to take a lot of time."

There was a knock on the door, Gregoir stood there with a few files. "I thought these might help," Gregoir informed them. "Signed request for the rare books."

"We are going to need more help," Michael sighed.

"What about Tony?" Gregoir inquired.

"Who's Tony?" Dani asked. This was not the first time

his name came up.

"He's a cyber-witch," Grant answered. "Alistair just got the approval today that he can work on the case. He should be here later."

"He's brilliant," Claire added. "He is the only one we know that can merge his abilities with computers. I know Alistair asked him to look over the break-in that happened here to see how someone bypassed the security."

"How have I never met him?" Dani asked.

"He sticks to himself, has a small circle of friends," Claire explained. "He has a basement apartment in Brooklyn and that's his base. He does some freelance work for a wide range of people and groups."

"See if he can figure out a way that could search through what we need without individually pouring through everything," Dani suggested. "We scan the log books every Friday. If he actually wants the physical tomes he will have to come here."

Claire started to speak but Gregoir came off the elevator that led to the lower floors. He looked paler than normal. "We have a problem," Gregoir stated.

They all froze, stopping what they were doing at the tone of Gregoir's voice. For a necromancer, Gregoir was a pretty calm individual. If he was agitated, then it meant something was serious wrong.

"What is it?" Dani asked standing up from her chair.

"I decided that since you guys were working on the log books, I would check on the Restricted Floor's logs," Gregoir explained.

"Do the logs not match up?" Claire asked.

"Worse," Gregoir. "One of the Black tomes is missing."

Dani and the rest got up, following him to the elevator that brought them down to level B. When they entered they all swiped their ID's allowing them to enter the secure vault. Gregoir walked toward the section for the spell casters and typed his code in. When the glass doors opened he motioned for Dani to enter. Dani walked in first and saw the problem immediately.

"How is this possible," Claire asked as she saw the spot the ancient tome should be.

"It shouldn't be," Dani stated.

The Restricted Floor was the hardest floor to gain access

too. The floor was one hallway with only the one elevator to come and go. Glass rooms lined either side of the hallway. Each room had a specific temperature for what the room contained. Every item had a chip that would set off a silent alarm if they ever entered the elevator.

Laying her hand on the pad to have it scan her palm she let out a scream. Gregoir dove across the floor as she crumbled to the ground.

He was surrounded in a red fog as he moved around the shelves. He was searching for something. Something that would help get the job done. He laughed as he thought of the reaction of the world to what he was about to do. Running his fingers along the edges of ancient tomes he couldn't help but appreciate the power these volumes held. A shame that it was locked away under the streets of Manhattan, hidden from the world.

When he was done, the world would know what he was after. They would know why he should be feared. But his power was fading, he was using too much of it to cloak what he was doing. He was going to need more soon.

Chapter 12

Dani was sitting on Dom's leather couch with Lucas holding her right hand. Tabby was studying the burn on Dani's left palm. It had reopened the one she had received at the Algonquin. Gregoir, Dom, and Sayad were pacing while Claire was helping her aunt. When Gregoir called the Jensen Clinic, Tabby told him not bring Dani there instead they would meet at Dom's place.

"Anything else in the vision?" Dom asked Dani finally

stopping for a minute.

"Just that it's the same red fog from the nightmares about the night my parent's died," Dani admitted. She hissed as Tabby began to slather a balm on the burn.

"That's not good," Sayad noted. He remembered the nightmares that Dani had about the night her parents died. The police believed she might have witnessed the crime, it was one of the reasons Helena brought her to their house.

"Towards the end, I got his train of thought," Dani recalled. "He was worried about using up his power, that he was concealing what he was doing with the power."

Tabby stopped and looked at Dani. "What do you mean? How was he using his power?"

Dani had to think. She hissed as Tabby tried a different ointment on it. Lucas went rigid as Dani winced.

Dom ran a hand over his shaved head and let out a frustrated breath. "The books on neutral locations were gone beside the Black Tome?"

"According to Sylvia those are the only ones that she can not locate," Gregoiranswered. Sylvia could locate items when they were missing using her fae abilities. "And no she can't locate them either."

"That rules out the witches," Claire stated. She handed the roll of bandages to her aunt. "We can't cancel out Fae magick."

"What of the burn?" Lucas asked as he used his ability to ease some of Dani's pain.

"It's the same poison that burned her earlier," Tabby said. "But to be sure I will take a sample and test at my home lab."

"Why not at the clinic?" Claire asked her aunt. The clinic had a state of the art lab that would be able to handle a test like Dani's.

Tabby finished bandaging her hand. "You need to be watched for twenty four hours, any sign of fever or hallucinations call me immediately," Tabby instructed. "Ointment every four hours until either I call you and tell you it's fine or it starts to heal."

"Aunt Tabby," Claire said in her warning tone. She knew her aunt was hiding something from her.

"Don't use that tone with me young lady," Tabby answered. She stood up and looked around the room, she noted the concerned look on her niece's face. "There was a break-in at the clinic last night. Or an attempt of one that is. Someone tried to get into the black cabinet in my office."

"You didn't report it," Dom noted as he watched Gregoir go very still. Often people would mistake a necromancer for a vampire, for they both had similar attributes but a necromancer was very much a witch despite being as still as a vampire.

"The black one?" Gregoir repeated.

"Yes," Tabby answered.

Gregoir immediately got on the phone stepping into Dom's office. "Someone want to explain the significance of the cabinet?" Dom inquired.

"It contains the most dangerous of herbs and remedies," Tabby explained. She thanked Sayad who handed her a glass of wine. Taking a seat in the leather recliner she continued. "Only the most advanced healers are allowed access to the cabinet which we keep in my office."

"Who knows what's in there?" Dom asked.

"With the exception of Claire, only five of us who work

at the clinic know the contents," Tabby admitted.

"This black cabinet, I take it the contents can be used for more than just healing?" Dani guessed.

"Yes, some can be used in very dangerous spells," Tabby answered.

"Like one's that could severe the neutrality of a place?" Dom suggested.   "Possibly, if they are willing to break several laws to do it," Tabby admitted. "I will give you the list of the five healers that have access. I will tell you that it would shock me if any of them are involved."

"I take it they weren't successful in the break in?" Lucas inquired.

"No, the wards and spells that protect it require an advanced witch to open it," Tabby assured them.

"I might be able to use what's in the cabinet but I don't have the power yet to open it," Claire added. "We're like vampires in that way. Yes we have power and ability but our strength increases over time and experiences."

"That actually helps in ruling out some people," Dom stated.

Dani yawned, she went to stand up but the world spun as she did. Lucas laid a hand on her back to steady her as she sat back down. "You need rest," Tabby told her.

"Crash here," Dom suggested.

"I'll grab Grunt on my way to Nick's place," Sayad assured her. "You stay here and rest. It will make mom feel better if she knows you are safe."

"Alright," Dani agreed.

"I'll take her to the guest room," Claire said standing up.

Tabby waited until Claire and Dani were both out of the room before she spoke again. "If she is still dizzy tomorrow she will need some blood to counteract whatever poison is coursing through her veins," Tabby informed the vampires.

"Greg also touched the pad earlier but it didn't effect him at all," Dom pointed out.

"I think it wasn't targeted for a spell caster, I think this poison can be made to only effect a specific victim" Tabby stated. She stood up collecting her things. "Watch her."

"We will," Lucas promised.

Gregoir came out Dom's office. "I need to get back to

the Archives," Gregoir informed them.

"I'll let Alistair know so he can inform the forensic team that you are coming," Dom told him.

Gregoir said his goodbyes, he then walked out with Tabby and Sayad. Claire came out of the back bedroom. "She's already asleep," Claire informed them as she collapsed on the loveseat. "Holy shit, this just got even more complicated."

"Dani said that whoever killed my parents knew them and they knew the killer," Lucas recalled. "If the killer knew what was in level C, as well as, targeted the Jensen clinic then we are dealing with a supernatural being."

"Which we believed was the case from the beginning, but this confirms it," Dom agreed.

"I'm not saying that my branch is not involved but we are bound by oaths that would kill us if we broke them," Claire stated. "Whoever is doing this, they are breaking many of those oaths."

"Which leaves: the Night Walkers, the Shifters, and the Fae," Dom answered. "We can rule out the Fae because most of them don't live in this realm."

Lucas ran his hands over his face. "I need to crash for a few hours, I have meetings all day tomorrow with lawyers, the elders, and Helena is meeting me to finalize arrangements."

"You are more than welcome to crash here," Dom told him. "You have somethings here anyway."

"I can bunk with Dani," Claire answered. "Someone should stay in her room."

"Alright," Lucas agreed. He would feel better being in the same place that Dani was.

* * * *

It was dawn when Dani woke. It took her a few minutes to realize she was spooning with Claire in the bed in one of Dom's guest room. She gently untangled herself from Claire, quietly she snuck out of the bedroom. Heading into the living room she walked right to the large floor-to-ceiling windows. Dom's apartment was located in one of the brand new luxury sky-rises located in Midtown. For a vampire the new high rises made sense because they often provided around the clock security, room service for when you had guests that needed more than blood, and access to the gym twenty-four hours a day.

Dom could afford it for two reasons, he was Lucas' second in command and second, he had been around for a few centuries which gave him time to save up money. For Dom, the place was perfect, some units offered special windows to keep the sunlight out during the day. Dom was fortunate, he was one of the vampires that didn't drop when sunlight came. Dani always felt weird watching the people down below, they looked like ants walking around. She didn't jump when a hand rested on her back.

"You slept?" Lucas asked quietly.

"Without any dreams or nightmares," Dani admitted leaning back into him. "You knew the moment it happened, didn't you?"

"Yes," Lucas admitted. "I dropped a stack of papers I was holding, it felt like my own flesh was burning."

"Our connection is getting stronger," Dani replied unsure what to think of it.

"I know, but it is too risky, with you being unbound, and with all that is going on," he admitted. Lucas looked out the window for a moment before speaking. "I spoke to an ancient while I was in Norway."

"About us?" Dani asked surprised. They weren't really even sure where they stood most days.

"He's a monk, he won't tell anyone," Lucas assured her. "But I explained the situation. He agreed that we have to wait until you are at least bound to a house. There are a lot of risks if we don't wait."

"And there is no harm in waiting?"

"None," Lucas assured her laying a hand on hers. "You are so young compared to me. I want you to be sure, to be certain, even if I have to wait a hundred years. And right now we both have so much happening, I have a House to lead, and this case it is getting more complicated each day. When it happens, I want it to be with few distractions."

"You are a rare creature," Dani commented as she looked at their reflection in the window.

"If this is true, then it is something most only dream of, why rush?"

Dani's phone vibrated. "It's my mother," Dani stated.

"Tell her I will meet her at my parent's at noon," Lucas

replied. He kissed her on the forehead before heading to the front door.

"Hi, mama," Dani answered the phone.

"Sayad said you were already asleep when he left," Helena stated. "You are alright?"

"Some pain," Dani admitted.

"Nick canceled his business trip in Boston. He is heading back now," Helena informed her. "Do we need guards on you?"

"I'm with Dom at the moment so I'm good," Dani assured her. She hated that her mother was worried. "Should I ask how Marcus handled the news?"

"Actually he was quite upset, he dropped his favorite brandy glass," Helena admitted. "Alexius even showed concern, as for Bartram, well he just laughed."

"Do you want to meet for dinner?" Dani suggested. "It might be take-out at mine and Claire's apartment."

"Yes," Helena answered. "Did Tabby say when she will know for sure what it was?"

"No, but the fact that I didn't worsen overnight is a positive thing," Dani reminded her mother.

"I will be with Lucas later today to help finalize things," Helena reminded her. "When I'm done I will text you."

"Lucas said that he should be there around noon," Dani told her mother.

They said their goodbyes. Dani headed into the kitchen and let out a short scream. Dom was in there, making coffee. "Shit," Dani said grabbing her heart. "Can you be louder."

Dom chuckled as he poured a shot of blood into a mug, followed by coffee and handed it to her. "Tabby said this will help and I know you've been taking some blood in your coffee from time to time."

"She talks too much," Dani sighed as she sipped the coffee.

"She talks in her sleep," Dom pointed out.

"She also spoons," Dani added. Dom chuckled at that. "I've found her spooning Grunt on occasion."

"She needs a girlfriend," Dom replied.

"Yea well unfortunately for both of us she is not might my type apparently," Dani answered which had Dom laughing.

They heard a low growl. Dom poured more coffee into a

mug and handed it to Claire as she stumbled into the modern kitchen. They both knew better than to try and talk to the witch before she was done with her first cup of coffee. So they each sipped their own coffee while Claire drank hers as if her sanity depended on it. Dom and Dani watched as Claire began to relax and her eyes actually opened up. She looked around the room as if just realizing where she was.

"Ok, I'm good," Claire stated. "What's up?"

"Alistair want's us at the precinct to go over what we have," Dom informed her. "I've also been informed by the council that Dani is now under my protection for the duration of the case."

"That will make mom feel better," Dani admitted.

"Though I think Lucas would rather be your personal body guard," Claire replied. When Dani choked on her coffee, Claire chuckled.

"We should head back to the apartment and get changed into clothes," Dani suggested after she recovered. "We can call Tabby on the way to update her on how I'm doing."

"Only after I check the burn and make sure you aren't

running a fever," Claire replied.

* * * *

The main precinct for the STF in New York City was located right by the Harlem 125th street station, which made it convenient for Claire to get to work. It was one of the perks to their apartment, Claire walked most days. Which anyone who saw her drive thought was a good thing.

Dom was waiting outside the doors to the precinct. He held open the doors when Dani and Claire arrived, the three headed into the main reception area of the precinct. The receptionist smiled at them as they entered.

"Anything we should know?" Dom asked her.

"The terrible twosome are in the bullpen," Audrey advised. "So I would suggest going right to your office."

"Sounds like a plan," Dom agreed. The last thing he wanted was for Jones and Hinderman to start in on Dani.

"Am I ever going to meet them?" Dani inquired.

"No." Dani raised an eyebrow at Audrey, Dom, and Claire. They had said it in unison.

"Alright then," Dani replied.

They took the back stairs that led up to the detective offices. Dom was head detective so he had his own office, though mostly Claire and the two other detectives under him hung out in his. Grant and Michael were already in the office looking at the crime scene evidence they had placed on the large evidence board.

"Where do we stand?" Dom inquired.

"Nessa and Tabby have confirmed that the poison that Dani has been in contact with is the same poison found in Josephine and Harold," Michael began. "They are running it against our system as well as the Jensen Catalogue to see if any of the ingredients will be flagged."

"So a poison that reacts only to Vampires?" Grant theorized.

"My aunt is looking into it as well," Claire assured them. "But Josie and Harold were elders, close to ancients, taking them down with a poison should have been impossible. Even if it was tailored made for vampires."

"Maybe the intent wasn't to kill them with the poison but to weaken them," Grant realized. "Weaken an Elder and you would be able to overpower them."

Dom leaned against his desk as he pulled on his chin thinking. "That could be the answer," he replied. "And how they took a bonded pair down as well.

"Meaning if he poisoned Harold then Josie would know or vice versa," Dani stated, Dom and Micheal nodded. "And if they were both poisoned then it would be like a double dose?"

"In theory, yes," Dom agreed.

"Which means our suspect knows enough about Vampires to know that if he poisoned both elders it would make them even weaker because of their bond," Dani noted. "He also knows how to break the neutrality of a spot, as well as, how to break into the Archives and the Vault within the archives."

"Which rules out that these were random killings," Michael sighed. "We're talking someone within our own community."

"Witches have been ruled out for the moment because of the oath's they make," Dom informed them. "But as Claire pointed out, that doesn't mean one of them couldn't be helping our guy."

"And not break an oath?" Grant asked. He was witch, a powerful water witch.

"Or hasn't taken the oaths," Dani suggested. Everyone looked at her. "Our main suspect has to be powerful to over take two elders even if they were weakened. A normal mortal wouldn't be able to do that even in their weakened state. If we go on what we know so far, they also have been around long enough to know the details of bonded pairs, neutrality, so we can state that he has to be an older vampire."

"That makes sense," Dom agreed.

"The oath a witch makes is binding to the law of nature," Dani continued. "If they break it not only are they cast out but they will die from it. So if we go with the theory that a witch could be aiding our guy that leaves us with two possible suspects. The first is a young witch who hasn't taken the oath which means they wouldn't be bound by the oath."

"And the second?" Claire asked.

"Someone who has nothing to lose," Grant finished for Dani.

"I'll ask my aunt for a list of those who haven't taken the

oath, see if she can think of anyone that would attempt this,"
Claire volunteered.

"I'll talk to my uncle as well," Grant offered. "Between
Vern and Tabby they should be able to come up with some
names."

"They'll both be discreet as well," Dom agreed.

There was knock on the door, Alistair appeared. "Is now
a good time?" Alistair inquired.

"We just got done with assignments," Dom answered.

Alistair nodded. "I had a meeting with our
commissioner," Alistair began. "It was quite tense as we did not
agree who should be leading this case."

"What did GQ want?" Dom asked.

"He wanted Hinderman and Jones on the case," Alistair
answered. He held up his hands before anyone could start arguing about the terrible twosome joining their team. "I said no. So
the four of you, with Dani acting as consultant, are officially in
charge of Josephine and Harold's death. I know I don't need to
tell you this, but there can be no mistakes, I put my neck on the
line when I told him no."

"We aren't going to let you down," Dom promised. "This is too personal for us."

"I know, which was why Holtzen wanted you and Dani off the case," Alistair admitted. "I reaffirmed to him that we need Dani, that without her we wouldn't know who the victims were, or how the murder happened. And if we need Dani then we also need Dom because he's her protector. He wasn't thrilled but he agreed."

"We've all been on cases where we knew the victim or even the criminal," Grant argued. "The Supernatural community isn't that large where we don't know at least the name."

"Guys, you don't have to argue with me," Alistair reminded them. "I just want you to know that this case is going to be watched closely by Holtzen. He is going to look for the smallest of reasons to throw all of you off the case."

"I take it than the conversation James had with my father did not go well," Dani said.

"My thought as well," Alistair agreed.

"Look, if me being on the case is going to be an issue..." Dani began but stopped when Dom growled and Alistair shot her one of his looks.

"I have never bowed to politics, I am not going to start now," Alistair informed her.

"Wait," Michael replied. They all looked at him not sure what he was going to say. "What if Dani publicly releases a statement that she has withdrawn herself from the case due to her close ties to the victims and their family. That she will still work with the investigators in her capacity as an Archivist."

"Why?" Alistair asked, curious as to what Michael was planning.

"It lets her father and James both think they got their way, which means they will think they won," Michael explained. "Dani though will still be involved because of the Archives, and she lives with Claire so it's not like Claire isn't going to share. We are already meeting most days at the archives anyway so it won't seem weird to continue to do so. We also know that this guy is going to attack again, when he does, the public will demand that Dani be asked to come back to the case."

"That is actually brilliant," Dom said.

"It would free up Dani to research the poison on why it

just targets Vampires," Claire added. "With the burn, her going to the Clinic won't be odd either. So we could add that she suffered an injury during the case and needs time to fully heal, thereby limiting what she can do."

"With her off the case, she could get to places we wouldn't be able to," Grant added. "Shit, it's brilliant."

"It really is," Alistair agreed.

"Don't I get a say in this?" Dani asked. She wasn't sure how she felt about the plan.

"What are your thoughts?" Alistair asked her.

"I think letting Marcus thinks he won can be dangerous," she warned them. "He is in rare form since Mom and Sayad left for Nick's. Playing into his need for control, it might not go well. But, I can understand the benefits to the deception and how it could help the case."

"So you'll do it?" Alistair asked.

Chapter 13

The call came at six in the morning. It came before any press announcement could be made, before Dani even had time to write up a statement. It wasn't a phone call or even a text but Dom knocking on the front door. Lucas was the one that answered the door as Claire and Dani watched from their bedroom doorways. Most of the inhabitants of the complex were not up or around at six in the morning. When Lucas opened the door and they saw Dom, everyone knew that what he was about to say was not going to be good.

"Al called," Dom told him. "We need to head to his

farm."

Claire wiped sleep from her eyes as the words hit home. Dani took the hand that Lucas extended toward her. "I'm acting Chief on this one," Dom then said in a grim tone.

"It's not Grey," Lucas said to Dani. Greyson Clarence was Alistair's oldest son and Dani's high-school into college boyfriend. The two were still extremely close.

"He left for Germany the day after the memorial," Dani told him but that didn't hide the fear that once again she might know the victim.

"I'll make the coffee, you guys get dressed," Lucas said.

The doors to the bedroom shut and Lucas headed into the kitchen where he began to prep the coffee machine. Over the past two weeks, he had learned exactly how Claire made it and was now permitted to man the coffee machine.

"She lets you make her coffee?" Dom asked leaning against the archway that led into the galley style kitchen that was common in New York.

"She taught me how to make it and supervised me before letting me alone with the machine," Lucas corrected him.

"We need to get you an apron," Dom teased as he accepted a mug that was half filled with blood and the rest with coffee.

Lucas flipped him off then got the two travel mugs for the girls. "How was the watch last night?"

"Report of a car that drove by two times, that has the morning shift going to look into it," Dom said. "It tipped them off because the second time it slowed down in front of the building. If it's reporters we'll take care of it, if it's more than that, I'll hand it over to Torres and Cooper to look into. We were hoping the press release would buy us time, but I think we just lost that time."

Dani was out first in jeans, a t-shirt, and sneakers. She took the travel mug that Lucas had just filled then added a few drops of blood to it before taking a sip.

"We are going to have to talk about you needing some blood each day," Dom informed her.

"But not today," Dani warned as she took her first sip.

They heard a door slam and then Grunt's nails as he ran into the cramped kitchen. After pets from everyone and Lucas filling his bowl with food, Claire emerged. Lucas handed her the travel mug knowing not to talk to the witch this early in the morning.

"I'll have them back by curfew, dad," Dom teased.

"Fuck off," Lucas replied. He then looked at Grunt. "Bed?"

Grunt spun in circles before racing to Dani's room. Lucas smiled as Claire flipped him off. He followed Grunt toward Dani's bedroom, Dom looked at Dani and she just narrowed her eyes at him. Grabbing her bag, Dani headed out out of the apartment with Claire and Dom following her. They were going have a two hour drive ahead of them to the Clarence compound on Long Island.

When they pulled into the drive that led to the main compound they were greeted by state police, the crime scene van, as well as, the medical examiner. Everyone was waiting outside their vehicles. Dom pulled in alongside Vynessa's car, Claire and Dani got out first. Vynessa walked toward them, waiting for them to get out of the car before she talked to them.

"I told everyone not to touch anything until after you got in," Vynessa told Dani.

"Thanks," Dani replied.

Dom spotted Alistair standing with his wife Evie and his sister Grace. Grace was the beta in his pack, they were one of the few sibling leaders. Most Alpha and Betas of packs were married couples, there were occasions where it fell to siblings. When Grace spotted Dani, she went right to her pulling her into a strong hug.

"Thank you," Grace whispered. She was trying to hold her emotions in so not to overwhelm Dani. It was hard for any were animal to keep their emotions tightly bound.

"It's Parker," Alistair told them, his voice cracking with emotion. "The cleaning crew found him when they went into his apartment. The door was unlocked."

"They didn't clean anything did they?" Dom asked as he took notes.

"No, they check all the rooms first just in case someone is still sleeping off a transformation or something," Evie answered. "When they found...him they immediately called Al. That was right before he called in you guys."

"Any idea of time?" Claire asked as Dani looked around

the area.

"Quick guess from Nessa was maybe early this morning," Evie replied. "She didn't want to touch anything because she knows it's harder for Dani."

"I'll go in with Dani," Claire told Dom.

Dom nodded. Dani didn't need directions to where they were going. The old barn had been converted into four apartments. Two on bottom and two on top. Grayson and his brother Todd had the larger of the two top one's, Parker's was next to theirs. Dani went up the outside stairs that led to the small deck that connected the two apartments. Crime scene tape was already up, marking off the area. Dani touched the door to Parker's apartment and immediately jumped back.

"It's the same guy," Dani realized. Taking a step into the apartment the world began to spin out of control.

* * * *

Dani opened her eyes then closed them immediately. Whatever she saw was not possible. Taking a deep breath she opened her eyes again and stood in disbelief. Red mist swirled around her, the apartment felt as if she had walked into a picture done in sepia tones. There were muffled voices somewhere but she couldn't tell where they were coming from.

"Claire?" Dani called out.

"Dani?" Claire answered unsure. Claire's voice sounded clear as day in Dani's mind.

"Um, so what's going on?" Dani walked around the combination kitchen and living area.

"I was going to ask you that," Claire admitted. "You are standing in the middle of the living room as if in a trance."

"Huh. I guess that makes sense."

Dani went toward where Claire said she was standing but felt a pull toward the hallway. "I think I'm in the astral plane," Dani informed Claire. "I'm getting a pulling sensation toward the hallway. So I guess I see what 'I' do on the other side."

"Alright," Claire agreed.

Dani headed toward the narrow hallway. There she saw a glowing line that led down the hallway toward the bedroom on the right. As she walked down the hall she saw images of Parker as he got ready to turn in for the night. She was following his final moments Dani realized. His astral ghost headed toward the bathroom, not really wanting to see him get to the bathroom, Dani turned to study the area.

"You just stopped in front of the bathroom then turned to face the living room," Claire stated.

"That's because I'm following his final moments," Dani realized.

"Shit. Has this ever happened before?"

"No, not like this, not with this much clarity," Dani admitted. "It's usually impressions, thoughts, imaged. This, this is like I'm right there with him."

The door to the bathroom opened as Parker stepped into the hallway. He headed into the bedroom, when he began to undress Dani closed her eyes. Once she heard him laying down on the bed she opened her eyes, Parker was sprawled across the bed with a sheet pulled over himself. He was flipping through the channels on the television.

"You think you are going to have to live through the entire evening?" Claire asked. "Cause you're staring at the bed."

"Don't tell me how bad," Dani warned. "Don't even think it."

"Closing eyes now so you don't see," Claire informed her.

The world shimmered around Dani as she realized that time was speeding up around her. The red mist that had greeted her when she first entered this world began to seep into the bed- room. It was coming in thicker until it was more of a dense fog than mist. Dani felt as if all the warmth in the room had vacated, rubbing her arms with her hands she watched knowing she was going to watch Parker be murdered. Knowing that she was help- less to stop it.

Parker sat up as he woke immediately. Rubbing sleep from his eyes he looked around the room as his night vision kicked in.

"You!" Parker yelled as he moved away from the bed. "How did you get in here?"

"I have my ways," said a voice. It was disguised by the mist.

"Why are you here?"

"To show that we are better than you, that we are better than all of you," he answered. "This is another step in the path

to greatness."

"Don't do this," Parker replied. "Dude, you don't want to do this. She's..."

Parker's voice was cut off as he grabbed at his throat trying to fight off unseen hands. Dani watched as he was lifted into the air by an arm made out of mist, he was flung across the room.

"The more you fight the better for me," the voice informed him.

Dani smiled sadly as Parker stopped fighting. His entire body relaxed as he was once again picked up. He was making his stand by not fighting back. Dani felt the fury in the room intensify.

"I will make you scream!"

Parker remained silent. Dani felt the tears run down her face as she watched what the monster did to him. When Parker was left broken and bleeding in the center of the bed the red mist began to recede. The fury that had encompassed the room began to fade. Soon Dani just stood there alone with Parker before her.

"I will find him, I will end this," Dani promised.

* * * *

Dani felt like her head had cleared as she opened her eyes to see herself standing in Parker's bedroom. The afternoon sun was coming through the window shining on the horror scene before her.

"You're back," Claire stated. She told someone to give them a minute. "And your nose is bleeding."

Dani instantly put her hand to her nose, when she pulled it away she saw it was covered in blood. Claire put a hand on her back then guided her from the room. She told Vynessa she could start, Vynessa tossed Claire a box of gauze. Claire caught it then escorted Dani outside. Dani gulped in the fresh air as Claire handed her gauze. Sitting down on the top step, Dani held it to her nose while she tried to come to terms with everything that she saw.

Dom came running toward them with Alistair closely behind him. "What happened?" Dom asked as he crouched in front of Dani.

"I went into the astral plane," Dani answered through the gauze. "I saw everything that happened."

"You can identify our killer?" Alistair asked in shock.

"No," Dani replied. They looked at her. "He appeared as this red mist, even his voice was distorted. I know it's the same person who killed Josephine and Harold."

"Did you get anything else?" Dom asked gently.

"He's doing this to show that 'we are better than all of you'. He said that Parker was just another step toward the greater good."

"A radical," Alistair stated gruffly.

"But from which branch?" Claire inquired.

"Not were's or he wouldn't have referred to himself as being better," Dom pointed out.

"Parker knew who it was," Dani informed them. They looked at her in surprise. "He didn't say his name but he tried to talk him out it."

"That is what Parker would do," Alistair said sadly. "He is, was, the peacekeeper."

"I think the guy gets power the more someone struggles," Dani realized as the bleeding stopped. "He said something to Parker as Parker fought back. That the more Parker fought him the better it was for him."

"He's able to use that energy to make himself stronger," Claire theorized. "That's really dark magick."

"Which confirms one of our theories," Dom answered.

Dani looked at Alistair. "The moment he said it Parker stopped fighting back. He wouldn't make this guy more powerful so he didn't fight back, he didn't scream."

"Which is why no one heard anything," Claire stated.

They had been wondering how no one, not even were's, heard anything. With how brutal the scene had been they had all figured there would have been some noise. If Parker had realized that if he fought back, that if he made a noise, it would make his killer stronger, then he would have stopped. He wouldn't have wanted anyone else to be hurt nor would he want to make a maniac stronger.

"Let's get you out of here," Dom said to Dani. "You're still pale."

"Claire, take her to your Aunt's clinic," Alistair suggested. "We'll call in Michael and Grant to help out Dom."

"I'm fine," Dani said. To prove her point she went to

stand up but the world spun. Dom caught her by the arm. "Alright, maybe getting checked over isn't a bad idea."

"Cap, I'm going to walk her to the car," Dom told Alistair. He then pointed at their captain. "No going in there. You are a civilian today."

"Vynessa already promised that she would kick me out if I entered the apartment," Alistair promised. Though it pained him knowing that he was helpless.

Dom put an arm around Dani's waist and practically carried her down the stairs as Claire and Alistair followed. Claire opened the door to Dom's jeep, he loaded Dani into the passenger seat.

"Not a scratch or ding," Dom warned Claire as he handed her the keys.

"I'll behave," Claire promised.

Dom snickered at that as he shut the door for Dani. Claire climbed into the driver seat as she called her aunt. Tabby told her to meet them at her place in Brooklyn.

Chapter 14

Claire had driven right to her aunt's house. This was Aunt Tabby's day off from the clinic which meant no one would see Dani with a nose bleed. The minute Tabby had opened the door to her row house, she quickly ushered the girls in, strengthening the wards that protected them as she needed. She sat Dani in the chair closest to the fireplace, and despite it being June, started a small fire to help with the chill that Dani had. She instructed Claire to make tea while she looked Dani over.

"Nothing hurts besides your head?" Tabby asked as she had Dani move her shoulder and neck.

"Just a massive headache," Dani answered. "Like leprechauns wearing wooden clogs and tap dancing out of beat."

"How about your stomach?" Tabby inquired as she checked Dani's pulse. She was pleased that it was returning to normal.

"It's fine."

"What about when you were in the astral world?" Tabby asked. That was the part she was more concerned with.

Dani was silent for a moment as recalled those moments. "I felt detached from my body," she realized. "But I didn't feel sick or in pain."

Tabby wrote everything down then took a seat on the ottoman across from Dani. "And this has never happened before?"

"Like I told Claire, I generally get impressions, images, thoughts, and feelings," Dani explained. "This was like reliving the whole thing."

"How was the hotel like?" Tabby inquired.

"Impressions, they were chaotic because of what had

been done to the wards," Dani explained. "But I stay in this realm while I get the impressions and images."

"And at Parkers?"

"I knew the moment I opened my eyes that I was in the astral plane," Dani replied. "I was following him as he went through his last moment's before he was killed."

"She was walking through the apartment like in a trance," Claire added. "We talked through the link."

"What are you thinking?" Dani asked Tabby.

The doorbell rang. Claire went to open the door. Lucas walked through the front door, when he spotted Dani he went right to her side. She shook her head before he laid a hand on her not sure if he would pick up on what she saw or felt. Instead he sat next to her.

"What did I miss?" Lucas asked as he studied Dani.

"My abilities are increasing," Dani informed him. "I walked the astral plane of the crime scene."

"Then had a bloody nose and massive headache," Claire added.

"I think this all but confirms that Dani is a Dream

Walker," Tabby stated before another word could be said. They all turned and looked at her.

"Shouldn't this have come to play when she was eighteen?" Lucas asked.

"In a witch, this ability tends to come out when they first start coming into their power," Tabby said. "By eighteen they would be assigned a teacher to help them learn to control their abilities. Sometime with seers we will start immediately but it depends on how it manifests."

"If that's the case why is it only coming out now?" Dani inquired as she felt Lucas slide his hand in hers.

"Because you are approaching thirty," Tabitha answered. "In the world of vampires, when you take your Oath that is when your latent abilities manifest."

"We don't start focusing on the individual's ability until after the blood oath," Lucas realized. "It's usually during that time of the ceremony that what they have to offer is highlighted."

"And once their talent is presented, like a witch, they are given a teacher to help them learn their skills," Tabby replied. "Dani is both a witch and a vampire, as with any like Dani, the vampire trait is deemed more crucial to develop because of what it involves to turn into one. While Dani has always shown abilities since she was thirteen, I believe the vampire trait hid her full potential and now as she readies for her next transformation it is coming out."

"Dream-walkers are extremely rare," Claire reminded her aunt.

"There are ten that I know of and only two in the America's," Tabby replied. "Both are mild in their abilities and what Dani is showing already surpasses what they can do. To walk the Astral Plane while awake is no trivial thing."

"If I don't learn to control it, what happens?" Dani asked.

"Your psychic ability will become unstable," Tabby informed her. "Those closest to you, those who share a link with you, will be at great risk. In some cases they have been able to alter and control minds. Create hallucinations, some fall into a sleep they never wake up from."

"Then how do we help Dani," Lucas asked Tabby. "Dom can help keep a person from dreaming."

"Having him around Dani will help," Tabby agreed. "He

will be able to pick up on the subtle shift from this plane to the astral before we will. But Dani needs to be trained."

"You said my ability have surpassed those who live in this area," Dani noted.

"I have reached out to one of the European Covens," Tabby replied. "I contacted Cassandra after Josephine and Harold were killed for I was already seeing signs of this change in Dani. Cassandra is the strongest seer and dream-walker that has been known for centuries. If anyone can train Dani, it will be Cassandra."

"Is the red mist part of this?" Dani asked Tabby.

Tabby shook her head. "No. That is your mind blocking you from something that it feels is a threat."

"The only other time I have encountered the red mist before now is when I dream of my parent's death," Dani admitted. "Before this case, I never encountered the red mist again."

"Then perhaps it is in your memory where the answer lies," Tabby answered.

"You have encountered this mist only three times," Claire stated. "When you recall your parents death, when you walked through the crime scene at the Algonquin and then at Parker's apartment."

"So, I unlock my memory and we solve the case."

"It's not that simple," Tabby warned. "If you rush to try and unlock your memories then it could damage your mind in the process. You are only just coming into this ability, an ability that is not well written about. You have already suffered a traumatic event as a young child. You are going to have to learn to control your abilities before you can risk unlocking the memory."

"Even if it means keeping a killer out on the streets," Claire demanded.

"I suggest a Council meeting," Tabby suggested. "You inform each branch of what is going on. Let them know there is a radical who is trying to undermine us all. That this individual is using dark means to do this. If we are on alert it will make his job harder."

"It's not a bad idea," Lucas admitted. "It will keep rumors from getting out of control and it might give you guys some more leads along the way."

"'I'll call Dom and Alistair, see what they think," Claire

replied. She got up leaving the room to make the call.

"In the meantime what do I do?" Dani asked Tabby.

"Fortunately for us, Cassandra had already planned on arriving tomorrow," Tabby replied. "I would suggest until then, you stay away from crime scenes, and dead bodies. Perhaps having Dom keeping you from dreaming tonight might not be a bad idea."

"I'll talk to him," Lucas promised. Dani shot him a look. "Let me do this. I can't help you control your ability, but I can make sure you are safe while you are learning to be even more amazing."

"Alright," Dani sighed.

"I also suggest we do not tell anyone about what Dani can do or what answers she might hold," Lucas stated. "It would paint a target on her, as well as, draw questions she does not need to answer at the moment."

"I agree," Tabby concurred. "Cassandra is here to study Dani's abilities as she has done with other seers. They will be working together to see if they can strengthen Dani's gifts and teach her how to control them so that she doesn't get nose bleeds or black out."

"We will have to tell Dom and Alistair not to say a word either," Dani replied.

"In the mean time, you need to rest," Tabby told Dani. "A trip to the Astral plane is exhausting to the body even when it is well planned. You might feel alright now but it could hit you at some point."

"I can take her back to the apartment," Claire suggested.

"No, the car circling the building were paparazzi," Lucas said. "I got the phone call while you two were doing your weird astral plane thing."

"I'm not sure staying at Nick's is the best idea," Dani said.

"We could stay at the apartment I usually live in when I'm in the states," Lucas suggested. "We can pick up Grunt on the way there, as well as, clothes to last a few days. Dom wants to deal with the paparazzi before we return."

"That would work," Dani said before anyone could make the decision for her.

"Claire, you might want to head somewhere for a few days or Dom can crash in Dani's room."

"One of us should stay there," Claire said. "I'm not letting them run us out of our home."

"I'll let Dom know that he should pack some things and head over," Lucas answered as he got up.

Tabby waited until he stepped outside. "The bond between you two, it will also help," Tabby told her. "It will keep you tethered to this realm even when the Astral Plane tries to entice you to stay."

"But will he be safe?" Dani asked.

"Yes," Tabby assured her. "You will not be able to draw him in with you."

* * * *

Dani walked around the apartment that Lucas stayed in when in the City. As long as she knew him he never had his own place. Instead he stayed at his family estate in Norway when in Europe or in one of the apartments in New York City that his parent's owned for visiting dignitaries. Grunt was already asleep on the balcony of the apartment where an outdoor bed of his lay.

The building where the apartment was located used to be an old factory. Now it had been converted into trendy apartments with around the clock security, a gym with pool, even a rooftop garden and bar. The price tag to get in was close to ten million dollars.

"Here," Lucas offered as he came out of the kitchen. He handed her a glass of white wine. "Food should be here shortly,"

"Thanks," Dani answered taking the wine from him. "Can I ask you something?"

"Sure." Lucas sat down in the leather armchair.

"How come you don't own your own place?" Dani asked as she sat in the love seat. "I mean, I get that you are always back and forth between Europe and here."

Lucas leaned back in the chair as he thought about it. "It's a lot more complicated, I'm picky," he answered. "I was mom's last child, the fact she had me at all is a miracle. There was about fifty years between Kerrina and me. They had already buried several children by then. I guess part of me wanted to give them what they thought they would never have."

"How many siblings did you have when you were born?"

"There were four," Lucas recalled. "Freddie, Graham, James, and Kerrina. They had nine that survived infancy, seven made it to adulthood. Three were stillbirths."

"That's a lot of death," Dani realized.

"We're vampires, Dani, we're surrounded by death."

"Is that why when you love, it's so passionate and complete?"

He nodded. Standing up he walked over to the balcony doors watching as Grunt chased something in his dreams. "As I got older I spent time with each of my siblings, learning from them, learning what I could do to help them with their roles and jobs. I thought about it when we moved here in the start of the nineteen hundreds."

"What happened?"

"The War to end all Wars happened," Lucas answered. "I fought. Came home and wanted to forget what I saw. We had lost Graham and James in the war. The country was different, grieving, pointing fingers. I wanted to forget it all."

Dani didn't say anything. He rarely talked a lot about his siblings. Vampires might live long lives but they didn't like to think of the past. As Lucas said, they were surrounded by death. Looking back meant recalling someone they cared for who had been long dead.

"Mom hit a dark time then, It was just Freddie, Rina, and me," Lucas continued. "Any thoughts of leaving vanished. Freddie was running the house while Rina took over the duties of mom. I helped dad take care of mom."

The doorbell rang. Dani got up, she went to the door opening it for the delivery man while Lucas looked out on the city. Lucas had already paid so she gave him a tip then brought her food to the island that separated the kitchen from the living area. Lucas joined her as she spread out her Indian fare. Grunt wandered in at the smell of food.

"We can change topics," Dani told him as he refilled their drinks.

"No, you should know this," Lucas replied. He tasted some of her tandoori before continuing on. "So anyway, by 1930 mom started to get better, she started taking back some of her roles. Allowing Rina and I to oversee the European branch of House Talon. We were there a few years. With me going between New York and Europe. Then by the late 1930's, we begun to hear whispers, rumors of entire population of supernaturals vanishing in the night."

Dani felt her gut squeeze as she realized what he was getting too. "I told Rina I would check out the claims while she stayed in Norway protecting our people," Lucas recalled. "I was in Germany on April 9th, 1940. That was the day that Hitler invaded Norway. It took me three months before I could get back, by then our estate had been burnt to the ground. The only thing remaining were the burnt remains of those who worked for my family. Rina was most likely one of the bodies I buried but there was no way of identifying them. I couldn't come back and do nothing. So I joined the resistance, becoming the leader of a team of supernaturals. I did not return to the states until 1950. After the War was over, I helped rebuild the estate, helped families get back to their loved ones."

"What happened too Freddie?" Dani asked gently.

"He blamed me for Rina's death," Lucas recalled painfully. "He said that if I had stayed, we would have made it out. Mom and Dad would hear none of it, she died because a mad man thought he could take over the world. Instead he changed it to the point we are still dealing with his actions. When I returned here, Freddie left. Refused to be anywhere near me. Freddie is why we know that taking blood from drug addicts can kill us. He got into the drug scene in California."

"So to answer your question, I never bought my own place because there never seemed to be a moment where I could think of what I wanted," Lucas answered her with a sad smile. "So now that I have bared my soul, why is that Brianna the Wise needs no offering from you?"

"What do you mean?" Dani asked. Very few had ever inquired as to why the Fae would appear to Dani with no offering or promises.

"Well, she treats you as if you are an equal," Lucas stated. "Not that she treats anyone poorly, but you don't have to go through the rituals that others have to do in order to speak with her."

Dani was quiet as she traded her wine glass for a glass of water. Taking a sip she wondered what to say. She had never really told anyone the story before, Claire and Dom knew parts of it and those parts were bad enough.

"I met Brianna when Claire was working on how to communicate with the Fae," Dani explained. "Not every witch has to learn, but with her being Tabby's heir she did. Just as Grant knows how to summon her as well."

"That makes sense," Lucas agreed. Having every witch know how to summon the fae would be tiring.

"Claire would drag me out of the library at college and bring me to Central Park, her thought was I could study from anywhere," Dani went on. Grunt had given up on food and was now curled up on the couch. "One day I was watching her and asked why did it have to be so complicated. Why not a simple request done politely and with respect, Brianna suddenly appeared, explaining that witch's like the ceremony and ritual."

Lucas chuckled as he poured himself a glass of red wine, it was a special blend that had blood in it.

"Brianna liked my questions, my way of seeing the world," Dani continued. "But being treated as her equal that didn't come until I was working on my masters in history."

"What happened?" Lucas inquired.

"I was doing some consulting for STF by this point, not a lot because I was in grad school and apprenticing at the archives," Dani answered. "The NYPD had contacted STF, Dom and Claire got the case. The police weren't sure if what was happening was supernatural or not, but they wanted the STF's take on it."

"So why bring in Claire and Dom?"

"To rule out the supernatural or confirm that it was," Dani answered. She held the glass in her hands. "Kids were vanishing. And I mean vanishing. No forced entrance, no ransoms, nothing on security camera's. Parent's weren't in custody disputes. These weren't parents that people would target for ransom. No pissed off employees that wanted revenge. These were average people who put their kids to sleep one night and the next morning their child was gone."

"That is terrifying," Lucas replied.

"Claire and Dom were brought in when the third kid vanished. They wanted to interview the first set of parents," Dani replied. "It's standard procedure when we take a case from the police. We re-interview everyone. However, when they went, the parent's were confused because they didn't have a child by that name."

"Confirming that it was supernatural," Lucas realized. "What happened?"

"They asked if I could do some research on beings that had this kind of ability," Dani replied. "I wasn't officially on the case but I worked in the archives so the information was there."

"You would get brought in eventually," Lucas assumed.

"The fourth one was a murder scene," Dani answered. "I got brought in on that one. All the doors and windows were locked from the inside. No footage on security, no silent alarms tripped. The kid was gone but the parent's were brutally slaughtered. I asked Claire, who had dealings with the fae before, if we could meet with Brianna. We met and what she had to tell us chilled all of us. There were rumors that a Changeling had been born."

Lucas stared at her for a moment before he felt the chill go up his spines. Changelings were rare, even rarer was one that survived birth. They were lethal, becoming only deadlier the older they got. A fae could mate with a human and be alright but when they mated with a member of the supernatural community there was a high chance of a Changeling. It was a risk that no one ever wanted to take.

"Was it true?" Lucas asked not even wanting to think what had been witnessed by Dani.

"When it was captured it was almost a five days old, twelve people were slaughtered," Dani recalled. "It bared no re-semblance to a baby or even a child. It's mind…"

"You touched it's mind!"

"And survived," Dani said simply.

The mind of changeling was so vile, so filled with chaos and blood lust that it turned people crazy if they were around them long enough. For an empath or psychic it could kill them just by a thought. If it didn't kill them it left them mentally bro-ken.

"I don't have to pay for service or promise a deed in re-turn because I helped stop the changeling," Dani explained. "That is why Brianna the Wise and the fae see me as an equal. They know what I saw, they are in awe it didn't break me."

"What of Claire and Dom?"

"The Fae worked their magick on those involved, in the eye of the law the killer had been caught but was killed in a shootout," Dani answered. "The kidnapped children had already been killed and their remains were returned to their parents. Brianna visits the families each year."

"The truth?"

"I surprised the Changeling when my mind didn't break, when I didn't answer it's call to kill myself, it went into a fit," Dani replied. "It allowed the Fae Guard to apprehend it in iron chains. You can't kill a Changeling. Their blood can actually carry their life to another vessel. Anyone older than thirteen would be killed, but someone younger would be able to accept the Changeling. They would slowly begin to turn into the monster."

"Would they live long?"

She shook her. "A born Changeling will live up to a week, but a child who takes in the essences of one is lucky to survive the next twenty four hours. There is no way to undue a Changeling taking over a body."

"So what do you do with a changeling when caught? I

would think to keep them in a cell would be a danger."

"You encase them in solid Iron then place them in an iron coffin, where molten iron is poured over it."

Lucas had no words. "Once you touch the mind of a changeling you understand what true evil is," Dani whispered. "There is no warmth in them, no ability to see anything that is good. They want pain and death. They enjoy suffering. There is no greater purpose for them, they aren't doing it to gain power over someone. They are doing it because they can. Because they want too. Because if they don't kill, they will end up killing themself to feed off the blood."

"How did it not break you?"

"Honestly, I don't know. But that is why Brianna sees me as an equal, why I don't have to pay tribute."

Chapter 15

The following day, they met at the archives. Grant was going to be late for he was bringing Anthony Vizzini with him. Dom and Claire were still talking after their sleepover without Grunt or Dani to run interference if one annoyed the other too much. The two bickered like siblings and both had bad tempers if pissed-off.

"Ok," Dom began. "I'll catch Grant up when he gets here. Until Alistair is back, I'm in charge of STF. So I am going to be heading over to the precinct once Grant and Tony get here."

"How is he holding up?" Michael asked.

"He's in leader mode," Dani answered. "Evie is stepping in for Grace until Greyson arrives later today. Grace, is doing as well as one could imagine."

"You picking Grey up?" Dom asked.

"Al is going to let me know after lunch," Dani said.

The doors to the main level opened. Grant walked in with a man about the same age behind him. The man in question had dark hair that stood up in various directions, he wore a blazer over a gaming t-shirt with dark jeans. Dani noted the cane and saw some of the charms vibrating off of it. Claire noted her look and smiled.

"He needs it but he also charmed it for defense," Claire whispered. "Not many pick up on it."

"Everyone," Grant began. "This is Anthony Vizzini."

"Inconceivable," Dani stated.

Tony turned his eyes on her and smiled. "Oh, I like her."

"You like anyone that catches on," Claire argued.

"Hey Red!" Tony exclaimed as he walked over and gave Claire a hug.

"Alright, before Claire kills Tony for calling her Red," Grant replied. "Tony has made some impressive progress."

"You mean you've made sense of all the chaos we threw at you?" Dom asked.

"I love chaos," Tony informed them all as he took a seat. He had given his subway seat to a little old lady and now needed to sit for a few moments.

He took out his slim laptop and Grant helped him hook it up to the projector. Gregoir and the rest of the archivist joined them to go over what he found.

"I'm going to start with the archives," Tony told them. "I made a system that organizes all the requests that come in to you by week, month, then year. Then it's sorted into categories based on branch and subject under the branch."

He pulled up an example. "I'm going to download it to your system after this because you will be able to access everything a lot easier," Tony replied. "I did the last three years to start with because I wanted a base to compare to this year."

"Makes sense," Sylvia answered. "You wouldn't know if there was a change in pattern if you didn't have a base."

"My thought as well," Tony said. "On the surface it looks normal. If you aren't looking for anything pertaining to this case, you wouldn't pick up on any flags. But when you start focusing on dark magick, rare poisons, bond mates, power rituals, and neutral locations things get a bit interesting."

"How so?" Dom asked.

"Well, access to level B start popping up a bit more frequently," Tony admitted. "And names start becoming a bit repetitive."

"Not just anyone can go in there," Dani replied.

"I know which makes my job so much easier," Tony admitted. "Right, anyway, I notice a pattern at the start of the new year."

"How so?" Dani asked leaning forward in her chair.

"We start getting a some repetition with names," Tony explained. "I talked to Greg and Sayad, and it could be theorized that someone was working on a family tree or research for a paper or coven. I get that. So I changed the program I was running. I wanted to see if I could figure out what books were being taken and by who."

"You can do that?" Dom asked.

Tony laughed at the question. "I can do anything."

Dom raised an eyebrow at the witch. "When it comes to technology, he's right," Claire sighed. "He can do anything."

"Just feed into his ego," Grant mumbled.

"What did you find with the new program?" Dani inquired bringing them back to the topic.

"Narrowing the search helped a lot," Tony replied. "So four names pop up quite frequently. The first is Savannah Morris."

"She still hasn't passed her apprenticeship," Claire pointed out. "What is she looking into?"

"Well that is an interesting question," Tony said with a smile. "Miss Savannah has been looking into books that could increase power."

Grant let out a whistle. "Shit."

"Who is Savannah?" Michael asked.

"She's a bitch," Claire said. "Her parents and siblings are well respected in the coven. And then there is Savannah who thinks she is entitled to whatever she wants."

"She also has yet to show an area she excels in," Grant added. "Uncle Vern things that she has just enough witches blood to test as a witch but might be weak enough to just be generic. Which is fine, because we need generic witches in the blood line. We can't all have specialization. The issue with Savannah is we can't find an element we can work with her on."

"So if she found books on power she would be wanting to learn how to increase it?" Dani asked.

"In theory," Greg responded. "It would be very short term and the books she would be wanting would require her mentor's signature."

"That would be Evelyn Gross," Claire replied. "She is a

powerful fire witch but is considered generic because she didn't find a specific path."

"I would be surprised if Evelyn signed off on any of them," Grant responded.

"She didn't," Tony answered. "There are ten denied requests. Now the interesting thing is Savannah had placed another request two weeks before the theft here. Then withdrew the request suddenly the Friday before the theft."

"Weird," Dom replied. He didn't like weird.

"First, Savannah kept trying to access the vault and each time she was denied. Before you ask, she submitted a form six times since the first of the year. Greg actually sent a letter to her mentor about her need to access the vault."

"That is unusual," Agnes answered. She looked at Claire and Grant. "Do you think your Aunt or Uncle would know of this? I would think that Evelyn might have told one of them because of the frequent attempts."

"I'll talk to Aunt Tabby about it," Claire replied. "If she doesn't then I'll text Grant."

"You said there were more than one name," Donovan recalled.

"See, here is where things get a little bizarre," Tony admitted. "A name for a Lambert Berger pops up. He has requested access to one of the tomes that was stolen. But I can't find anyone by that name in any of the houses, I put in a request to a god-talker I know to see if maybe he knows the name. I'm waiting to hear back from that."

"Maybe an academic?" Greg suggested.

"If it was academic an institution would be listed," Dani argued. Yet the name seemed familiar to her, she just couldn't place it.

"And none are," Tony confirmed.

"Tony," Lars asked, he was the archivist for the God-Talkers. "Who did you reach out too?"

"The city rep," Tony answered.

"He'll know, I'll look at my records as well," Lars said.

"But the name doesn't stand out to you?" Claire asked the archivist to the God-talkers.

"No, I mean it's definitely German, but that's it," Lars answered.

"He's right, I'm not familiar with it either," Sylvia added.

"Tony, did you figure out how they broke into the restricted floor?" Dom asked.

"Yes," Tony replied. He changed the images up on the screen. "If he hacked into the system I would have been alerted. I looked through all the fire walls and safety nets that were in the system and none were tripped. I think our thief used a variety of charms and spells to manipulate the system. Now to do that we are talking a lot of power being used. So much that the person was probably drained at the end of it."

Dani froze in her seat. "He was," Dani said. "I heard him

mention in the vision that he used more power than he wanted to avoid leaving a trace."

"We have been tossing around the idea that this might not be a Spellcaster," Grant began. "Would a non-spellcaster be able to this?"

"I think only a non-spellcaster would be able to do this," Tony answered.

"Isn't that a little bias being that you are one," Michael pointed out.

"No," Tony said. "Just like what happened at the Algonquin, you're talking someone who has broken several of our cardinal laws. Which means Tabby or Vern or both would have known immediately, as well as run the possibility of dying on the spot."

"What about an apprentice?"

"When we turn 18 and are tested to see where we start our apprenticeship we take an oath to harm none, to maintain the laws of the coven, and to not use false power to improve our standing," Tony replied. "It's a sacred oath, not only would Tabby and Vern feel the break of oath but so would their Mentor. What was done here, it harmed Dani, it violated the laws of the Coven, and they used dark magick to manipulate the system."

"He's right," Claire replied.

"Of course I'm right," Tony said.

"Were there any other names?" Grant asked.

"They checked out to be academics," Tony answered.

"Can you send me all of this so I can show Al when he's back?" Dom asked.

"Yea," Tony replied. "Actually Dom, can I talk to you for a moment."

"You can use my office," Dani told them.

"So what do you want us to do?" Sylvia asked Dani.

"We still need to know what poison is being used and where it's coming from," Dani said. "Traces of the poison was found on Parker but the components varied a bit. It can help me research this Hebert Berger guy with Lars. Claire, you, Grant, and Greg can contact Evelyn and look into the books she wanted. The rest can keep going with the original assignments."

"I need to make a phone call real quick," Michael said. He then looked at Grant. "I'll meet you when I'm done."

Grant nodded. He looked at Dani. "We're meeting with Vynessa to go over the poison in both cases," he told her. "I'll send her report to you once we have all the information."

"Sounds good," Dani said, relieved that she didn't have to go to a morgue.

"I already have it," Claire told Grant. "I finalized it with her late last night. The amount of Silver and Mistletoe in Parker's version was much higher than in what was given to Josie and Harold and what burned Dani."

"Well that would make sense," Gloria said, the archivist for the shifters. They all looked at her. "Silver and Mistletoe are both more lethal to a shifter than to a vampire."

Well, shit," Grant said staring at Gloria. "That's why this poison is impossible and why Claire can't get a read on it."

"The ingredients are the same but in different dosage..." Claire began. She grabbed her bag and jumped up. "Grant I'm coming with you."

"Got it," Grant said as he grabbed his stuff.

* * * *

Sayad, Dani, and Lars had hit a dead end with Hebert Berger. When five o'clock rolled around, they were glad to be able to just leave and start again in the morning. Claire and Grant were still with Vynessa, Micheal was at the precinct with Dom looking through old case files that dealt with weird poisons. Dani was heading to the airport to pick up Grayson. She had Claire's jeep, Dani ignored the two cars following her. Alanna was in the front one, so far her team had been good at staying out of sight. Lucas had explained to them that Dani hated having to have security so to stay back as much as possible. And they had. It wasn't an issue when Dani was with Dom or at her apartment, it was everywhere else that was the concern. Greyson was flying into LaGuardia, they were then going to grab food at Never and Dust before he grabbed the train to Long Island. Dani was willing to drive him but like Lucas, Greyson was also concerned about her safety.

Dani pulled into short-term parking and found a spot, she then waited for the other two cars to pull in. Alana was the only one to come out of the car, so the two walked in silence toward the arrival doors. Greyson had already told her he would be in street clothes, he didn't want to be noticed in his fatigues, he just wanted to be out of the airport with minimum fuss. Alana milled around a coffee stand while Dani waited at the international arrivals gate. His plane had already landed and was going through customs. Dani spotted him immediately when he came through the gates, his light mocha skin stood out against the plain white shirt he was wearing. He wore a N.Y. Yankees baseball cap and jeans. A duffle bag and back pack were slung over his shoulders, his eyes were hidden behind sunglasses.

Dani walked to him when he was through and he pulled her into a hug. They stood there for a moment before moving out of the way. They walked to the coffee stand Alana was at and Dani introduced her to Greyson who was ordering coffee.

"You keeping her out of trouble?" Greyson asked after he took a sip of coffee.

"Not sure anyone can actually keep her out of trouble," Alana answered as the trio headed out of the airport. "But we are trying."

"Good," Greyson said. "Tell Lucas, we appreciate what you guys are doing for us."

"Your pack did the same when we needed time," Alana answered.

At the car, Greyson was introduced to the rest of the security detail before he loaded his gear into the back of Claire's car.

"We are going to split off once you guys are on your way to Never and Dust," Alana informed Dani. "You are safe with him and you both need time to grieve together."

"Thank you," Dani said.

"Text when you have dropped him off at the train station," Alana reminded her.

"She will," Greyson promised as he appeared. Dani stared at him. "Were hearing, just as good as Vampires."

Alana chuckled then looked serious. "You have our condolences, Mr. Clarence."

"It's Grey," he told her before sliding into the passenger seat.

Dani rolled her eyes as she headed into the driver's seat. Greyson got comfortable in the passenger seat as he moved it back a bit.

"Your body guard is hot," Greyson informed Dani.

"She can kill a person in 200 different ways," Dani answered.

"I might have to compare notes with her," Greyson replied.

They fell silent as Greyson drummed to the radio. When they got to *Never and Dust* the family dinner crowd had left. Gloria ran and hugged Greyson when she saw him come through the door with Dani.

"Tell your father, whatever he needs," Gloria said when they parted. She looked at Dani. "I kept the back booth clear for you."

"You are the best," Dani told her.

"I'll get your usuals," Gloria told them before leaving them alone.

Greyson looked around the bar, he recognized some of the people in there. He respected the fact that they had nodded to him when he entered but letting he be by not coming over to give their condolences.

"Alright, what the hell is going on?" Greyson asked Dani once they were seated in their booth.

"Well that's a question that can be in reference to a whole lot of things going on," Dani pointed out.

"Danika."

"Parker's death is tied to Josephine and Harold," Dani explained finally. "They were lured to the Algonquin, there they were given a poison that was lethal to Vampires. It subdued them so that as they died our killer could drain them of their power."

"The same poison that burnt your hand," Greyson noted as he looked at the fresh pink scar of where the burn had been.

"Yes," Dani confirmed. "Parker also ingested the poison but here's where it gets weird. The doses for the ingredients changed. There was more silver, more mistletoe, in his than what was in Josephine and Harolds."

"Because silver is poison to all were's and mistletoe is poison for cats," Greyson realized. "So this poison, it can be altered depending on the target?"

"That's the working theory at the moment," Dani replied.

"Did Parker know who it was?"

Dani nodded. "He...was so fucking brave," Dani said as her voice cracked.

Gloria emerged with their drinks and food. They felt a bubble go up around them as the banshee left. Dani took a long sip of the beer she had.

"He woke up to his murderer in the room with him," Dani explained. "The killer, who was able to cloak his scent and his presence from the pack. He tried to reason with him, I think he knew it was pointless."

"Parker was the peace maker of all of us," Greyson said as he took a sip from his own beer. "Fuck, Dani."

"I think Parker knew I would be there, that I would see what happened, I think he wanted to get information from the killer, so that I might hear it," Dani replied.

Greyson paused before taking another sip. He thought for a moment. "Parker would, if he knew that it would give you an edge, he would do that."

"Grey, this killer, he killed my parents," Dani said. "He was at Josie and Harold's memorial."

"That explains the detail Lucas has on you," Greyson replied.

"It was the only way to keep Nick from begging me to leave the case," Dani answered. "Lucas promised guards and I can still work the case."

"Lucas hasn't asked you to step down?" Greyson asked carefully.

Dani arched her eyebrow at him as she leaned back in the booth. "Lucas likes where his head is too much to ever think of asking me to step down," Dani commented.

"He is a smarter man than many," Greyson said with a grin. "So you and he?"

"It's complicated."

"That's a social media status," Greyson replied.

She ate one of her fries before answering his question. "We're mates."

"I know you'er friends....wait, shit, seriously?" Greyson asked understanding what she meant. "Have you bonded? I mean you're not a full vampire."

"No we haven't bonded, because no one knows what would happen if we did especially since I have yet to take the Oath," Dani said.

"Well that has to be frustrating," Greyson realized.

"You have no fucking idea how frustrating," Dani answered with a groan. "We share a bed, we kiss, anything more and it's like walking through the other's mind. And I have enough shit going on right now."

"So not even foreplay?" Greyson asked. He dodged the fry that got thrown at him. "Okay, we won't talk about your sex life. We'll talk about mine."

"You suck so much right now," Dani replied.

He went to tease her right back but froze when he saw who just walked through the bar door. He grabbed her hand in his in case the bubble wasn't enough.

"Bartram, I believe you were informed on your last visit that you are banned from this establishment," Gloria stated as she came out from behind the bar. Her accent getting thicker toward the end of the sentence.

"But dear Gloria, can't we make amends," Bartram said in a voice filled with charm and seduction. "After all, with everything that is going on in our community, shouldn't we be sticking together."

Gloria walked right up to the vampire who towered over

her. "And I bet you know exactly what is going on," she all but growled. "You have ten seconds to leave my bar before I have the wards kick your ass out into the river."

The whole bar was silent, for everyone knew better then to challenge the banshee. Power radiated from her in waves, those sitting close to where she was were already moving out of the way incase she made do on her threat to unleash the wards.

"10, 9, 8..." Gloria began counting.

"I heard my dear sister was here," Bartram explained with his hands held up as if he was innocent of a crime. "I wanted to see how she was doing after another person she knew has died so tragically."

"And you're an asshole, leave now," Gloria replied.

"Have you seen her?"

"1," Gloria said.

Everyone ducked as the wards that defended its inhabitants were turned on Bartram. The look on Bartram's face as magick spun around him was priceless. Dani almost laughed as she watched the magick throw him out of the bar. A loud splash was heard letting them know that he landed where Gloria warned he would.

"Round on the house," Gloria announced as the wards went back into place.

She walked toward where Greyson and Dani sat. "Let's go," Gloria replied.

They slid out of the booth and followed Gloria through a door next to where the kitchen was. They went down a narrow set of stairs into what looked like an old basement that had been forgotten about.

"I don't know what the hell is going on, but your adoptive brother is involved in this," Gloria informed Dani. "The wards, one of them reacted to blood magick. And he's gunning for you."

"I know," Dani said. "There was a warning from Parker

when I entered his mind at the crime scene. That I have to unlock the doors in my memory."

"Do you know who?" Gloria asked.

"Tabby has been in touch with a Dream-walker named Cassandra to come train me," Dani replied.

"Tell Tabby I'm going to work with you and Claire," Gloria answered. "The Mediterranean pantheon has rumors of a traitor who is selling names to not the nicest of people. Cassandra is one of the names that have come up possibly being a traitor."

"I'll tell her," Dani promised, shocked at what Gloria was telling her.

Gloria nodded. There was a knock from somewhere. Gloria walked toward a moss covered door that appeared out of nowhere. When she opened it a very confused Alana stood there.

"That was amazing," Alana said to no one.

"The two of you go with Alana," Gloria replied. "Name your destination and you'll arrive."

"It's a fae portal," Dani realized. They were rumored to exist and most people never lived to see one.

Gloria winked at her before she closed the door on them. Power pulled all around them as Alana named the destination.

Chapter 16

"And she is certain that Cassandra is one of the suspects?" Tabby asked as she paced in Claire and Dani's apartment.

"She said that she would train Claire and me," Dani answered.

"Why do I need to be included?" Claire asked as she handed Dani a mug of tea.

Dom went with Alana to drive Greyson to Long Island. With Bartram showing up at the bar, no one was taking chances.

Unknowing, he had just placed himself on the top of their list of suspects.

"Actually, it makes sense," Tabby said. "For the most part Dani will need to learn how to use her talents without help. But there will be circumstances, like what happened at Parker's apartment, or even the Algonquin, where having you understand how it works will be beneficial."

"Would I better understand what Dani needs?"

"Yes, I believe you would," Tabby replied. "Banshee's are extremely powerful. They are believed to be the first of the Fae, for Bean Sidhe translate into woman of the fairy. They slowly became associated with death, being warnings of death, after a great battle accrued in their realm. Some say seeing one is an omen of your own death, other's see them as spirits helping them grieve the lost of a loved one. There are many Banshees that prefer life here in our world then in their own."

"How come?" Dani asked.

"While Banshees are wise beyond their years, they are seen as a bad omen, even among their own people. They also look the most like humans so blending in is not an issue for them," Tabby explained. "They don't look like the monsters of fairytales, so they can live a normal life pretty much. Most live near water for they are related to the Water Fae."

"And Gloria?"

"She will be an excellent teacher," Tabby answered. "I'm a bit annoyed with myself that I did not think of asking her to begin with. Water Fae are extremely gifted with dream magick, and with her being a Banshee she has a connection to death as well."

The door to the apartment opened with a warning growl from Grunt. Lucas walked in, closing the door behind him.

"I will call Gloria to let her know what my thoughts are on your training and then the three of you can set up a schedule," Tabby said as she stood up. She paused for a moment. "It might not be a bad idea for Lucas to be in on some of the training as well. I'll talk to her about it."

Tabby hugged Dani, when she hugged Claire it was tighter, as if she was also afraid for her niece.

"I'm fine," Claire assured her aunt.

"Just... don't be stupid," Tabby replied as she kissed

Claire on the cheek and left the apartment.

Claire waited a few moments before turning to look at Dani. "So what didn't you say in front of my Aunt?"

"That when the wards threw Bartram out on his ass one of them detected blood magick," Dani replied.

"Well shit," Claire said almost sorry she asked.

"You don't seem surprised by this," Lucas noted as he watched Dani.

"In some horribly twisted way, it would make sense if Bartram was involved because ... well none of it makes any sense," Dani replied. "We've been looking at this as what a person has to lose, but maybe we need to think about what do they have to gain? Bartram is going to ignore the negative. He is going to see the ability to gain power and take it, the ability to outsmart my father and Alexius, and to pull the ultimate power move would be priceless for him."

"And killing?" Claire asked.

"Josie and Harold weren't his first, and neither were my parents, if Alastair's cold cases say anything," Dani replied.

"And you don't think Alexius is involved?" Claire asked.

"Alexius is an ass who hates anyone who isn't a vampire," Dani began. "But, image, public opinion, those all matter to him. His biggest rationale for me taking the Oath is because it is improper for an unmarried woman to be living on her own."

"She's right," Lucas agreed. "I don't think he has a heart but he would never do anything that would damage his family name. He wouldn't risk it for ultimate power."

"And Marcus?" Claire inquired.

"If he is involved it would be the cover-up," Dani answered.

"So do we tell the others?" Claire asked.

Dani took a sip of the tea. "Dom needs to know," Dani answered. "I don't want to keep Grant out in the dark, but ...."

"You don't trust Micheal," Lucas realized.

"He took an Oath to my House, it would place him in a difficult position," Dani admitted. It had nothing to do with the fact she trusted Michael with her life. This was about the oath. "I mean he hates Bartram with a passion and he can't stand Alexius or my father. So it's nothing like that, but I don't want to put him a position where he has to choose career over his house."

"That is a valid concern," Lucas agreed.

"But we didn't have that concern with Dom," Claire pointed out.

"Because my parents don't treat our house like we are back in the time of Feudalism," Lucas pointed out. "With the lower ranking vampires in Marcus' world, he does."

"Look, this is a huge what if," Claire began. "Shit, you really think it's Bartram?"

"I think it could be, or he is majorly involved in this," Dani said. "Look, Not many people know about the red mist in my memories. I refuse to believe that is a coincidence since I have never seen it at any other crime scene. I also felt it at the memorial service. If it's not Bartram then it's someone who movies in our circle. I know there are a lot of what ifs but focusing on him might not be a bad place to start."

"Okay," Claire sighed. "Just, let's fill Dom in, and then when you are at the archives maybe work on the Bartram angle. If we can find a solid trail then we go to Alistair."

"Deal," Dani said.

"I could put some feelers out on the Berger and Son company that Tony found," Lucas suggested. "And yes I will do it discreetly, Red."

"I really hate that nickname," Claire reminded him. She let out a huge yawn. "Alright I'm going to bed. Grunt you want to sleep with Aunt Claire tonight?"

Grunt got up from his spot at Dani's feet and followed Claire into her bedroom. Lucas looked at Dani. "You should go to bed too, the next few days are going to be a bit intense."

"Lay with me before I fall asleep?" Dani asked.

Lucas smiled and took her hand helping her off the couch. They headed into what was now their bedroom. His clothes were now hung up alongside hers. In her bathroom, his things were mixed with hers. This apartment felt more like home to him than any place he had lived in a very long time. He changed out of his dress shirt, and pants, pulling on basketball shorts and a tank. While Dani went through her own routine, he took off his watch and leather cuff that he wore and sent them down on the nightstand he had claimed.

Dani smiled at him as she came out of her bathroom.

Taking his one wrist she turned it so she could the see the raised scars that encircled his wrist. She kissed the one just above his veins. He tensed as she did, Dani reached up on her toes to kiss him.

Lucas wrapped his left arm around her, pulling her closer so that their bodies were lined up. He knew they should stop, they both knew they should stop. But tonight, with Bartram turning up at the bar, with what Gloria discovered, he needed to know she was okay.

"I want to forget," Dani whispered as she kissed just under his chin where stubble had started to grow.

"We can't," Lucas groaned as he leaned down to kiss her again.

"I know," Dani whispered. Lucas found a sensitive spot behind her ear that had her melting. "I just...I need to feel you, feel us."

Lucas stopped and looked down at her. "You know what's at risk?"

"Whenever you have been in my head it's been this calming presence," Dani replied. "I'm not afraid, Lucas."

"I am," he admitted as he held her close for a moment. "You terrify me, Danika. You are this light, this energy and I am so afraid that when you see what I have done, what I have been through, you'll turn from me."

"I won't," Dani promised.

Lucas saw the truth in her eyes, he held her close to him before kissing her. "No sex, but we can do other things," Lucas said with a glint in his eyes.

"Like what?" Dani asked with a mischievous grin on her face.

* * * *

Lucas was standing in the living room looking out the windows. He was wearing dark jeans and a black dress shirt. The sleeves had been pushed up to the elbows already. He heard movement as Dani stepped out of her bedroom with her hair already curling madly. She was wearing cotton shorts and a tank.

"I have coffee going for you," Lucas told her with a hint of a smile.

"Thanks," Dani said with a yawn and a shy smile.

She headed into the kitchen and found a mug sitting next to the counter. Pouring the coffee into the mug she opened the fridge and saw mini vials of blood in the one shelf. Taking one she dumped it into the coffee then added cream. With her coffee in hand she walked to where Lucas stood.

The door to Claire's bedroom opened and Grunt was the first to come out. He ran to his food bowl, that Lucas had already filled. Claire then stumbled out and went right to the kitchen. She paused then walked back into the living room.

"You two had sex," Claire realized.

"Technically, no," Dani said as she sipped her coffee.

"I need coffee."

They watched as Claire stumbled back into the kitchen to get her coffee. Lucas smiled and kissed Dani lightly.

"No regrets?" He asked.

"None, you?"

"Only that we couldn't go farther," he admitted.

She knew she was blushing as she smiled. "Lucas..." she began but then stopped as an image slammed into her. The coffee cup fell from her hand as she fell backwards.

Lucas was chained to the wall of a dungeon or something. He was trying to break free of the chains that held him. Across from him someone was laying on a table, while a surgeon explained, in German, what he was going to do. The pain was so intense as he screamed out at the guards to use him instead.

"Dani," Lucas gasped pulling her from the scene.

She looked at him and saw confusion in his eyes. "What just happened?"

"What did you see?" Lucas asked as he sat down in on the couch. He pulled her into his lap, needing the contact. Claire was there on her other side, checking Dani's pulse while Grunt was trying to climb onto Dani's lap.

"You were chained to a wall, a man was on a surgical table of some sort, this surgeon was talking to him but I think it was in German."

Lucas sighed leaning his head back. That was not one of the visions he would want anyone to see.

"Do you guys want alone time?" Claire asked. She hadn't had a full cup yet so her brain wasn't really working right.

"You can hear this too," Lucas said. He moved so Claire could join them, knowing that having Claire there would also help Dani.

"I told you I fought in World War II?" Dani nodded so he continued. "I was part of an elite resistance fighters group, we were all supernaturals. We worked with all the different resistance groups, France, UK, and others. When our estate in Norway was seized, I was in Germany working out the logistics of how we would operate."

"And what I saw?" Dani asked

"My squad, we were captured," Lucas recalled. "It was

toward the end of the war, the Nazis were desperate. Their "doctor death" wanted as many supernaturals as he could get to experiment on, see how much we could take before we died. How he could replicate our DNA in human's without having to be beaten or bred. Bjorn, the man on the table, he was an extraordinary witch. He was a berserker."

"A what?" Dani asked confused.

"They're a branch of God-talkers," Claire recalled from her studies. "Each group of gods have their fighters here on earth. They deal with those who break the laws of their people. Berserkers answer to Odhin and the Norse gods."

"And Bjorn was one of them?" Dani asked Lucas.

"He was amazing in battle," Lucas said with a faint smile. "He was an entire unit on his own. Hitler wanted to see how he could harness that power, make super soldiers that were linked to Odhin."

"Well he was fascinated with Norse mythology," Dani recalled. "He twisted it to serve his purpose."

"The scene you saw was the start of another torture session with Bjorn," Lucas explained. "We were close. I had ensured that his wife and kids got to America before he would join our group. I used my title as a Talon to get them past the immigration issues. He knew that was not something I did often. He was the only one that knew that Lucas Haroldson was actually Lucas Talon."

"What happened to him?" Claire asked the question. She knew it was dumb, knew that the answer wasn't going to be a happy one.

"He died," Lucas said softly as he rubbed his wrists absent-mindedly. "I watched him die. Watched what they did to him. Some of the scars I have are from me trying to break free of the chains they used on me. They were a silver compound, I didn't care."

Dani kissed his forehead as she held him close. He had

seen so much death, so much horror, yet when you met him he was easy going.

"What of his family?" Claire asked.

"My parent's made sure his wife and kids were taken care of, I could get them to New York City because my parents were here," Lucas replied. "They declared them as under protection of House Talon. I brought his ashes home with me, gave them to his widow. She thanked me for bringing him home."

"Lucas, they both knew the odds of him coming home were slim," Dani said. "You gave her closure by bringing him home. She didn't have to wonder."

"It took me a while to figure that out," he admitted.

"So what did you see?" Dani asked.

"Parker," Lucas replied. Both Dani and Claire grimaced at that. He looked at her touching her face with his hand. "How do you do it? How do you walk into murder scenes knowing you are going to experience everything?"

"I keep asking her the same thing," Claire replied.

"If I don't then who else will?" She asked them both.

"And how can you argue with that," Claire replied.

"Don't you have somewhere to be?" Dani asked Claire.

"Yes, I can refill all our mugs because this shit is too deep to be dealing with in the morning," Claire said. She got up and headed into the kitchen.

"Did we see these images because of last night?"

"I've slept the death sleep in a bed with you, was completely defenseless," Lucas theorized. "You trusted that I would keep you safe, not wanting to be alone. We were both defenseless but knew the other would keep the other safe."

"Strengthening the link between us," Dani realized.

"Plus we also took our intimacy to a new level," Lucas said with a knowing smile. "Something we had never done before. A few stolen kisses isn't going to cement a bond."

"What now?"

"Now we are going to have to figure out who our killer is, unlock your memory, go to Parker's funeral, and get you Oathed," Lucas said.

"And after lunch?" Dani asked.

Lucas couldn't help but smile as he bent down to kiss her.

"NO SEX ON THE COUCH!" Claire yelled.

"It was a kiss," Dani replied.

"I know, but I'm just saying, no sex on the couch," Claire replied. "It's the new house rule."

"She's no fun sometimes," Lucas chuckled causing Dani too blush.

Chapter 17

The armored SUV carrying Lucas and Dani pulled through the gates of Clarence Farm just as dusk was setting. Alana was driving with Dom following in the SUV behind them. When Alistair had extended the invitation to Lucas, the vampire had been floored. He knew that Dani would be invited for she was practically an honorary pack member. She and Greyson had dated for the last two years of high school and her first year of College. The distance, what they wanted to do in life, the realization they had become better friends than lovers had ended their relationship. Now the two were like siblings. Lucas knew that Alistair felt fatherly toward Dani, as he had been there the night her parents were killed. But when the invitation was extended to him, that was a surprise.

The funerals for Were's were private affairs held within the confines of the pack and close friends. It was rare for Heads of other branches to be invited. But Alistair was not like many other pack leaders.

The SUV rolled to a stop and doors opened. Todd Clarence helped Dani out of the SUV while Alana held the door for Lucas.

Todd pulled Dani into a hug. "You're going to find him."

"I am," Dani promised.

Todd nodded. He then shook hands with Lucas. "I'm Greyson's middle brother," Todd explained. "Drake is helping with final preparations."

"Greyson, Todd, Drake," Lucas said out loud. "Batman fans?"

"I think he wins the reward for figuring it out the quickest," Alistair said as he appeared. "Lucas, thank you for coming. It means a lot to us to have you here."

"I was honored when I got the invitation," Lucas admitted.

"Todd, go help Drake," Alistair instructed his middle child.

They watched Todd head off toward where his brother was. Alistair motioned for them to walk with them. Lucas had been to the ranch a few times over the years, it was usually full of life and noise. People were always coming and going. But now the voices were hushed, black banners with silver accents hung from the buildings. Candles were lit in the windows, and torches lined the pathways.

"About a hundred and fifty made it here," Alistair informed them. "Others who couldn't, have sent what they could. Parker... he was loved by a lot of people. He hated being Grey's second, but he did it because Grey asked him."

As they walked Lucas noted that many of the Weres nodded to him as if he was one of them and not an outsider. As they neared the home where Grace and her family lived they spotted a large group of women. The women were standing near the porch wearing white dresses, wreathes of flowers encircled their heads as they whispered amongst each other.

As they past the last of the buildings, they headed up a small incline that led to a large area that had been cleared of trees. It was stunning, Lucas could picture on a night of a full moon how amazing the view from here would be. He noted that a large pyre had been constructed in the center of the clearing. Men were adding last minute items to it.

"We have a special license from the state and federal government," Alistair informed Lucas. "Every pack has at least one person licensed to do cremations and burials."

"This is ...." Lucas failed for words. "Thank you."

"I think it's time we put all the old stories to rest, don't you," Alistair said.

"Yes," Lucas agreed.

Alistair nodded. "Dani, you can take him toward where the family will stand," Alistair instructed Dani. "Things will start as the sun starts to set more."

Alistair then headed toward a small stone house near the edge of the clearing. Chanting could be heard as he opened the door. Lucas followed Dani toward where people had begun to gather.

"They focus on their loved one returning back to nature," Dani explained to Lucas. "When the full moon rises, their ancestor's will rise and run with them in spirit."

"Like the Fae, in a way," Lucas noted.

"Except they aren't seeing Parker in a new flower, or the first rain of spring," Dani answered. "The women wear white, those unmarried where the flower wreathes, they begin the processional. Then the men who are related to the deceased will carry him on a litter to the pyre. The family then comes out and, well, you'll see."

Lucas nodded, now understanding why she told him not to wear black, and to wear comfortable shoes. Dani had worn a light purple cotton dress that fell to her ankles with comfortable flats, her hair was loose, and she wore little makeup. He dressed in gray slacks, with a purple dress shirt, and his black motorcycle boots. He had pulled his hair back into a plait so it wouldn't blow in his face during the ceremony.

He heard singing before most of the others did. Soft female voices singing in a mix of latin and english. People began to form a large circle around the pyre, all dressed similar to how Dani and he were dressed. No ties, no suit jackets, no black. As the singing got louder, Lucas noted the torches that several of the women held as they came up the hill to the clearing. Some who knew the song joined in as the circle opened to let the women in, they then formed a half circle at the head of the pyre.

Lucas then heard drums from somewhere. The doors to the cottage opened and several men wearing leather kilts, and white button down shirts filed out, banging on the drums as they joined in the chant the women had begun. Instead of joining the women, they form a small half circle at the foot of the pyre. A female carrying a torch walked to one of the drummers and handed him her torch. She then rejoined the choir of women.

Slowly the singing and the drumming came to a stop so that all one could hear were their heartbeats and nature around them. Lucas gripped Dani's hand as he took it all in. Those that were elderly were given chairs to sit in, the young who were too small to stand were carried off to Alistair's where they would rest or play games. A slow drum cadence began and the door to the cottage opened, this time a dozen men, some Lucas recognized, carried a beautiful wooden litter on their shoulders. To the cadence of the drum, they marched to the pyre. Greyson, Todd, Drake, and Parker's brother Miles were the first four of the men. They wore all black with silver arm bands that had a panther etched onto it.

It was all well choreographed, as they moved with the drums, positioning the wooden litter, men moving from where they were to help slide it onto the pyre. When it was finally in place, Greyson, Todd, Drake, and Miles joined Dani and Lucas. Then a blonde female from the choir came to join them. Dani introduced her as Gwen, Parker's youngest sibling.

Another drum cadence started and Alistair emerged from the cottage, with his wife, then followed by Grace and Arthur. He paused by an elderly man, they hugged briefly before continuing toward where Dani stood with Lucas. Greyson stepped forward and took his mother's arm, while Miles took Grace's. Alistair nodded then walked toward the pyre, from his pocket he pulled out a small match box car and set it down. Next, each family member came to place an item that reminded them of Parker.

Lucas saw Grace knees buckle before most, and was there on the other side of her before she could fall. He helped her husband straighten her up, staying there with her, supporting most of her weight so that her husband could grieve. Grace patted him on the arm as he helped her return to where the family stood. Arthur followed them and pulled Lucas into a hug thanking him.

Once they were all back, Alistair stood at the head of the Pyre and nodded to the drummers to stop.

"Tonight we are here to send a child of the moon back to his ancestors," Alistair began. His voice trying to be strong. "Parker Riley will be remembered with each full moon that rises, he will be remembered as we run through the night to slay the monsters that prey on us."

Alistair went to speak again, but no words came out. He turned to Lucas and gave a simple nod.

Lucas let go of Dani's hand and, surprising many including Dani, stepped to where Alistair stood. He placed a hand on Alistair's shoulder.

"Lo, there do I see my father," Lucas began his voice

strong and clear. "Lo, there do I see my mother, and my sisters, and my brothers. Lo, there do I see the line of my people back to the beginning. Lo, do they call to me. They bid me to take my place amongst them, in the halls of Valhalla! Where the brave may live forever!"

Alistair walked to the Choir and took two of the torches, he handed one to Lucas, then another to Grace, the third went to the old man in the chair. Alistair took the one from the drummer. He waited until Lucas was at the head of the pyre and he took the foot, with Grace and Ben Riley in place.

"May we see you on the next full moon," Alistair said as he lowered his torch. "May you walk with our ancestors and be in peace."

Locking eyes with Lucas, they both lowered their torches to the pyre followed by Grace and Ben.

* * * *

Lucas stood leaning on one of the porch railings, listening to a story about the last full moon run. Now the ranch was filled with laughter and music and noise. Gone was the solemness, replaced with a celebration for the life of Parker. Many had thanked Lucas for being there for Alistair when he needed a voice. Most were touched that he selected a prayer from his people.

"It has blood in it," Greyson said as he handed him a beer.

Dani was across the way laughing at something that had been said to her. "You know if you hurt her the pack will tear you apart," Greyson informed him.

"If I hurt her, I will deserve whatever pain is bestowed upon me," Lucas replied.

Lucas watched as Miles was walking over with his grandfather. "Lucas Talon, this is Ben Reiley," Miles introduced them. "Gramps wanted to talk to you."

"I can talk for myself," Ben stated. One of the guys got up from the porch chair so that Ben could sit down.

Miles rolled his eyes as he sat on the step. He had no clue what his grandfather wanted to talk to Lucas about, but since he saw Lucas arrive the old man had wanted to talk to the vampire.

"You were in World War II," Ben stated to Lucas.

The beer froze to Lucas lips at Ben's statement. The others paused as well. "I was," Lucas confirmed.

"You were part of one of those mixed units," Ben continued. "You rescued people."

"I did," Lucas said. He noted that Dani had stopped talking and was watching him closely as if she was picking up on his unease.

"Gramp," Grey warned. He could pick up on Lucas' tension, many soldiers didn't like to talk about war, especially those that survived World War II.

"Before they tell me to shut up," Ben continued. "Thank you."

Lucas looked at the old man, confused for a moment. "I'm not sure..."

"I was ten, the orphan train I was on, the tracks had been messed with," Ben began. "They were sweeping the cars for any supernatural kids, though they didn't phrase it that way."

"No they wouldn't," Lucas replied then lowered his beer as he remembered. "You were in one of the cars that been knocked over. You were trying to keep your sister calm, telling her that superhero's would rescue you."

Ben chuckled. "She was five at the time and liked my comics," Ben replied. "But I was right, you came and saved us."

"It wasn't just me," Lucas answered.

"No it wasn't, but you are here now, so thank you," Ben said. "Lettie and I got to live our lives because of your troop."

"Wait," Miles said as things started to click into place. "How is this possible?"

"When we rescued the children from the train we sent them to safe homes," Lucas explained. "If I remember, we sent your grandfather, his sister and a few other's to a farm in Ireland. The Rileys."

"The five of us took their last name," Ben confirmed. "We had lost all our paperwork in that crash. They gave us a fresh start while keeping true to our different heritages."

"Does dad know?" Miles asked.

"No, I just came here to tell a stranger something I didn't tell your father," Ben answered.

"Are we jewish?" Miles asked.

"No, my parents were sent to the camps because they

protested against Hitler," Ben explained.

Dani walked over and laid a hand on Lucas' arm. "What am I missing?"

"Just how bad-ass your boyfriend is," Miles answered.

"He's exaggerating," Lucas said.

"No he's not," Ben and Greyson said at the same time.

Lucas rolled his eyes as he pulled Dani toward him to hide his embarrassment. This just caused Greyson to laugh even more.

Chapter 18

White boards had been set up in the conference rooms at the archives. Case notes pertaining to crime scenes and victims were on the two side board, the bigger of the three held the notes discussing the working theories. Once a day they would all meet up in the conference room, either in person or via speaker phone to go over everything they had found. There were many different aspects of the case that made a straight forward answer difficult.

Claire came running into the conference room late for the meeting. She slammed a notebook down causing them all to jump. "I found it!" Claire exclaimed with triumphant smile.

"Found what?" Gregoir asked as he picked up his reading glasses that he had knocked to the floor.

"The poison, it's history," Claire said with a huge smile for that had been their biggest issue.

The room fell silent. "The amount of digging and cross referencing I had to do is mind numbing, but I found a few references to it," Claire said excitedly. "The one that broke it open for me is from the 1850's, in London. There were news articles dealing with an apothecary who was arrested for the killing of three prominent lords, all who were vampires as well."

"Did he know they were vampires?" Tony asked. Even in Victorian Society when the occult was all the rage, the supernatural community had to be cautious about who they trusted. Many of their laws today were based on that time period.

"According to the apothecary, the concoction was only to purge the person's stomach not kill them," Claire read from her notes. "Now in a regular person that would be true, though it was a very extreme mixture that would leave the person sick for days. In extremely high dosages given over a length of time it could kill a mortal. Because of this it was usually used on enemies, political opponents, or jilted lovers."

"What else does the apothecary say?"Dani inquired.

"He writes that a wealthy man came in and inquired about the concoction, he had been warned that it would leave the person quite ill for several days. That if this was for a stomach ailment there were other mixtures the apothecary would recommend. The lord was insistent and paid in full."

"What happened to the apothecary?" Dani asked. "Did the detectives believe him or was he charged?"

"Thankfully he had two shop assistants who recalled the lord and were able to verify that the man was warned. The shop was given a fine for handing out a dangerous remedy and the lord was never found."

"I guess it would be safe to say that this lord knew his victims were vampires and he knew the poison would kill them," Grant stated. "Even if the apothecary knew of vampires he wouldn't tell the police that."

"My thought as well," Dom agreed. "Even back then we were cautious. We never stayed in a place for more then a decade or two."

"How easy is it to find?" Lucas wondered. "Is this some-thing I could find on the internet or in an herb book?"

"It's not," Claire replied. "I have only found it in one book of herbs which is buried in the back of the Dark Arts section. You would also have to understand old Latin. I can tell you that I was never taught how to make it."

"Ok, but what about Parker?" Dani asked. "I gather it was a different poison?

"Same potion just different levels of the contents," Claire stated. "I had Vynessa break down the poisons found in all the victims and Dani. She confirmed, that for Parker, silver was added at a higher dose as well as mistletoe because he transforms into a cat."

"So what's the concoction made of?" Grant asked.

"Silver, Holy Water, Mistletoe, and Deadly Nightshade."

Dom let out a whistle as they all went silent. Claire went on. "Mistletoe, as we know, is poisonous to felines and Parkers's a were panther so it would be enough to make him severely ill, then increase the liquid silver in it and with his already weaken system it would kill him."

"What about for Dani and my parents?" Lucas asked. He felt Dani rest her hand on his thigh under the table.

"Very little silver," Claire said. "But a heavy mix of Holy Water, Mistletoe and Deadly Nightshade."

"Is there an antidote?" Tony asked Claire. She was the antidote queen.

"No," Claire said. "Trust me I've been trying to figure one out but I can't counteract both the silver and the holy water."

"You said there was another time this was mentioned," Dani remembered.

"This is where things get a bit weird," Claire warned. "For those not part of the research club, we've been researching the Joseph line."

"That sounds like fun," Tony said dryly. "I'm kind of glad I'm part of the tech group."

"Your missing out," Dom joked as he leaned back in his chair. "Do you know Helena met DaVinci?"

"Is she the inspiration for the Mona Lisa?" Tony replied trying to keep his geekiness in check.

"Are you two done?" Claire asked. They both nodded.

"So this is all from third hand accounts but it's around the time of the end of the crusades."

"So the 1200's?" Grant asked. He was never good with history.

"More like the 1400's," Dani commented. "In the year 1453 the Ottoman's take back Constantinople and in 1492, which is considered the end of the Crusades, the Spanish win Granada from the Moors."

They all looked at her. It always amazed them how much history Dani actually knew and that this was her area and not criminal investigation.

"Thank you Professor Joseph," Dom replied.

Dani flipped him off. "Wrong Joseph, that's Sayad."

"Are we done?" Alistair asked.

"Anyway," Claire said as she continued. "Not a lot of names are given in the account that I was reading."

"To be fair, back then, names of supernatural's would not be written down for fear of being found out later on," Dom explained. "The Accords aren't even around then."

"Can Claire finish with this," Lucas suggested as he refilled their drinks. He had been invited because of his knowl-

edge .

Claire shot Lucas a thankful look. "Okay, so as Dani

said, in 1452 you have what is referred to as the Fall of Constan-

tinople."

"And we know a white person siding with the Crusades

wrote that title," Dani commented. Claire arches her eyebrow at

Dani. "Sorry, continue."

"They get wind of a rumor that is spreading from camp

to camp. Rumors saying that an Ancient was killed while he

slept and no evidence of foul play was found."

"You don't just walk up to an Ancient and kill them,"

Dom pointed out.

"If you let me finish I can explain," Claire said annoyed.

Sometimes the fact that they acted like family made it hard to get

through briefings. "Most thought it was just rumor and dis-

missed it. However, there's a journal entry in the Centurion

House archives that is an eye-witness account from a captain. He

states that a messenger arrived at their camp with troubling news.

Pretending to not overhear what was said in the tent, he found out that an elder was killed using a poison mixture. The messenger was killed so no one could hear what had been said."

"Kill the messenger and no one knows a poison can take down an ancient or an elder," Dom stated.

"Who was the person that received the messenger?" Dani asked.

Claire looked through her notes. "A man by the name of Catigernus," Claire answered.

The vampires in the room went silent at the name. Dani stood up grabbing her tablet. "I have to go," Dani said.

She rushed out of the room. Dom went to follow but Lucas shook his head. "Let her be," Lucas replied. He had a feeling he knew exactly where she was going.

＊＊＊＊

The Metropolitan Museum of Art was busy with summer tours as Dani entered it. One of the security guards immediately recognized her, he waved her over to his section that was for employee and volunteers over.

"Hello, Miss Danika," he said as he had her go through the metal detector. "Here to see your mom?"

"Is she in her office?" Dani asked.

"She is. You go on back there."

Dani nodded and took the badge he handed her. She headed toward one of the "employee only" doors. Her mother worked at the MET as their expert on the byzantine era, as well as, other areas of ancient history. Heading to where some of the offices were, Dani smiled at the secretary for the antiquities department.

Dani knocked on her mother's door than entered. Helena looked up from her computer, she smiled when she saw Dani.

"Well this is a surprise," Helena said getting up from her desk. Then she noted Dani's face. "What is it?"

Dani closed the door then looked at her mother not sure where she should even start this conversation. "I need to know the truth," Dani began. "About everything. About the night my parent's died, about your father Caius Catigernus. About Marcus."

Helena stared at her for a moment then slowly sat back

down at her desk. She turned off her computer then looked at Dani.

"Then my fears are correct, he is involved," Helena realized.

"Mom, I can't protect you if you don't tell me what is going on," Dani informed her.

Helena nodded. "Perhaps it is time it all comes out anyway," Helena sighed, for the first time truly feeling her age. "Lies can wear on a person's soul after a time."

Helena got up from her desk and walked to one of the bookshelves. She took a frame picture off of one of the shelves smiling at it. It was of their estate in Istanbul.

"My father had lived a long time before I was born," Helena began. She looked at Dani. "You know the legends about our line?"

Dani nodded. "That we descend from the Centurion who ended Jesus' life on the cross with his spear."

"And if I told you that it was true?" Helena asked.

"Explain."

"My father never spoke of who he had ended the suffering for," Helena began. "Only my brother's and I were ever told the story and even then he wouldn't say the name. But he was a marked man after that."

"Pissing off Roman Emperors was usually bad for ones health back then," Dani agreed.

"After escaping Jerusalem he went all over the world, well, as much as one could at that time. His name was a hated name, one linked with traitor," Helena started. "He changed it to Caius, which was a common Roman name. He went to the lands of the Vikings, then to the British Isles. By then he realized the curse bestowed upon him for ending the suffering of a prisoner was true. He hadn't aged at all."

Dani watched as her mother moved around the room. "He looked to all sorts of scholars to find if there was a way to end his curse," Helena continued. "He had fled his homeland to escape from his actions. Now he was determined to find out what had been done to him and if he could change it."

"He found it?" Dani guessed.

"He was alone, Danika," Helena stated so that her daughter would understand what was coming next. "There was no one like him."

"Let me guess he made a deal with the devil," Dani said sarcastically. It wouldn't be the first time.

"Nothing that dramatic," Helena assured her. "A simple potion that would allow him to breed, to turn his curse into a blessing. If made wrong then it would cause excruciating death but he didn't care. If it worked he could have a family, if it failed then death would finally find him."

"So what happened?"

"It worked, obviously," Helena said with a sad smile. "He gave his blood to those he thought deserving. He fell in love had four sons. Moved to Istanbul where he could live a nice life as a farmer and merchant. By the 1400's he was a respected land owner. He married his third wife, for the other two had died in either child birth or from the plague. And I was born in 1440."

"Did your brother's fight in the battle for Constantinople?" Dani asked.

"Yes, one was killed during it," Helena smiled sadly. "Ari doted on me. They all did, I was the only girl."

"Did you know who he was? What he had done?"

"He rarely spoke of those years," Helena replied. "When he did it would be just the five of us. We knew we were what people called Vampires. That if known we could be hunted. But many thought we couldn't walk in the light, so the fact that we could, helped hide the truth. My father was strict, if you were to drink from a human you could not drain them nor leave them for death. He would not tolerate monsters."

"Something changed, though," Dani noted.

"The crusades happened," Helena sighed as she sat back down at her desk. "So much bloodshed. I remember when our people took back our City. Sayad, who your brother is named after for he was the youngest of my four brothers, he had been kept from the battle to protect our home, our workers, as well as my mother and me. I was thirteen when it began."

"What happened?" Dani asked.

"My father returned home in the dead of night. He woke Sayad and myself up, needing to talk to us. He was very agitated, worried. An ancient had been killed from another tribe of vampires near the Carpathian Mountains. A poison had been used."

Dani sat up straight at this. Helena went on. "I had never heard of a poison that could kill us, I said as much to my father. Knowing that one existed, that it could be used to hunt us down, I understood why my father was troubled. But his answer was not what I had expected."

"The poison, it was a stronger version of the potion he had made to alter himself," Dani realized.

"Yes," Helena confirmed. "He cried as he swore he had destroyed all evidence of that potion. Knowing that it could be used against us, that it could kill us. He knew that he was going to have to kill everyone who handled the message so that once again it could be forgotten about."

"And he wanted both of your forgiveness for what he was about to do," Dani said.

"Life had value to him, he didn't see us as a superior race but more as protectors," Helena explained. "Ari and Yustaf were soldiers they would see it as the consequences of wars. Sayad and I were the thinkers. To my father all life was sacred, as vampires our role was to preserve and help the innocent. We fought in wars because we could handle more than humans. We could handout larger rations of food during famine because we didn't need to eat human food to survive. Even though it was to ensure our survival, he felt guilty that he would have to kill those who were simply doing their job."

Dani stood up and walked over to the side bar in her mother's office. There an electric tea kettle stood ready to boil. Giving her mother time, Dani turned the kettle on then got two mugs ready. Smiling, she took one of the tins of teas that had come from Josephine and put the right amount of leaves in the strainers. Once the water was boiled she poured it into the mugs then handed her mother one.

"For the fact Josie hated tea she had the best taste in flavors," Helena said with a smile. "She preferred Coffee and Hot Chocolate."

"I told Lucas I would help him sort through her tea cabinet," Dani said as she waited for her tea too steep.

"How is he doing?"

"He is focused on keeping me safe, on finding out who is behind all of this," Dani said.

Helena nodded. "And you will tell him all that I am

telling you."

"Mom, I..." Dani paused. She then looked at her mother. "He's my other half."

Helena sat back and looked at Dani. She had suspected, she even commented on it a time or two. But to hear it, to know that it was real, she felt her body warm at knowing Dani had finally found happiness.

"Your father, he was your mother's mate even if he was a witch," Helena informed her. "They would be thrilled to know you have found yours."

Helena took a sip of the chamomile tea before she began. "Back to my tale. My father trusted all his commanders. He believed that his words would be followed. You can guess that things did not go as my father had planned. Of course we did not know this until centuries later. One of his commanders was supposed to kill the messenger when he reached him. My father had been careful and only used one messenger to send to those who needed to know. Lambert Berger. He was a scout, knew the lands, the quickest routes. The message that Lambert delivered to the last captain had one additional line, to kill him."

"I take it the Captain thought differently," Dani replied.

"Lambert was quite skilled, so they struck a deal, in it Lambert got a new identity, a new rank," Helena answered. "And by all accounts Lambert was killed. He was already a vampire at that time so there wouldn't have been much of a body to leave behind."

"Besides living, what did Lambert get out of it?"

"Revenge on the person he blamed for his parent's and siblings death," Helena said. "You see my father was a large land owner. He had overseers. One was very cruel, those that lived on the lands lived the life of a serf. Lambert had watched his parents and siblings die from illness and starvation. By the time my father learned the truth about the overseer, Lambert had left, for his family lay in shallow graves."

"He blamed your father."

"He did," Helena agreed. "In return for his life he would get a knew name and would be recommended to serve in my fathers elite guard. The deal was struck that once Lambert had enough pull he would seize our estate and the captain would become the knew head."

"Let me guess, the captain was Marcus."

Helena smiled over her mug. "No. Marcus had the Captain killed shortly after he was betrothed to Caius' only daughter. He didn't want anyone to know of who he was before he had become Marcus Joseph."

"Well shit," Dani said. "So he knew about the poison, about what it did to our kind. Did he know how it was connected to your father?"

"No, only I knew that," Helena replied. "I married Marcus because I loved him. I believed he loved me. And for centuries he played his part well. Doting husband and father."

"So what changed?"

"Avelina," Helena replied. "Or Ava as she went by. Ari and Yustaf had been killed in the final two battles of the crusade, there was a brother I had never met for he died before he had a chance to become a vampire. Ava was my brother Sayad's youngest."

"Why did she change everything?" Dani asked.

"Because the family that Yustaf and Ari had left behind were all dead by the 1600s. And not from battle or disease," Helena explained. "My father had died as well, leaving Sayad and I running our house and bloodline. Sayad began to be suspicious that there could be a threat to our family. Your brothers were already born by this point, but still young. When Sayad's two oldest died in their sleep he knew he had to protect his wife who was pregnant. Dianna died during childbirth, and he said the child had as well. Instead he sent Ava away with her nurse. I had no idea she survived until she found me in New York City in the early 1900s. It was a chance meeting but we knew the minute we saw each other."

"How did Marcus react to her?"

"On the outside he welcomed her into the House," Helena said. "But she scared him. She had your abilities, and Sayad never liked Marcus that worried him. He wasn't sure what Ava had been told, if perhaps my brother left her a diary with everything in it."

Helena paused and looked at Dani. "You and Ava were all I had to connect me to my brother. She knew I would protect you with my life."

"Why was Marcus there that night?" Dani asked.

"Honestly I didn't know for sure if he was there at the times of the murder," Helena answered. "He called me from the scene but he was head of house and it was a murder of one of ours so it made sense that he would be called. Especially because Ava and I were related."

Helena stopped, then looked at Dani. "I'm just thankful that your memories are locked away," Helena admitted. "I fear what will happen when those memories are unlocked."

"Mom," Dani said. "I am going to make my Oath to House Talon."

Chapter 19

Claire found Dani and Grunt on the roof. Dani was standing looking out on their little slice of Harlem. The flowers and plants were in bloom making the roof look more like a slice of a fairy tale than being in New York City. There was a glass green house to keep plants during the fall and winter months. Tables, chairs and a few grills were nestled around the space, with June being mild so far they had a few late grill-outs with neighbors when everyone's schedules matched.

"Was it my mom or Lucas that sent you up here?" Dani asked as Claire joined her.

"Neither," Claire answered. "I felt a disturbance in the force."

Dani couldn't help but chuckle. They stood there in silence for a few moments. "What are Lucas and Dom doing?" Dani asked.

"Arguing over Dom going to talk to their old mentor," Claire answered. "Dom doesn't think he has to but Lucas is pretty sure that the old guy might have more information as well."

"You mean Abe?" Dani inquired looking at Claire.

"No clue," Claire admitted. "Dom referred to him as a hermit, so old he probably predates most religions."

"That's Abe," Dani confirmed. "He's an Ancient, some think he might be a Sage actually. Dom is fiercely protective of him even though they don't get along."

"They were arguing in Old German when I left," Claire answered.

Dani was quiet for a moment. Lucas didn't seem agitated so she relaxed a bit. "How did thing's go after I left?"

"Sayad came to help with some things," Claire replied. "Can I ask where you went, Lucas seemed to know."

"I went to see my mother," Dani answered. Claire looked surprised at that. She had wondered who Dani had gone off to see. "Caius, the vampire you mentioned, that's her father."

That Claire was not expecting. "You know what the records say about him?" Claire asked shocked. In her research she had learned about the tales about the Centurion/Joseph line.

"I know," Dani answered. "Did you recognize the other name as well?"

"That it matches the name of the company Tony discovered?" Claire inquired. "We talked about that as well. There is no record of a vampire named Lambert Berger."

"That's because by all account's he died in battle in 1453," Dani answered. "He didn't. He changed his name then married into a prestigious bloodline, where he had four sons."

"Oh shit," Claire replied.

"He knew about the poison, knew it could kill," Dani went on. "I really was hoping that he wasn't involved in the murders. That maybe at most he was just going to be a cover story for Bartram."

"Dani..." Claire began.

"I mean he's an asshole," Dani replied. "But that doesn't make him a criminal. Him being a racist, bigot, who things everyone should bow before him, and covers up his criminal derelict of a son, that makes him a criminal."

"What do you want to do?" Claire asked.

"I have to tell the team," Dani replied. "They have to hear it. We can't hide this from them."

"You know it's not enough to get warrants," Claire warned her. "It does allow us to question your father, but we have nothing solid that ties Bartram to any of this."

"If I unlock my memory?" Dani asked.

"It would have to be witnessed by several elders," Claire reminded her.

Dani nodded. "And if Lucas sees it through the Bond?"

"That would count if you can prove the bond," Claire answered.

"When do we train with Gloria?" Dani asked Claire.

"First session is tomorrow night," Claire replied. "We're going to meet her at my Aunt's."

* * * *

Dom had forgotten how fast Lucas was, and how strong he was. It was something that most people didn't expect from the tall, lanky vampire. But the bloody lip and broken nose that was already healing was a reminder that Lucas could be more danger-ous when provoked. The three hour drive would help cool him down, something he would need as he went to see Abe. The grumpy old vampire was still pissed when Dom moved him to America. And that had been thirty years ago. Dom had found him a place nestled in upstate New York that at one point had been a small monastery. The monks that had lived there were moving to a new location and had been reluctant to sell to a vam-pire. Dom told them Abe had been raised amongst monks, and that becoming a creature of the night had not been his choice. The monks agreed to sell. Of course, Abe found the whole thing hysterical.

Dom pulled his car through the old iron gates that opened

when he punched in the pass code. The drive was lined with overgrown trees that hid the brick and stone building from view. Dom still had no clue what he was going to say or even why Lucas asked him of this. Pulling the car around the back of the house, Dom got out of his car and saw that a figure was standing in the back doorway.

"I heard the gates open," The deep gravelly voice said.

"Aren't you supposed to be getting weaker," Dom challenged as he walked to the door.

"That's what they say," Absjorn answered.

The two men hugged, Dom now a good head taller than his old mentor. Absjorn moved to the side so that Dom could enter the house.

"I see Lucas can still best you," Absjorn noted as they walked through the kitchen.

Without talking they both headed toward the library which was where the ancient vampire spent much of his days.

Dom took a seat in one of the leather chairs as Absjorn poured them each a drink. He handed Dom a glass then took his own seat.

"It's not a holiday or an anniversary," Absjorn stated. "What brings you here so late?"

Dom studied the amber liquid in the glass he held. "Lucas sent me."

"And how is Lucas doing?"

"His focus is on us solving the case," Dom answered. "He... found his mate."

"Ahhh," Absjorn said. "The young Danika?"

Dom looked at the ancient vampire. Absjorn chuckled. "It always disturbed you when I knew things that I shouldn't know. I liked to think it was being raised by monks that made you doubtful of seers."

"I was more fearful of what humans would think when they realized you weren't a crazy old man," Dom countered.

"And have you told him about your mate?"

Dom set the glass down and stood up heading to the fire-place. It was summer so no fire but he needed to stand up and move about. He hadn't come to talk about Rena, about the child that she carried.

"Did you blame me for not knowing that her going out that night would end in their death?" Absjorn inquired.

Dom shook his head resting it against the cool stone man-tle. "No, never."

"Really?" his mentor asked surprised.

"If you had the slightest hint that something would have happened to Rena, you would have never let her leave that night," Dom answered. "Besides we both know that Rena would not have listened and still gone to help a patient."

Rena had been a midwife in their small village in eastern Germany. One of her patients was having a difficult pregnancy and Rena wanted to be there the moment the water broke. It didn't matter that a highwayman by the name of Peter Niers was preying on women, leaving them dead. Rena was a born vampire but had yet to turn, she was also Dom's Bond-mate. She was pregnant with his child. Rena was also Ab's youngest child.

It had been Dom that had found her the following morning. When she had not returned to their home, he decided to bring a basket of food to the cottage she was at the night before. Rena had never made it to the cottage. Dom should have died when she did as this was the way it worked with Bond-mates. He fell ill, weak, ran a high fever, but by the next full moon he was healthy again. It was thought that because their bond was so fresh, that she wasn't a full-blooded vampire, that is what had saved him. He felt it was more of a curse, because he would walk the rest of his days knowing the one person that fit him was dead.

"Does Lucas know of her?" Absjorn asked, though he knew the answer. Dom shook his head. "And I take it he is not finding much information on having a bond-mate that is not a

full vampire?"

Dom was silent. "Dominykas, I am disappointed in you,"

Absjorn snapped. "So would Rena."

"Don't, old man."

"No, I am not stopping," Absjorn said. "What happened

to Rena, to you, to the child you both created is horrific. How

you walk each day as you do is amazing to me. But to not help

your friend, your blood brother, that is unlike you. You can help

them in ways no one else can."

"I know!"

"Then what is stopping you?"

"Because if I say it, if I tell him, then it's knowing that af-

ter all this time, the pain is still there, that she is still gone, that I

am mate-less," Dom finally admitted. "And I will have his pity."

"Not pity," Absjorn replied. "You will have his respect

for walking each day knowing what you know. Talking about

her will not bring her back, but it will give you peace."

"I didn't come to talk about this," Dom informed him.

"No you came to talk about the murders to see what I know," Absjorn replied. "So ask your questions."

Dom stared at him then took his seat. This time he took a sip of the liquor. "There is a poison, it was used on Josephine and Harold, it was also used on Parker Clarence, and Danika has come in contact with it."

"I take it that the poison is altered to deal with the different class of supernatural?" Absjorn asked as he stood up from his chair.

Dom watched as he walked to one of the floor to ceiling bookcases that lined the walls. "Yes," Dom confirmed.

"It's a complicated potion," Absjorn stated. "The ingredients are not difficult to get if you know where to go. Especially today. But if the amount of a single ingredient is wrong it will be the most violent of deaths or completely ineffective."

"Yes, that is what Claire and Vynessa said," Dom replied. He ran a hand over his head not sure what to think.

"Now if it's made in a certain way, which is the hardest use of it, it will stop the heart completely," Absjorn went on. "Then when death has just about embraced you, life will surge through your body. But it will change you, what you could once eat will no longer sustain you."

"How...do you know this?" Dom asked.

Absjorn found what he was looking for. He took the book off the shelf and handed it to Dom. "This should help Miss Jensen come up with an antidote for the poison."

"How do you know it will help?"

"Because they are my notes."

Dom felt like someone had just been hit a second time that night. "That's impossible. Caius, the head of the Centurion Line, got it from an apothecary."

"He did," Absjorn confirmed. "We had known of each

other for a few decades, almost a century I think. We went by different names, but it didn't matter for we still recognized each other. I at first thought he was a vampire, like me. When we met up in London in the twelve hundreds, I finally asked. And he told me his tale. He had met other vampires in his travels. For him, he felt kin with us, especially those of us who did not choose this life."

It was Dom that refilled their drinks. Absjorn continued after a sip. "I had asked why he never asked one of us to turn him so that he could become a vampire and then be able to turn others. He informed me that he had tried it about a century ago but it failed. The scientist in me wanted to see it, so he allowed me to attempt to turn him. He stayed at my place so I could watch and observe. The notes are in the book you hold."

"It didn't work?"

"We watched as my marks vanished from his skin as if they had never been there," Absjorn answered. "I saw his anguish. While yes we were similar, he could not create a family. He could take one as a lover and they would not be able to have a child. His curse prevented him from that."

"So for him to live, he had to die," Dom realized.

"The issue is the curse prevented death from happening," Absjorn replied. "Which meant it had to be something that would trick the body, the curse, allowing him to die and then be reborn."

"But how?"

"See that is the part that we never wrote down," Absjorn stated. "I mixed some of my blood in with the drink that contained his poison. This way his body would know my blood. Then I waited for the heart to still, once it did, once he took his last breath I slit my wrist and allowed him to drink a few drops of my blood. We knew the potential the poison had, and we ensured that the only copy of the experiments was in that note book you hold. Anything else was burnt to ashes."

"Then how did it re-appear in the 1500's?" Dom asked.

"I had an apprentice," Absjorn replied. "He was arrogant and furious with his maker who was an ancient living in what is now Romania. I never trusted him alone with my personal notes, nor was he allowed in my personal lab. But one night, I was not there, for my wife had gone into labor and I did not wish to leave her side. When I returned to my lab, he had vanished and my notebook was laid out on the worktable. I sent word to Caius that my apprentice most likely copied down the formula to the poison. We agreed that if it were to surface all those involved would be silenced."

"And when it did appear, Caius issued those orders but the messenger made a deal," Dom said.

"I terrify Marcus Joseph more than any other being because he knows that I am aware he knows what the poison is," Absjorn answered.

"Then will you be there for when Danika takes her

Oath?" Dom inquired.

"Why would Marcus Joseph invite me to Danika's Oath? I am not of their house."

"Because Danika will be taking her Oath to House Talon," Dom said with a slight smile.

"Oh she is a very brave and intelligent girl," Absjorn said with a chuckle. "The fates did well matching them. Tell Lucas I will be there and make sure Miss Jensen treats my notes with care."

"I'll return them when she is done."

Absjorn shook his head. "She may keep them," he informed Dom. "You may also invite her to come see my library. Someone with her talent will be impressed with what I have here."

Chapter 20

They were all silent as they stared at Dom. He had called

a meeting at his apartment with the whole group. Even Tony had

been invited to hear what Dom had to say. No one spoke while

he explained what Abe had told him, Claire kept staring at the

velvet wrapped package that sat in the center of Dom's glass din-

ing room table. His apartment was in one of the newer high rises

that had pretty everything one needed, concierge services, room

service, around the clock security. It was modern and all glass, metal, and leather. There was nothing that said Dom lived here.

"You had a bond-mate?" Lucas asked his voice void of emotion.

Dom nodded. "We were only bound for two years, it's why I didn't die with her."

"And she wasn't a full-blooded vamp?"

Dom looked up at the man that was like a brother to him. "I'm sorry."

Lucas said nothing, he looked at Dani then left the apartment. The tension was thick. "You said that Abe was the one that created the elixir that would help Caius become a vampire?" Dani recalled trying to ignore the anger she had.

"Yes," Dom replied. "They both knew how dangerous it could be so any copies were destroyed as was some of his equipment."

"If it was dangerous why keep any notes on it?" Tony asked.

"They didn't know what was going to happen to Caius, how long the elixir would work, if the change would be permanent, would there be any ill effects later," Dom explained. "Abe kept his notes so that if anything arose he would have his notes to fall back on."

"And that is his notebook?" Claire said, the excitement clear in her voice. The thought of reading the notes that no one else had seen before, that could answer so many of her questions about the poison, it was thrilling.

"Yes," Dom replied. "He, uh, is gifting it to you Claire. He heard about your talents and believes you would benefit greatly from everything that lies in there."

"Did Abe ever say what happened to his apprentice?" Grant asked.

"He vanished," Dom answered. "Both Caius and him kept their ears open for any sign of him but he was smart and kept off the radar. It wasn't until he killed the ancient that he resurfaced."

"And after the killing?"

"Vanished again until his body was found several years later in Russia," Dom answered.

"So not our guy," Grant replied.

"I had thought the same thing," Dom assured Grant. "But no, Bartram is still on our suspect list."

"Tony, any more information on Berger and Son?" Alistair asked.

"Some shady real estate deals in the last decade," Tony replied. "Several have been stalled by zoning boards or because permits were wrong or not approved. I can't find any way that shows how they are making money yet in the last two years they showed a profit of millions."

"Any names?"

"An L. Berger is listed as the President of the board," Tony replied as he flipped through his notes on his tablet. "Can't find a trace of him or the name that Dani gave me, but if he faked

his death then that explains why there is nothing. Any other

names just lead to dead ends."

"Can you send me the list?" Alistair asked. "Dom and

Michael can look through them to see if they might recognize

some alias from before we all went public."

"Sending the file to you now," Tony told him. "It's en-

crypted so I'll send the password in another email."

"Paranoid?" Michael commented.

"Always," Tony answered. "I'm going to get up and pace.

I need to move a bit."

"Go right ahead," Dom told. "In the future, don't ask."

Tony nodded. He knew that vampires were not fans of

people pacing in their spaces but he appreciated the fact that

Dom understood he would get stiff sitting and needed to move

around.

"Dani how does your mother know that Marcus was

Lambert Berger?" Alistair asked Dani.

"Her brother Sayad," Dani replied. "He had overhead a conversation after Marcus and Helena were married. A man had approached Marcus, informing him that he knew who he really was, that he would expose him as a fraud."

"I bet Marcus loved that," Michael commented.

"It didn't go over well when Marcus realized the man actually spoke the truth," Dani replied. "My mother was pregnant, Sayad didn't want to stress her out so he kept the secret to himself. He hid the truth in a journal that he sent with his daughter and her wet-nurse."

"Because if he left it, Marcus would have found it and destroyed it," Claire figured.

"Pretty much," Dani agreed. "My mother gave it to Helena shortly after they met."

"Why not give it to her before or tell her after she gave birth?" Michael wondered.

"Helena wouldn't have believed it, not at that point in their marriage," Dani answered. "She admitted she would have sided with her husband at that point."

"And why Bartram?" Michael asked. "I mean I get that he is a total asshole who is creepy but this seems a little grand for him."

"Right now it's more theory," Alistair reminded him.

"But even you just explained why people won't think it's him," Dani pointed out. "Josephine and Harold would think he was capable of black mail, but not murder, not to this scale. They would not fear meeting him alone, they also would know if they mentioned it to anyone word would get to my father. So they would keep it quiet until they knew for sure."

"But Parker, no one sensed or smelled him?"

"True," Claire said. "But Grant and I have been working on what was in those text's that were stolen. One of them contained spells and charms that would allow a supernatural to be unseen in sense to another supernatural. Now unlike a Neutral spot, this would only last for a few hours and it drains the person of their energy. It also is extremely dark and requires blood."

"You think that Bartram would use this spell to sneak onto Alistair's property to kill Parker?" Michael inquired. "I mean that seems like a lot of work for anyone."

"Then how do you explain someone getting on to my property, by passing about twenty Weres and security?" Alistair asked. "We know he used a spell to conceal his crime from the security system here and that was before... Parker."

"Okay but why Bartram?"

"Because everything is going back to Berger and Sons," Dani reminded Michael. "Alexius is an asshole but he won't do anything that would tarnish the family name and shell company's do just that."

"And we don't think it could be someone else?"

"It could be," Dom answered. "But right now things are

pointing at Bartram. If you can find us another lead then show us and we'll look into that too."

Dani was impressed that Alistair and Dom both didn't let it slip that there was more, that there was what Gloria had told Dani about Bartram. Right now they were keeping that quiet, it would put Gloria at risk as well as the bar.

The group talked for a while more, going over plans. Claire almost drooled when Dom handed her the velvet wrapped book.

"It's like Christmas morning," Claire whispered. "I...I'll visit him once the case is over and thank him. This is amazing."

"Dani, Claire and I will meet you in the hallway," Grant said knowing Dom was going to want to talk to Dani. "And Michael has places to be."

"I do," Michael asked oblivious then realized what was going. "Right, I do."

Dani rolled her eyes as they all headed out the door with

Alistair behind them. Dom waited until the door shut.

"I'm...Dani, I don't even know what to say," Dom said as he slumped down in a chair. He rested his head between his hands. "Talking about her, about what happened, it brings it all back. Knowing what I almost had and what I lost."

"Tell me about her," Dani said. Dom looked up at her as if she hadn't heard what he had just said. "You want me to understand, you want me to talk to Lucas. Then you need to tell me all of it."

Dom sighed. "It's a long story," Dom warned her.

She sent at text to Grant telling him to take Claire home, Dom would drive her back when they were done talking. "I have time," Dani said and slipped her phone in her pocket.

Dom got up and headed into his kitchen he grabbed a beer, a bottle of blood, a wine glass, and a bottle of white wine. He poured them each a drink adding blood to his beer.

"I was left at a monastery when I was barely a week old,"

Dom began. "The monks took me in, not sure what to do with me but there was a convent nearby. They made arrangements with the nun's and those that worked for them, so that when they were in their studies or prayers I would be looked after. It was once suggested perhaps I should be moved to the convent, but the monks had grown attached to me. I was their ward, they would protect me and educate me. They never forced the religious path on me."

"What did you do there?" Dani asked.

"I was one of the few children, some of the workers would bring their's from time to time," Dom recalled with a far off look. "We would help with chores, harvesting the garden they had. Cook would have things for me to do. When I was of school age, they took turns tutoring me in their best area's. To me it was like having a dozen uncles. The workers taught me their trade while I would teach their children what I learned. I was good with my hands, so I began to apprentice with a local carpenter. I moved out of the Monastery when I was twenty but not off the property. I moved into the old caretakers cottage."

"It sounds peaceful," Dani admitted.

"It was," Dom agreed. He took a long sip from his beer. "The Monks, they took in many travelers who needed a night to rest or a storm to wait out. They never took money, instead the guest would just have to help with chores that they could handle. There was a terrible thunderstorm one night, one that made you fear this was the end. That the earth would split in two or that Devil was breaking through the ground with his army of demons. A couple came to us, their carriage was stuck in the mud, and they were soaked through their clothing. We brought them right to the kitchen and Cook sat them down in front of the hearth giving them bowls of warm soup. I went with two of the youngest monks, and two workers to get the horses and see about moving the carriage. "

"And you alone pulled the carriage out of the mud," Dani

said sarcastically.

"I wish," Dom said sadly. "The carriage was where they said it was but the horses were no where to be found. The wife had asked if we could bring back their bag so they could dry some of their things. The one worker looked in the front of the carriage while the other went to the back of the carriage. I heard a whistle from the back and went to see what he needed. He had moved the canvas covering on the back of the carriage. There were two bodies there, one male and one female. Their throats had been torn open. We had heard rumors of vampires, and we felt dread. We alerted the others, told the other worker to head to the nearest inn with the two monks, alert them to the carriage, that there are highwaymen loose. They wanted to come with us but we argued that we would be faster with just the two of us. The monks did a quick prayer for us and for those back home."

"Dom..." Dani whispered.

"It looked like a slaughterhouse," Dom said. "We split

up, thinking it would be better than staying together, that one of us might have a chance at catching them. It was Jonah that found them. He sent up an owl hoot, no one would think anything of it but I would know it was him. They were having sex with bodies around them, blood covered them but they didn't are. The female noticed him first, she laughed as she licked her fangs. I watched in horror as she called to him in this sweet song like voice. I wanted to yell to him."

"But it would alert them to where you were," Dani realized. She had rested a hand on his.

"They liked to play with their food," Dom replied. "I thought his screams were horrible but the silence after, that was worse. I had picked up a sharp knife in the kitchen, and I was gripping it in my hands waiting for them to be vulnerable. I was so happy when it was she that was distracted. She was humming while the male tried to see about opening up a chest he hoped was filled with gold. When she finally heard my approach it was too late for I had slit her neck with the knife then stabbed her in the chest. He heard her fall to the ground. He was on me so fast, it was a blink of the eye. The knife had fallen from my hand and slid away from me. He was impressed with me. They had no clue I had been there, the fact I had managed to take her out astounded him. Instead of killing me, he was going to turn me. I refused, I tried to fight him, but he was so strong. What he did to me, it's why I will never doubt a victim. After he drained me nearly of all my blood, after he forced me to take his blood, the pain it was unreal."

Dani was silent as he took a moment to continue. "I remember gentle hands, and a voice telling me it will be alright," Dom replied. "I was given liquid to drink but I had no clue what it was. I was delirious. When I finally woke, it was one of the younger monks that had come with us to the carriage. Charles. He looked relieved when I woke up. He promised that I would be alright, then he left the room I was in. I was so overwhelmed with what I was hearing, what I could smell, it was confusing.

When Charles returned it was with a man in his fifties. He was

called Absjourn, it was his home I was recovering in. Charles

left us, Absjourn then thanked me for killing his son and daugh-

ter-in-law. He then apologized for what had been done to me,

Charles had explained to him who I was. He then explained that

he was a Vampire, but unlike his son and daughter-in-law, he

called them rogue, he took his blood from those willing and nev-

er left them for dead. That we did not require much blood to sur-

vive but those who over indulge, it becomes like an addiction."

"Bloodlust," Dani replied.

Dom nodded. "I stayed there for a few months, until I

was strong enough to be shown around the village that Abe lived

in. He introduced me to his family, his youngest daughter Rena

who was close to my age. Abe explained to me that she was born

a vampire, that at some point she will need to finish the change if

she chose too. For us the connection was instant. I felt more

Castro - Sacred Dark

333

whole than I have ever felt before. It shocked everyone at how fast it happened."

"Lucas and I have known each other most of my life but one day he was just Lucas and the next day I saw him and we both paused as we felt like something clicked inside of us," Dani replied with a smile.

"It is the most amazing feeling in the world," Dom admitted. "When you find the person that balances you. Anyway, Abe explained that while it was rare to occur with someone not a full blood vampire it had happen. Even rarer were bond-mates that were best-friends not lovers. There was a pair of siblings once recorded, and no, it was not intimate relationship. But they were powerful in battle and stubborn as hell."

"None of this is written anywhere," Dani informed him.

"I will make amends," Dom promised. "And I will write down all I know and will have Abe add to it. Bond-mates used to be more common, bloodlines didn't spread far apart. Our numbers were also higher in the 1500's, the witch hunts hadn't happened yet. I don't think any of our communities ever fully recovered from the witch-hunts."

"You said Rena died," Dani replied.

"We were married within a year, she was pregnant that spring," Dom answered. "She was a midwife, an amazing healer. Even pregnant, she wouldn't stop seeing her patients. Even with rumors of a killer preying on women. She went to check on a patient who had a difficult pregnancy, when she didn't return that night, I made a breakfast basket to bring to the home. I...she never made it to the cottage. She had been murdered and left there, just off to the side of the road to be found. Abe figured I would follow her within the week as the bond drained me of my energy. Instead I raged with fever for a month. The elders believed that our bond was brief, so our energies had not fully blended with the other yet. I wish they were wrong, I wish I had died with her. The pain, knowing I found that person, knowing I had that, it's a pain I can't explain."

"I'll explain it to Lucas," Dani promised.

"If he wants me to resign, I will," Dom told her.

She smiled softly then hugged the big vampire. Instead of stiffening up like he usually did, he found himself hugging her back. He ignored the tears that he hadn't shed in centuries.

* * * *

He walked toward the Hudson River, where no one would be able to hear his conversation. The waterways were places where the supernatural could talk and not worry about mortals or other supernaturals to hear.

"Yes?" A voice asked on the other end.

"There's a situation you need to be aware of," he answered.

"And what is that?"

"They know who Lambert Berger really is and that Berger and Son is a shell company."

There was silence on the other end for a moment. "What else do they know?"

"That dark and forbidden magick is being used to conceal the identity of the killer, as well as the name of a Witch that might be willing to risk it all."

"This is much sooner than I expected," the voice on the other end admitted.

"They have also traced the poison back to Marcus."

"And how the hell did they do that!"

He wanted to say Helena, that Danika had learned it from her mother but his vow prevented him. "Absjourn informed Dom about it."

"That old hermit is still alive?"

"He had Dom give Claire his personal notes on the poison so that she might be able to create an antidote."

"Fuck!"

He had to hold the phone away from his ear as the other

man cursed and yelled. "Do you know where she is keeping it?"

"She was heading home to study it," he answered.

"Alright, we are going to have move up the time-table of the next phase," the man replied. "Are you up for this?"

"I am."

"Then I will notify the other two and we will start the next phase."

The call disconnected and he looked out across the river. He crushed the phone in his hand so that nothing could be found on it then tossed it far into the river.

Chapter 21

Dani was curled up in her unicorn sheets while her mother finished her story for the night. Her father was in the kitchen doing the dishes from dinner while his girls, as he called them, did their nightly routine. Mom had the night off so she got to read Dani her story, and play games with her. When they heard her dad call her mom by her name, Ava paused in the story.

"Alright Little Duck, you stay right here in your bed," Ava said kissing her daughter on the forehead. "Look through the book while I see what your father wants."

Dani nodded as she yawned. Ava smiled as she brushed

a dark curl out of her daughter's face. "And no following me with your mind," Ava warned.

It had only been in the last few months that Dani had started to travel with her mind. Elliott had already put a phone call into Tabby for help on how to teach Dani how to handle this gift. Ava could handle the mind reading, the reading of emotions, but dream walking- that was out of her league.

The moment Ava stepped out into the hallway she knew something was not right. Heading into the kitchen Ava stopped short when she saw the head of her vampire house sitting at their tiny farmhouse table.

"Lord Joseph," Ava stammered.

"Tonight it is Marcus," he assured her. He looked around the 'quaint' kitchen as he accepted the tea from Elliott. "I know it is late and I should have called but this is a delicate matter."

"I don't kill anymore," Ava reminded him. She had been an assassin once, many centuries ago.

"Actually I am here because of your husband," Marcus admitted.

Elliott and Ava stared at each other not sure what to

think. They both sat at the table waiting for the vampire to talk again. "I find my self in a very unusual position," Marcus admitted.

"Marcus, I am honored that you would come for aid from me," Elliott began. "But I am not sure how much help I can be to a vampire."

"Hear me out and then make your decision," Marcus asked.

"Is Helena sick?" Ava asked. She had never seen Marcus look desperate before.

"No, and I should have prefaced that before I started," Marcus assured her. "This is about one of my sons."

"We're listening," Elliott said.

"Bartram has always been the child that pushes the limits, test the boundaries," Marcus began. "Perhaps because he is the youngest we allowed him to get away with more things, didn't pay enough attention."

"He's drinking tainted blood again," Ava realized. Marcus nodded. "I am so sorry."

"Tainted blood?" Elliott asked.

"It's an expression meaning blood that is not pure," Ava explained. "In this situation, Bartram is taking blood from drug addicts. He is getting a high off of the drugs that are in the blood stream of the addict."

"I was thinking more along the lines of a blood bourn disease," Elliott stated. "But those can't harm you."

"But drug laced blood can," Ava answered.

"It can also prove fatal," Marcus added. "We need blood to gain nutrients that our body can no longer produce."

"Drink enough drug laced blood and you start depleting your body of those nutrients," Elliott replied. "Similar to a drug addict. The drug becomes your focus, you forget to eat, drink, care for yourself. Your body can start shutting down."

Elliott studied the elder vampire across from him. "What do you want from me?"

"I have heard that you can create a potion of sorts that can erase the effects of the drugs," Marcus said. "Erasing the craving for it, even the memory of ever using it."

"I have never done this for a vampire," Elliott warned him. "I have only done it in extreme scenarios. Even then it's

dangerous and can be fatal."

"We are desperate," Marcus admitted hating that he had to beg. That he had to be here in this hovel asking for help from a witch.

Elliott leaned back in his chair thinking about if it would work. "I would need a vial of his blood," Elliott informed Marcus. "And not for any type of binding or mind control. First, I would need his blood to test out the potion see if it could even work. Second, I need it so that the potion would work for a vampire."

"You will destroy whatever blood is left over?"

"Yes," Elliott promised. "Trust me I don't like asking for blood nor do I like working with it."

"I understand," Marcus.

Ava went to say something but froze. "I need to check on Ava and someone is coming."

Ava got up and headed out of the kitchen hurrying into her daughter's bedroom. She knew that Dani had been listening in on the conversation even if her daughter wasn't even aware of it.

"Dani, take your unicorn and I need you to hide in the spot in your closet where no one can find you," Ava began trying to keep her voice calm.

Dani took her stuffed unicorn and followed her mom to her tiny closet. "No coming out unless it's me or daddy, Aunt Josie, or Aunt Helena," Ava instructed. She hugged Dani tightly then kissed her on top of the head taking in the scent of the shampoo they washed her hair in.

Once Dani was settled in her closet Ava headed back to the kitchen.

"Well well, so glad you could join us," a new voice said as Ava entered the room. The man smiled at her as he motioned for her to sit. "Now let's all have a conversation about what we were all talking about a few minutes ago."

****

Someone was slowly brushing their hand through her curls, while telling her she was safe. A rough tongue licked at her face bringing Dani out of the dream she just had. Opening her eyes she saw Grunt sitting to one side of her looking worried and Lucas to the other side of her. She immediately wrapped herself around him and let the tears and pain go. Dani was exhausted, so tired of trying to be strong, to not let this case, this hell to get to her.

"I'm here," Lucas whispered as he held her tight, kissing her hair.

"I know what happened to my parents," Dani gasped in between sobs. "I know it all now."

Lucas said nothing and just rocked her in his arms. There were no words he could give her right now. When he had heard the scream in the apartment, he had never known fear until that moment that something could have happened to her. With Claire and her work with Gloria, Dani's dreams had become more vivid. Gloria warned them that whoever the red mist was in her memory might have a mental hold on her, and that was what Lucas had thought for a moment. Instead, when he entered the bedroom he smelled heartbreak. He quickly texted Grey and Claire to let them know, Claire was on a date with some woman she met at the occult store in the basement of their apartment building.

Dani took several deep cleansing breaths like Gloria had taught her. "Can you make that tea that Gloria brought me?"

Lucas nodded. Dani followed him out of the room, she went to their couch with Grunt climbing right up in her lap.

"You know you're not a lap dog," Dani informed the mutt. He just licked her face and whined softly.

Dani smiled softly as she heard Lucas walking around in the kitchen getting the tea ready. His laptop was open on the coffee table with some paperwork spread about. Claire and she had both told him if he wanted to buy a desk they could figure out space for it or he could use Dani's room. But he said he was fine with his set up and worked mostly when both Claire and Dani were asleep. Lucas only needed a few hours of sleep each day.

Lucas came back with two mugs of tea, he handed Dani hers then sat down next to her.

"Marcus had gone to my father to ask for help with Bartram," Dani began. "Bartram had fallen off the wagon again and was drinking from drug addicts."

"And my brother wasn't the perfect reason as to why that was a bad idea?" Lucas asked. Freddie had been a hard blow to the vampire community, not just because it meant that Lucas was now the last Talon heir but that even Vampires were vulnerable to hard drugs.

"Bartram has always believed he is the exception to the rules,"Dani reminded him. She sipped the tea, feeling calmer as she did.

"Why did he go to your dad?" Lucas inquired. It was well known that Marcus was not a big fan of asking for help from other supernaturals.

"My father was a healer," Dani explained. She wasn't sure how much Lucas knew of her biological father. "Apparently a very well known one. He had created a tonic that would not only counter the effects of the drugs but also help erase the cravings and the memories of being high."

"A fresh start," Lucas replied. "And if Bartram get's murderous when taking tainted blood then going to your father would be something that Marcus would deem necessary. Did your father agree?"

"He warned Marcus that he had never tried it on a vampire and that it could be fatal, it had only been used a few times and in extreme circumstances," Dani answered. She reached for Lucas' hand knowing she would need their connection. "He never really got to the point of agreeing because Bartram showed up."

"Dani where were you?" Lucas asked.

"Mom brought me to my closet with my favorite unicorn, she told me to stay there, but I could hear them and I could see weird color out lines of them," Dani told him. "I now know that was their aura's that I was seeing."

"They were both there that night," Lucas said. He didn't ask if she was sure it was a memory and not a dream. Gloria had been teaching her how to recognize the differences.

"I mean, I know we've been suspecting Bartram's involvement in both cases," Dani began.

"But knowing that you have been living with your parent's killer and the person that covered it up is different."

"It's sickening," Dani corrected him.

"What do you want to do?" Lucas asked.

"I want to meet with Sonja, my mother and two brothers, you, and the other's and start my Oath Ceremony," Dani said. "We can't move on with the case until my memories are unlocked."

"Dani," Lucas said turning so the he was facing her. "I don't want oathing for a case. I know what is at stake, but I want you to do it because you want to."

Dani set her mug down and laid a hand on his cheek.

"You are one of the most amazing people I have ever met," Dani informed him. "And you heard Gloria the other night. My senses are getting to the point that I can do the Oath whenever I am ready. Having the memory unlocked, it's time Lucas. I want this, I want to show people that I am my own person. That I am not going to oath to Marcus just because that is expected. I am going to oath to the Talon House, that will be the best at helping me grow."

"Wow," Lucas whispered. He kissed her lightly. "Just so you know, I think you are amazing too."

"I still think we are right in not rushing into the bonding, with everything going on, it isn't the right time," Dani admitted. "No matter how frustrating it is."

"We'll talk to Abe about it," Lucas agreed. He kissed her forehead. "Why don't you try to sleep out here while I work. I can email everyone on our list and get that started. And you won't be alone."

"Okay," Dani agreed.

He grabbed a blanket off the back of their couch and laid it over her as she curled up on the one side of the couch. Grunt moved to lay on the floor at her feet, Lucas smiled and went back to the work he was doing. Nicholi and Sayad were going to have his head on a silver platter when they realize how his thoughts on their sister had changed.

Chapter 22

They met at House Impuldulu, the email from Lucas had

not contained much information just that Dani requested a meet-

ing with them about something important. Sonja was thrilled to

host them all, and with it being a bright sunny day she had them

all enter the interior courtyard of the House. It was a hidden oa-

sis with tastes of Africa around the outdoor area. It also had a

glass ceiling that had been charmed so no conversations could be

overheard.

Dani and Lucas were the last to arrive, both nervous as to how her brother's would handle their news. Their hope was that Sonja, Tabby, and Helena would keep any bloodshed to a minimal. There were two people surprised by their invitation and that was Greyson and Todd. Sonja had welcomed the two into her home with warm hugs and promised that she had meat on the menu for their late lunch.

Dani was holding onto Lucas' hand when they entered the house. They could hear everyone talking in the courtyard, but due to the charm the words were indistinguishable. Lucas looked at her, nervous. Dani rolled her eyes at him as she took the lead following the butler. When the doors opened to the courtyard the conversation stilled as everyone watched Dani come in holding onto Lucas' hand. Dani watched Nicholi's nostril flare as he took in the scent. She let go of Lucas with enough time to move to the side as Nick almost flew across the room.

He had Lucas pinned to the bright yellow cement wall,

his elbow pressing against Lucas larynx.

"Nick!" Sayad and Dom both yelled at the same time as they shot up from their seats. Greyson and Todd quickly took Dani to the side, as Claire was shoved behind her aunt.

"He smells of our sister," Nick growled. "She reeks of him!"

Helena shook her head when others went to step forward. "Nicholi Caius Centurion-Joseph, release him now."

"He's touched our sister!" Nick challenged even as Lucas exposed his neck.

"He is her bond-mate!" Helena stated so that they could all hear it.

Nick turned and stared at his mother. But Dani stepped forward much to Greyson and Todd's dismay. "We kept it a secret because of everything going on," Dani explained. "It's one of the reason's we called all of you here."

"You are too young," Nick told her.

She snorted at him as she raised an eyebrow. "You really think Lucas is the one to de-flower me, as you would say, that happened way before this."

Grayson got really still hoping neither brother would look at him. "Release him, Nick," Dani instructed. "Or I'll try a trick Gloria taught me and lull you to sleep only you'll wake up with the worst headache you can imagine."

Nick let a low growl before he stepped back from Lucas. "I...apologize," Nick said as he extended his hand.

"I was expecting worst from the both of you, to be honest," Lucas admitted as he shook his hands.

"Sayad was never one for confrontation in public, he'll wait until you're alone," Nick informed him.

"No he won't because I'll remove his access to the archives," Dani said as she took a seat next to Claire. Sayad glared at her.

Sonja raised a flute to Dani. "A woman after my own

heart!"

Dani clinked her champagne flute with Sonja's. "Alright, entertainment portion is over, everyone sit and behave," Dani instructed.

Dani waited for everyone to get drinks and sit. "We called you here because you are the people we trust most with the information we are about to tell you," Dani began.

"You each were also selected to help with a few stages of a plan," Lucas added.

"And this plan?" Dom asked pretty sure he wasn't going to like it.

"With the help of Gloria, I am gaining better control of my dreams and my memories," Dani explained. She sipped the champagne before setting the flute down. "With this new ability I have begun to recall what happened the night my parents were murdered."

"The dream last night," Claire realized.

"Yes," Dani answered. "I now have a clearer picture about what happened."

"And you called us here to tell us?" Nick said.

"In a way yes," Dani replied. "With the memories un-locking and with Gloria noticing that my senses linked to being a vampire are becoming stronger, I think it's time for me to take the Oath."

"And you think that it's wise to do this? Marcus will see that you remember," Nick pointed out.

"She is not going to take the Oath to our house," Sayad said understanding. "Dani has always been her own person and she will chose the house that would allow her to blossom with her talents instead of trying to hide her away."

"I will only allow it with your blessing," Lucas told them. "Which Dani is not too happy about."

"Of course you have it," Helena said standing up. "Quiet, Nicholi."

Nick closed his mouth before he could say anything. Helena went and hugged Dani before going and hug Lucas. "Your parents, they would be so thrilled, so happy for you," Helena whispered.

"Thank you," Lucas replied.

"Can a vampire switch the house they were born too?" Grayson asked. He felt better knowing that Dani was not going to pledge to Marcus.

"It's been done, it's not common," Sonja answered. "It usually is done because of a marriage, or a bond mate, or because the person feels a different house will offer more protection or better education. We all offer different skills, different abilities so if a person from another house fits our skills better they might switch so we can better teach them."

"And where would you want this to take place?" Nick asked.

"Not at House Talon," Lucas replied. Everyone look startled. "Marcus will know something is up and we want him in the dark as much as possible. Same with Alexius and Bartram. No offense, Helena."

"I wouldn't want them there either," Helena assured them. "House Joseph is out of the question as well."

"We were wondering if we could have it here," Dani asked Sonja.

Sonja looked shocked. "Of course," she said. Then paused. "But I have a better suggestion. We haven't done a ceremony there in decades, not with the Houses now having places here in the city."

"Oh, it would be perfect," Helena agreed, realizing the place Sonja was thinking of. "And Marcus would never think anything of it."

"Do we know what they are talking about?" Nick asked everyone else.

"I believe they are thinking of the Cloisters," Tabby

replied. "The supernatural groups had made arrangements with certain officials in New York City long before we came out to the public, so we could hold rituals at certain places throughout the city. Money and land were used to keep their mouths silent about our existence."

"I don't know if the Cloisters would do it, it has been a long time," Sonja replied.

"One of our coven members works there," Tabby informed them. "I will call her and see what she can do for us. The Summer Solstice is in a few days, that would be the ideal time to do it but would we be ready?"

"Dom, Gray, and Todd, do you think you could set up a security plan in that short of time?" Lucas asked.

"Ah, that's why we are here," Greyson replied. "If Tabby can get us into it today then yes we could be ready by the Solstice. But I want Alana to help because Dom, I'm sure, will be part of the ceremony."

"I wouldn't bet on that," Dom answered.

"Don't be more of an asshole," Lucas said to Dom. "Of course you're standing up with me."

"When isn't he an asshole," Claire inquired. She got a look from her Aunt and instead sipped her champagne.

"Would this be okay with you, Dani?" Helena asked.

"It would keep all of us safe from whatever wrath Marcus will unleash when he learns," Dani agreed. "And I love that place."

"Let me call now," Tabby said. "Sonja, could I use your office?"

"Of course, just let Darius know that you have my permission and he'll show you," Sonja told her. "I know you know where it is, but he likes to know where we all are."

"I will," Tabby said.

"I hate to bring this up, but outfits," Claire stated.

At this the vampires all chuckled. "That is not something

to worry about," Helena assured her. "Next to a marriage or death, the Oath is one of our biggest ceremonies. Dani's outfit has been in the works for several years. One final fitting and it will be ready in time."

"So just I have to worry," Claire replied.

"Right because you look horrible in everything you where," Dani teased.

"Ha ha," Claire answered.

"You will wear your formal ceremonial robes," Tabby told her as she entered the room. "You will be standing up there with me as my heir, just as Grant will be up there as he is his Uncle Vern's heir, and we are the ones that help conduct the ceremony."

"Well, shit," Claire mumbled.

"And when you take my place you can change what we wear," Tabby informed. "Trust me, the robes we have now are more flattering than the ones my predecessor made us wear.

They were truly horrid."

"They had the gold fringe, if I recall," Helena replied.

"Please, I still have nightmares about those things," Tabby admitted. "And we are set for the Summer Solstice, it will be at sundown."

"I'll let Abe know," Dom answered.

"Will he come?" Helena asked Dom.

He nodded. "He said he would when I saw him a few days ago."

Lucas looked at Dani and squeezed her hand. "You ready?"

"Yes," she promised him. "Just realizing I am going to be center of attention."

"And that the entire supernatural community will realize you are bonded pair," Helena added.

Lucas and Dani both looked at her. "What do you mean?"

"When you take the Oath, especially because it will be Lucas who is delivering the oath, bonded pairs have been rumored to glow gold, signaling the strengthening of their bond because of the Oath," Helena replied. "It lasts for a few moments."

"Can someone please write up a rule book?" Lucas asked to no one in particular.

"That is not a bad idea," Helena admitted. "We write everything else down, it is odd that no one has taken the time to write this information down as well. I'll talk to Abe about it, he knows the most about it."

Dom gave a nod to Helena, appreciating that she did not mention his name in that. Helena had the ability to sense bonded pairs, and had sensed that he had once been part of one but survived the tragedy. It was an ability that she did not share publicly with anyone because every vampire would be asking her to play matchmaker.

"I have an amazing caterer that will do anything, "Sonja

informed Dani. "Actually let's eat, because they prepared much of what we are having. And we can discuss other things, with it at the Cloisters we don't have to decorate or really worry about floral arrangements."

"Floral arrangements?" Dani asked.

"It's alright," Helena assured her daughter. "Sonja and I will handle it."

Dani just nodded not sure what to think as they followed Sonja out of the courtyard and into a less formal dining room where a buffet was set up for them. The food smelled and looked amazing. Her mother, Sonja and Tabby began to discuss the ceremony while the rest of them just let the women plan.

Chapter 23

They had closed the Cloisters earlier, notifying visitors that a private event would be happening. Greyson and Alana had their teams already at the Cloisters working in janitorial outfits so guests wouldn't suspicious. Sasha had led Dani and her mother to private rooms where they could change into their outfits. Dani walked into the small attached bathroom and stared at herself in the mirror. Her world was changing forever after tonight. Dani was filled with so many emotions. She was excited yet terrified at the same time. Part of her felt like she was a bride on her wedding day. In away she was, this wasn't a normal oath ceremony. She was pledging herself to Lucas' line.

There was a gentle knock on the door then her mother telling her they were ready. Stepping out of the shower she grabbed the thick towel and dried off before wrapping herself in it. She walked into the room and stared at her gown that now hung out of the bag.

When one went to their Oath ceremony they wore the traditional style of their line. Even though she would be swearing her oath to a different House, she would wear the style of her ancestors.

The Kaftan gown was done in a deep green hues. Gold and silver embroidery covered the bodice and trim of the gown. It would fall to her ankles. Laid out on the bench was the decorative gold and green belt that would finish off the gown.

Dani went behind the dressing screen and pulled on the underwear she would be able to wear under it. Once she was ready she took a deep breath and came out behind it. Helena had the gown ready for her. With the help of Sonja who had arrived while Dani was collecting herself in the bathroom, they raised it over Dani's head and helped maneuver it down her body. The material felt cool against her skin as it settled around her. The heavy embroidery sparkled in the light as the carefully placed beads and pearls picked up the light when she moved.

Helena picked up the belt and smiled at Dani. Without saying a word she fastened the belt to the dress showcasing Dani's narrow waist. Sonja helped Dani slip into gold heeled slippers.

"Can I look yet?" Dani asked.

"Not until we are done with hair and makeup," Helena replied.

Sitting on the ottoman, Dani let Sonja tackle her makeup. It would be kept simple, a subtle smokey eye to enhance her eye color, darkened lips, and a hint of bronzer on her cheeks. Her hair was twisted into an elaborate crown of curls with gold and green pins accenting the twists.

When they were finished, Helena helped her stand up. When Dani faced the mirror she gasped. The gown was a work of art, her hair and makeup was subtle so that the gown did all the work. Helena opened a jewelry box and handed her a pair of earrings. The gold was old, in the center of the drops were emeralds, instead of diamonds the emeralds were surround by citrine.

"They are the only jewelry you need," Helena said Dani placed them on her ears.

A knock came on the door. Sonja went and opened them to see Dom wearing a formal black suit.

"We've just finished," Sonja informed him as she let him in the room.

"The last guests are being seated," Dom told her. He then froze as he saw Dani. "Lucas is going to pass out when he sees you. You are an absolute vision."

"I'll go make sure that Nick is ready," Helena said as she smoothed her hand over her pale gold Kaftan that she wore.

Sonja followed Helena out. Dom smiled as he took Dani in.

"You sure clean up nice," Dom replied.

"Shut up," Dani said. "You know how heavy this gown is?"

"I don't want to know," Dom admitted. He held out his arm. "Your chariot."

Rolling her eyes she took his arm and they left the room. The ceremony would be taking place in the 12th century apse from the Church of Saint Martin in Spain. The doors were closed to the Apse, as Dom and Dani approached. Helena smiled and motioned to Nick to turn around, when Nick turned to look she watched his eyes widen in surprise.

"We will honor and cherish her," Dom promised his old friend. Kissing Dani on the cheek. "Next time we talk you will be a Talon."

Dom then headed to the double doors that led into the ballroom. Helena took both of Dani's hands and smiled at her.

"My little girl," Helena whispered. "Your parents, they would be filled with such pride today."

Nick heard the music. "It's time."

Dani let out a breath then took both her brother and mother's arm so that she was in the middle. Nick had almost cried when she asked for him to escort her down the aisle with Helena. It traditionally was the role the father played.

Nick gave a single knock on the doors and then they were opened. Stepping through the doorway, Dani took in the the me-

dieval space. Sonja had outdone herself, candles were lit everywhere, with flower garlands hanging from the ceiling. It looked
as if one stepped into a fairy garden. There were whispers as
Dani walked down the aisle to the alter that waited. In front of
the alter stood Lucas and Tabby and Grant's Uncle Vern. Claire
and Grant stood behind them.

Dani couldn't help but smile as she focused on Lucas in
his formal tux. His eyes hadn't left hers since the doors opened.
He was trying to keep a neutral face but the grin was slowly win-
ning. When they finally reached him he was beaming at her.

"Nicholi Caius and Avelina Helena of House Centurion,"
Tabby began surprising everyone that she used the original name
of the house as well as Helena's real name. "Do you present to us
Danika Magdalena Grace Centurion to us today?"

"Yes," Helena and Nick said together.

"You understand that this is not the end but the
beginning?" Tabby continued. "Tonight we witness the merger
of two lines which strengthens all of us as we remember where
we came from. Tonight is not about the past but of embracing the
future. A reminder of our own oaths and vows we have given

through lifetimes."

"We do," Nick answered.

"Then stand with us as we begin this new journey," Tabby declared. She then looked at Dani and couldn't help but smile. "You truly are the light, my child. You shine wherever you go, beating out the darkness."

Taking the chalice that had been used for hundreds of years, Tabby held it high. "This chalice has seen much since it was created," Tabby began. "It represents renewal, loyalty, commitment, family, and unification. For all that it represents one would think that it would be adorned with the most precious of stones, made of the finest material. But often such things can be a distraction from the truth. And the truth is simple: we are each different but we are all one. United together we are stronger than when alone. Together we grieve, we celebrate, we live. And today we come together to witness a new member of our community."

Placing the simple metal chalice on the alter, Tabby uncovered a small dagger. "Helena," Tabby said handing the dagger to Helena.

Helena walked forward and took the blade. Upturning her wrist she made an incision then let a few drops fall into the chalice.

"With this blood may you remember the past that has formed who you are today," Helena recited. "May you grow stronger with knowing the foundation that has been built for you."

Handing the blade to Tabby, Helena stepped back. Tabby doused the blade in a silver bowl to purify it then looked at Lucas.

"Lord Lucas Haroldson, Lord of the House Talon," Vern began. "Before you stands a new oath giver. She comes on her own free will, with the blessing of her family and her ancestors. Do you accept her and all that she brings?"

"I do," Lucas said with a smile as he stared down at Dani.

"In return do you honor to protect her, guide her, teach her, nuture her, and except the gifts that she will bring?" Vern asked.

"I do," Lucas answered.

Vern and Tabby turned to those assembled and together

spoke. "To the elders and ancients of House Talon, do you accept the oath giver that stands before you?"

"We do," they said.

"Do you promise to honor her ancestors as she honors yours, do you promise to protect and guide her? Do you promise to accept her for all that she brings?"

"We do."

Tabby took the blade from the bowl then wiped it on a clean cotton towel. She handed the blade to Lucas. "Lucas."

Lucas took his jacket off and handed it to Dom who stood behind him. He then undid the cuff of his dress shirt rolling it up to his elbow. He took the blade from Tabby and slid his just below his elbow for the scar tissue on his wrist did not allow him to cut through it. Turning his arm, he let the blood flow into the chalice.

"With this blood, it will connect you to our ancestors," Lucas recited. "As it connects you to your future. With this blood you vow to House Talon that you will honor our ways, value our teachings, and fight alongside us as a sister of the blood."

Tabby took the chalice from Lucas and set it on the alter.

Placing a cloth over the top of it she laid her hand her just above it.

"The blood that rests in this chalice unites these two houses, the blood in this chalice brings forth Danika into our covenant with nature, with magick, with all that come before and all that come after. Once accepted it can not be broken. For what is bound in blood is bound forever."

Tabby took the cloth of the cup and offered it to Danika.

"Do you Danika freely accept what is before you?" Tabby asked.

"I do," Dani said with a huge smile. She had a feeling she was bouncing where she stood.

"Do you accept that link that will be forged between you and your house?"

"I do."

"Do you accept the knowledge that will be given to you as they receive the knowledge from you?"

"I do."

"Then Daughter of Night and Blood, may you drink your past and future and join us," Tabby stated.

Taking the chalice Dani beamed at Lucas. "Gladly," Dani said. Some of the crowd laughed at her excitement.

Dani sipped the contents of the chalice. She prepared herself for the head rush that would happen. It had been explained to her that this would awaken many of the vampire traits that lay dormant in her blood. Her heart began to race as her blood accepted the contents. She felt Lucas' hand on her back to steady her as the world spun around her. Smells became intense as she heard the heartbeat in Lucas' chest.

She went to speak but the pain came as her blood felt as though it would boil. Dani heard a scream but wasn't sure if that was her own scream or someone else's. She tried to move but then it all went black.

****

He stood with a telescope pointed at the Cloisters. The security was tight with no way for him to get close to the place. The wards that had been placed around the place for the night also prevented anyone not invited from getting any closer. All he could do was watch the ceremony unfold. When he saw enough to confirm what his informant had told him, he folded up his telescope and approached the car waiting for him.

"My building," he instructed his driver.

The driver nodded and pulled into the street. There was no conversation, small talk was for the weak minded. It was to fill the space because mortals didn't like silence. But he did, he liked what secrets the silence held. He relished in the calm before the storm just as he enjoyed the chaos that could be created. The car pulled along a sleek looking modern building near midtown, it was one of his more recent acquisitions that he bought in the last decade. Turned it from an empty department store into luxury apartments with spa, gym, and a round the clock security.

The doorman simply nodded as he strolled in through the doors. He walked through the lobby heading to the offices. There he took his own private elevator up to one of the apartments. The doors slid open, he heard a gasp as he stepped out into the walk-in closet from the hidden door. The blonde was just coming out of the shower. Smiling he snapped his finger and the towel she clutched around her chest fell to the ground.

"I wasn't expecting you," Savannah said with a smile as she walked toward him naked. She ran a finger down his black dress shirt.

"I wasn't planning on coming," he admitted. He pushed her toward the bedroom as he unbuttoned his shirt.

He watched as she climbed onto the bed, she was on her knees as she watched him undress. He climbed onto the bed then wrapped his hand around her neck as he licked her cheek.

"The books?" he whispered as he bit her ear.

"Translated," Savannah admitted. "I finished the last passage today."

He pulled back and looked at her. "You didn't call me?"

"I was going too after my shower," she answered.

His eyes narrowed as he pushed her onto her back. His hands roamed over her body as he studied her with the eyes of a predator. He smelled fear and deception coming off of her, smiling he tightened his grip on her neck.

"Oh we are going to have fun tonight," he hissed. "Or should I say I am."

Chapter 24

Dani woke to her phone ringing. Her head was pounding, Lucas was laying against her back with an arm wrapped tightly around her. Grunt lay at their feet snoring away. They did not get back until close to three in the morning, and when she looked at her phone she saw it was only seven. Whoever was calling either had a death wish or it was important. Slowly she removed Lucas' arm from her and slipped out of bed, when she headed out of her room she saw that Claire was on the phone coming out of her room.

Claire held a finger to Dani as she finished the conversation, when she hung up, Claire looked grim. "Evelyn was found dead this morning by her cleaning lady," Claire told Dani. "They think she's been dead for three days because that was the last time the cleaning lady was there."

"Savannah?" Dani asked.

"Grant is trying to get a hold of her now," Claire answered. "Also, Michael is mad that he wasn't invited to whatever party we had last night."

"Well when it hit's the newspaper he will understand why," Dani said as she headed into the kitchen to make coffee. "What does Alistair want us to do?"

"Hang tight for the moment," Claire answered. "Right now the others can handle it. Nessa is there looking to see if it was natural or murder. He's waiting until she knows before calling us in."

They both sighed as the coffee machine began to brew. They heard Grunt come out of the bedroom and Claire filled his bowl with his food while Dani went about to make breakfast. Since they didn't have to rush to a scene, they could actually prepare a meal instead of grabbing something quick.

"So, how you feeling?" Claire asked Dani after she took the coffee mug from her.

"Weird," Dani replied. "Knowing so many people saw that memory, it's a bit weird."

"Alistair was having them all write it up, Grey and Todd will collect them then bring them to the Accords Building to be reviewed," Claire told Dani.

"I think I vaguely remember that," Dani admitted. "Last night, after the ceremony, it's a bit hazy."

"Alana said it's like being high but still knowing what you are doing," Claire told her.

"That is kind of how it feels," Dani admitted as she sipped her coffee while getting the eggs ready. "So did we glow?"

"Like neon gold if that is even possible," Claire replied. "Everyone was in awe."

When the eggs were done and plated, Lucas stumbled from the room. Dani reached into the fridge and handed him a bottle of blood. They were all up earlier than planned.

"Why are we up this early?" Lucas asked after he drained the bottle dry.

"Evelyn, Savannah's mentor, was found dead this morning," Claire informed Lucas. "We're waiting to find out if it was natural or not."

"Not how I planned to spend today," Lucas said as he joined them at the small table.

"Sleep, sleep, and more sleep," Dani replied. "That's how I planned it."

"Ditto," Claire said as they clinked their mugs.

The knock on the door had Claire groaning. She got up and opened it to see Dom standing there looking as tired as Lucas but in his usual detective outfit. Black pants and a dark shirt.

"Murder," he answered. "There were signs of a struggle but no obvious signs of foul play so she's rushing a tox screen with our poison in it to see."

"Are we going there?" Claire asked as Dom headed to the fridge.

"No we are waiting on Grant. He can't get a hold of Savannah, so he is going to call her siblings to see if any can get a hold of her."

"It is 7 a.m. on a Saturday," Dani pointed out.

"Yes but she was supposed to be at the herb gathering at six this morning and she hasn't shown up," Dom answered.

"Herb gathering?" Lucas asked.

"After the solstice, people selected from the coven go and

harvest fresh herbs from our farmers," Claire explained. "They then begin the process to dry them out."

Lucas nodded, understanding. He took a sip of Dani's coffee before stretching, an arm going around the back of Dani's chair.

"So what's the plan?" Claire asked.

"We hang here until we are told otherwise," Dom informed them.

★★★★

It was noon when Alistair told them that it was time to look into where Savannah was. Grant was on his way to the apartment to go over what he had learned from her siblings. Micheal would be meeting them at their location.

Grant arrived ten minutes later looking annoyed. "Do you know how many pissed-off witches I have had to deal with?" Grant asked them. "They were trying to get me to take her place and do the harvesting."

"Did you explain that you were working a case," Dom asked.

Grant shot him a look as he headed to refill his travel mug with coffee. "Yes, of course, why didn't I think of that?"

"Where are we going?" Claire asked him before him and Dom could get into an argument.

"Calipso Towers in midtown," Grant answered after sipping his coffee.

Dani let out a whistle. "That's a pretty exclusive place," Dani commented.

"You know about it?" Grant asked as they headed out of the apartment leaving Lucas and Grunt behind.

"It has a ten year waiting list, the cheapest condo is about a million," Dani replied. "And for that million all it get's you is a studio that could fit in mine and Claire's place."

"Why the hefty price tag?"

"Security, there's a spa, 24 hour concierge service, room service, a health center that is state of the art, as well as a rooftop lounge with garden and lap pool."

"How do you know so much about it?" Claire asked Dani. They all crammed into Dom's SUV because it could fit all of them.

"Marcus wanted to buy into the property when it was still being developed," Dani answered. "It was one of the few times that Mom not only fought with him but won."

"Your mom was against getting involved?" Grant asked.

"There were a few reasons," Dani said. "The first was that the building was originally going to be converted into a home for supernatural teens. Instead this group came in and greased enough palms to bury that project and let them build a luxury condo instead."

"Because the city needs more luxury places," Claire said dryly. "What's the other reason?"

"Nick could find very little information on the group that was funding the project," Dani answered. "Mom didn't like that. She didn't want our name to be tied to a project that had kicked out our own kind."

"And Marcus listened?"

"Remember a large part of our money comes from my

mom," Dani reminded him. "The buy-in was more than what Marcus could liquidate from his own assets. He needed to borrow from Mom which he can't do without her permission."

"How large was the buy-in?" Claire asked. "I mean that had to be exorbitant if Marcus couldn't get enough cash together."

"And risky if the place didn't sell," Grant added.

They pulled up to the old department store near 5th avenue that was now Calypso Towers. They were all surprised to see that cop's were closing off the entrance to the building.

"This is not a good sign," Dom stated as they climbed out of the SUV.

They spotted Micheal talking to another cop closer to the building. Showing their badges, they were allowed past the tape. Michael spotted them and waved them over.

"What's going on?" Grant asked his partner.

"Cleaning called in a murder in one of the upper floor penthouses," Michael explained. "The cop I was talking to was about to call us when I showed up. Trent Donavan is lead on this and has been dealing with a pissed-off building manager. I haven't spoken to either."

They followed Micheal past the revolving doors and stopped as they looked around the marble entry area. It was a large space with sitting areas positioned around the open floor, there was a gas fireplace against two walls, and a large fountain in the center of the room.

A middle aged man with silver hair was talking to a few of New York's finest, he was running a hand through his graying hand when he noticed the three of them.

"You called in more cops?" he asked.

"Detective Donovan requested that we call in the STF," one officer stated.

Dom raised an eyebrow as he headed over. "I'm Detective Talon, this is my partner Detective Jensen, as well as Detectives Cooper and Torres, and our consultant Doctor Joseph," Michael introduced them.

"I'm the building manager Richard Smythe," the gray haired man said in an annoyed tone. "I would like to know why you were called here without my knowledge."

"I called for them," a deep voice said from behind

them. Trent appeared from the elevators. He approached the three shaking their hands. "Thanks for coming. Mr. Smythe, if you remember a murder has occurred on your property. I called these three here because your tenant is part of the Supernatural community which means it falls under their jurisdiction, as well as, mine."

"Just get this over with," Richard growled as he stormed away to his office.

"Well he seems cooperative," Claire noted.

"You have no idea," Trent answered. "Follow me."

They headed to one of the elevators. Trent waited for the elevator to start moving before he spoke. "You got here way too fast," Trent stated.

"We were coming to check on a possible witness to the case we're working," Dom answered. "This can't be a coincidence. So what do you know?"

"The apartment is owned by the group that built this place," he explained. "However, the tenant that lived there is not part of the group."

"Is it an apartment used for visiting guests?" Michael

asked. Many of the Vampire houses owned apartments that they used for guests that were visiting for long periods of times.

"From what I have been able to figure out, this tenant has always lived in the apartment," Trey answered. "There was some confusion because her name is only on the mailbox, so it took some time to figure out who actually owned the apartment."

"Do we know who the victim is?" Claire asked.

"She's a witch," Trey replied. "Hence me wanting to call you guys in. We just found her ID before I called over to your place. Her name is Savannah Morris."

"Well shit," Michael mumbled.

"You know the name?" Trent inquired.

"She was to be a potential person of interest in our current case," Claire answered. The Morris family were going to be distraught over this.

"And now she's dead," Trent realized.

The elevator dinged and they all got off. There were only two doors on this floor, Trent directed them toward the one with the cop guarding it. They entered the apartment.

"This takes opulence to a whole new level," Michael

declared as he looked around.

"This is over the top," Claire agreed.

Dani studied the large open area which had been done in whites and faint gold accents. "It feels empty," Dani commented.

Dom arched an eyebrow as he looked at Dani. "That's not good," he replied.

"Why is that?" Trent asked.

"I should be picking up on some violence, anger, some-thing," Dani explained as she pulled on a glove and ran a hand along the marble foyer table. "There should be something for me to pick up. But it's nothing, like it was wiped clean."

"Like the Algonquin?" Claire asked.

"Smoother then that," Dani said. She touched the couch hoping for some impression but nothing. "If Savannah lived here there should be some trace of her here."

"Savannah was a witch," Michael replied. "Claire, could Savannah wipe the place down to erase her being here?"

"There are some witches that will cleanse their home in such a way," Claire answered. "But it's not easy and not something you would even do more than once a month if that much."

"You guys ran into this at the Talon murder?" Trent asked.

Claire nodded. "But we could even feel the effects of it," Claire told him. "Whoever did it had made a mess of the spell. Anyone with supernatural talent or blood in them felt odd in the suite."

"Meaning if this is tied together your guy learned from that," Trent suggested.

"Or he didn't come in the front door," Grant replied.

"How did he get in? Parkour up the side of the building?" Claire asked.

"Maybe we have a hidden entrance," Dani stated. "One that didn't make it on the blueprints."

"Lead the way," Dom said to Dani.

"You know there are times when I think you guys see me as a bloodhound," Dani replied.

She headed down the hallway noting the garish modern art that hung there. "Someone has worse taste than Marcus," Dani noted.

"None of you siblings call your father 'dad'," Trent realized as they entered what looked like a home office.

Michael laid a hand on the lap top. "Cold."

"No we don't," Dani replied to Trent statement.

"My dad would be hurt over it."

"And would your father throw you out a second story window because he didn't like your choice in boyfriends?" Dani inquired. Trent just looked at her in shock. "The killer wasn't in this room."

Trent watched as she headed out into the hallway. He then looked at Dom "He didn't?"

"If he did then it was when Helena would have been away," Don answered. "And yes, I can see him doing that to Dani if he was in the right mood."

When they joined Dani in the hallway she was standing outside the double doors that led into the master suite. "I really don't want to go in there," Dani said in a weary voice.

"That bad?" Claire asked.

"More tired of walking into scenes where one of us knew the victim," Dani replied.

Sighing, she put her gloved hand on the door handle and even with the glove she can feel all the emotions that were waiting for them on the other side of the door.

"I really hate my job at times," Dani commented as she opened the door and walked into chaos.

Chapter 25

The master suite was enormous, it was composed of three three rooms. The sitting room was done in elegant pale gold tones with some antique pieces. It was a far departure for the modern decor of the rest of the place. There was a gas fireplace with a Persian rug laid out before it. Dani felt the chill of the death, but studied the furniture.

"Some of these pieces should be in museums," she noted as she looked at the Louis the Fourteenth writing desk.

"This was decorated by another person," Claire added.

"A female. Definitely feels like Savannah."

Dani nodded in agreement as she ran a hand over the settee, a shiver ran down her spine. "There's a faint impression of him here," Dani replied.

"Meaning what?" Michael asked.

"She knew the killer just like Josie and Harold did," Claire concluded from the look on Dani's face. "Dani is picking up on faint imprints of him that aren't tied to the murder."

"Will that be harder for her?" Trent asked.

"No," Claire answered for Dani as her friend wandered the room. "It might actually help her focus. The imprints from the murder will be different, they'll be filled with raw emotions, a kind of blood lust feeling."

"You sound like you speak from experience," Michael noted. He knew that while Claire had her own unique abilities they weren't on the level of Dani's.

"We were linked once when she came across a scene," Claire explained. "I had a few seconds of knowing what it's like for Dani."

"What's it like?" Trent asked almost immediately regretting the question even as he spoke it.

"A weaker person would be locked in an asylum," Claire stated. She then followed Dani into the small office alcove. "Hey, those are coven books!"

"I think some of these are the ones that were stolen," Dani said as she gently picked one up from the old bookcase.

Michael grabbed a camera out of his backpack and began to snap pictures of the books. While Dom grabbed his phone and Grant went to look at them with Claire. Claire and Grant went through them carefully before placing them each into evidence bags. Claire pulled out a collapsable bag from her backpack and they placed the bagged tomes into it.

"I think we should get these out of here," Grant said as he felt a chill around him.

"You want to run them to the archives, have Greg confirm them?" Dani suggested.

"I'll go with you, then we'll bring them to the precinct, and fill Alistair in on what's going on," Dom added.

Claire took the books from her bag and handed them to Grant. "Once Greg confirms, notify my aunt," Claire said quietly to him. Grant nodded then grabbed his own book bag.

"We'll take my bag," Dom said. "I'll swing back after, you guys will still be here?"

Claire told him she would call if this went quicker than planned. Dom and Grant made their goodbyes and headed out of the apartment. Trent radioed down to the officer on the ground that the two would be leaving with evidence and to have one car follow for security.

"If you guys want to keep looking, I'll nose around here to see what she was doing with them," Claire suggested. "It's not like you're going far."

Dani nodded. The trio headed out of the office space and into the large bedroom area. A huge antique four poster bed sat in the middle of the room. Delicate fabric hung down from the ceiling framing the bed. The linens were done in silver, with the bed in light wood. The only thing that marred the bed was the blood stains from where Savannah's body was.

"Vynessa moved the body already," Trent explained. "She said that with the blood on the sheets you would be able to work with that. She also said once we were done we needed to bag the sheets."

"She's right," Dani said. She wondered what made Vynessa hurry to move the body before Dani got there. "She suggested to call us?"

"She did," Trent confirmed.

Dani nodded then walked around the bed. "They were lovers," Dani realized as faint images played out in her mind. "More than lovers, well, well, well."

"What?" Claire said coming from the office.

"He's a vampire," Dani said confirming what they had suspected. "He took blood from her."

"That's pretty deep, taking blood during sex," Michael stated. "That's like proposal of marriage almost in our world."

"Not to him," Dani commented as she touched the head board. "She would know the intimacy behind it so he used it to control her, to make her think this was more than what it was."

"Which was her getting him information," Claire said filling in the blanks as she joined them. "I found her journal and book of shadows."

"Why help a killer?" Trent asked.

"Savannah comes from a long line of powerful and influential witches," Claire explained. "But there was a lot of problems with trying to place her. She had just enough power to pass the ceremony at eighteen but not enough for it to be focused."

"Let me guess, he offers her eternal love and power," Michael guessed. Claire nodded. "I hate guys like him, they give the rest of us a bad name. Let me drink your blood and I will give you the world. Ugh."

"If you two are done, I know where our hidden entrance is," Dani stated.

They all looked at her. She smiled as she headed to large dressing area. "This is the size of my bedroom," Claire noted as they stepped into the mammoth size room. There were shelves for purses, shoes, boots. Clothes were arranged by designer and season.

"No men's clothes," Michael noted as he looked through the clothes. "He didn't leave anything here."

"He didn't want anyone to find out," Trey suggested. "If it was found that she was staying here he could say he was helping her out. But if he left things here then that would be a different story."

"But they were in love," Claire reminded him in a sarcastic voice.

"But still kept their relationship secret because they knew it would cause issues," Dani replied. She then laid a hand along the side panel of the mirror. "Here we go."

They all stood back and watched as an elevator door appeared. "Well now isn't that interesting," Trent stated. "I wonder where it goes?"

"Who wants to go and find out?" Michael asked.

"I should go," Dani replied. "Bloodhound, remember. I can tell if this is the right path."

"I'll go with her," Trey suggested.

"Alright," Claire replied. "Dan, are you sure about this?"

"I'm fine," Dani assured her.

Dani pressed the elevator button and they waited a few moments for it to arrive. When the doors opened Trent stepped in after her with hand on his gun just in case. Claire watched the doors close.

"We might as well look around while they are off finding where the rabbit hole leads to," Michael suggested.

"Bet it's not at interesting as Wonderland," Claire replied. "I could use help in the office."

They headed to the office where Michael saw that Claire had still be going through drawers. They both work in silence for a few moments.

"So what's up with the secret shindig that you were at last night?" Micheal inquired as they looked around.

"You didn't see the papers today?" Claire asked as she ran her gloved hand along the walls and furniture looking for hidden buttons.

"No, why?"

"Well there was an Oath Ceremony last night," Claire explained. "Grant and I are heirs so we had to be there."

"Which house had the ceremony?"

Claire headed toward the office the books had been in. There had to be more here. "House Talon."

Michael looked at her shock. "Lucas already had his first Oath, that's awesome." And explained why Dom would have been there. "Why was Dani there?"

Claire stopped searching and looked at Michael who was studying the altar that Savannah had set up.

"Dani was the one that took the Oath."

Michael almost dropped the dagger he had found by the altar. "She betrayed her house?" He said in shock.

"What?" Claire asked as she went to look at the dagger he had held.

"She changed houses?" He replied like that was what he had originally said.

"Her and Lucas are Bond mates," Claire informed him. "I'm surprise you couldn't spot the glow of their bond from here."

"You're serious."

"Of course I'm serious," Claire said. "And this a coven ritual dagger. Can you get me another evidence bag."

Micheal went to his book bag and grabbed one out. He handed it to her, Claire thanked him then studied him.

"You okay?" Claire asked. "You look pale for a vampire."

"I think the blood soaked sheets are getting to me," Michael replied. "Witches blood, it can sometimes smell sweet."

Claire had never heard that before but stopped when they heard the elevator doors slide open and headed into the bedroom. Dani stepped off followed by Trent. "So?" Claire asked.

"A closet that is usually locked near the back of the main floor," Trent stated. "Our buddy the manager was very surprised when he heard us knocking on the door to let us out of the closet."

"No one knew it was there?" Michael asked.

"And he has assured us that no one will know it is there," Trent replied. "What about you guys?'

"A ceremonial dagger, a journal, and some other things," Claire answered. "The dagger is definitely from the coven."

"I think all that is left is to bag up the sheets," Michael replied.

"Can I just go through the office one more time?" Dani asked.

"I'll go with her," Michael answered as he glanced at his phone after he felt it vibrate.

"We'll bag the sheets," Claire replied.

Michael and Dani headed across the bedroom space, she heard the crack then the splinter of glass. Michael grabbed her by the waist and pushed her against the wall so that she was covered by him. Trent had grabbed Claire and pulled her down the side of the bed.

"Active shooter!" Trent called into his radio.

Michael moved Dani to the doorway as another round came through another row of the floor to ceiling windows. He hissed as one went through his right shoulder. The wound was already turning black.

"We got silver bullets," Dani informed Trent. She heard him radio in for any supernaturals on site to wear their special armor. Michael let Dani help him to the floor so she could look at his wound. He handed her his bag from him, there would be a medical kit in there.

"All Supernaturals wear silver protection," Trent ordered over the radio. STF wasn't the only force that had supernaturals on payroll.

"We're sitting ducks," Michael noted as he tried not to focus on the pain. "This place is all windows from here to the front door."

"Can we get to the elevator?" Dani asked as she pulled out the silver kit. Michael hissed as she poured in a counteractive liquid that would stop the silver from spreading into his blood.

"Our shooter will have a clear shot all the way to it," Trent noted as he studied the lay out of the place. "And the manager deactivated the hidden one."

They all crouched as another round of bullets tore through the windows and drapes. Trent heard his radio crackle and held it to his ears.

"I'm going to butterfly it," Dani told Michael. "That way it can be stitched properly later."

He nodded. As gentle as Dani could be, she pulled his skin together to use the butterfly bandages. Then he helped her take off his shirt so she could wrap the wound that would help with the bleeding. He was sweating by the time she was done. The medicine she used would keep the poison from spreading but it did nothing to speed up the healing process. The silver would still slow that part down as new skin and cells would re-grow to replace what had been damaged by the silver passing through his body.

"If that was Dom, I would be passed out from pain," Michael noted as Dani finished.

"Dom wasn't taught by Tabby Jensen," Dani noted.

"That is very very true," Michael agreed.

"No dying over there," Claire called over to them.

"We're good," Dani answered. She then looked at Michael. "You have your gun right?"

"I do, why?" Michael asked. "The guy is…"

"Across the street, three floors up, on a balcony," Dani answered for him.

"Did you do a scan?" Claire asked. "Danika."

"Possibly," Dani commented.

"I'm lost," Trent replied.

"So am I," Michael assured him.

Dani ran a hand through her side. "So sometimes and for very short time period, I can look for heat signatures of beings," Dani said. Gloria had actually been teaching her how to control it and have it last longer without draining her. "It takes a lot out of me, so I don't do it a lot. But in this case I thought it might be a good idea to know what we are dealing with."

"How long is the balcony?" Trent asked after he radioed in what Dani had told them about the shooter's location.

"It goes from the bedroom to the start of the living room," Dani replied.

"So we just have to get to the hallway," Michael noted. "We can maneuver around the open doors, but if he can't see into the living room that gives us an exit route."

"Dom is sending a team up to the floor of the shooter. He left Grant at the archives when he heard about the shooting and is here with two teams," Trent informed them. "He also said don't do anything stupid."

"Who us?" Claire said sarcastically. "Never."

Michael chuckled. Then he watched Dani pale. "What?"

"A second shooter just showed up," Dani said. "Good news is living room is still free, but he's above our current guy."

"Dani, don't drain yourself," Claire warned.

"It's not like we have a lot of options," Dani pointed out.

They felt the building shake for a moment. "What now?" Michael asked.

There was radio silence for a moment. "A small bomb went off in the emergency stairwell when SWAT entered to come get us," Trent informed them.

"He planned on us finding Savannah," Dani realized. "So he set traps that would only go off in case of rescue."

"I'm pulling back the teams from entering this building," Trent stated. They all nodded in agreement. "They can help get people out of this building as they evacuate."

"Dani and I can get to the hallway but you two are…" Michael began.

"… Sitting ducks," Trent finished.

Dani cursed, then looked at Michael. "I need your gun."

"Why do you need my gun?" Michael asked. He knew that Dani was allowed to use a gun in situations like this. From what he heard she had yet to miss the center at the range.

"Do you trust me?" Dani asked.

"You are asking me for my gun and then do I trust you, that is the set up for a bad horror movie," Michael informed her.

But he was already putting his thumb on the indent on his holster. The indent read his print then unlocked the holster. He pulled it out then carefully handed it to her. "I really don't want to know what you are going to do."

"Trent, can you fire off a round just to distract our guys?" Dani asked.

Trent looked at Claire, who nodded despite looking pissed. He grabbed his gun then aimed for the shattered window, firing off two rounds. Out of the corner of his eye he saw Dani move out of the doorway.

Taking a deep breath Dani focused her mind on the one with the better aim. This was going to hurt a lot, but zeroing in she calculated the distance and the angle the shot would have to be. Ignoring the wetness she felt above her lip she closed her eyes focused on the path before her and fired the trigger. She stayed there for a moment to make sure she got their guy. And she did, she had disarmed him by hitting his right shoulder.

Michael caught her as her knees gave out and pulled her back under cover. It was enough time for Claire and Trent to get across the room. Trent handed Claire his gun and pack then took

Dani from Michael.

"Piggy Back time," Trent said. Claire helped get Dani on his back.

"You are done," Claire told Dani as she hoisted Trent's backpack on her front.

"I am so done," Dani said with her voice slurred. "Like rainbows dancing in front of my eyes."

"This is going to be fun," Claire mumbled. "I'll take lead, Michael you take the back."

She crouched low so that the furniture in the office would cover them as they made their way to the double doors. When they all reached the doors, Claire headed out first, holding up a hand if she had to think about an upcoming path where a window would be. No one spoke as they made their way to where the hallway met the living room. They all took a deep breath knowing that they made it past the wall of windows.

Michael went to say something when they heard an explosion, the floor before them shook. Claire and Michael each steadied themselves while Trent tried to find balance with Dani on his back.

"I'm going to set you down for a minute," Trent said to Dani.

"I can stand," she promised her voice a bit more steady than it had been. "Nose not bleeding."

Trent helped her down then leaned her against the wall. He stepped away, trying his radio.

"Trent?" Dom's voice came through.

"We're in the apartment still," Trey told him.

"A bigger bomb went off when an elevator was accessed," Dom explained. "Bomb team is here."

"I've got one injured," Trey stated. "Dani pushed herself as well, so we need to get out of here."

Whatever Dom said was cut off by static. The lights flickered around them then finally everything went dark.

"Well, we have cover now," Claire replied. "But if stairs and elevators are rigged we are still stuck."

"They were probably all linked," Michael stated as he thought about it. "They would only be activated if one went off. Then that would trigger the rest so that if the right door was opened, or elevator door opened the device would go off."

"They also probably vary on size of radius," Trey added. "I would wager not one single blast would take this place down."

"But if enough go off the structure might no longer be sound," Claire finished.

Dani closed her eyes and took a deep breath. "Would the devices have a heat signature?" Dani asked.

"What do you mean?" Trey asked.

"Could I pick up on it?" Dani said.

"No," Claire and Michael said at the same time.

"Michael is still bleeding through the bandage," Dani noted. "Which means holy water was probably in the bullet. He needs medical attention sooner rather than later."

"Can you see through walls?" Trey asked her.

"Possibly," Dani replied. She never really pushed her abilities with meshing the astral plain onto real life. Gloria had a theory she might be able to.

"It isn't going to leave a heat signature but you'll notice an object that is out of place or bulkier then it should be," Trent explained. "Think of it like an x-ray, you are looking at the bones, and trying to find the break. We don't need details just enough to let us know if we can go down the stairs or the elevator shaft."

"I can do that."

"Your nose starts bleeding or anything else starts bleeding then you are done," Trent continued. "No passing out, no getting spacey."

Dani nodded. "This is a bad idea," Claire commented.

"You have a better one?" Dani asked.

Once they were settled, Michael took the lead. With the lights out they needed his vision to lead them through the dark hallway. The emergency stairwell door was already open so they all agreed to go down it. As they neared the next floor and door, Dani put a hand on Michael's shoulder to stop him.

"Avoid the step right there," Dani said. "There's a trip wire right at the edge."

Michael nodded, kneeling down he used a penlight to see that Dani was right. Studying the one right before the landing he saw that it was clear. He jumped to the landing then with his good arm, helped Dani down. Claire came next, followed by Trey.

"The door is hot," Claire noted. "Hot doors are never good."

Michael and Dani both sniffed the air. "Smoke," they said in unison.

"Stairs it is," Trey replied.

They made it down three more flights before they took a break. Doors were either locked, blocked, or hot to the touch. They found five more stairs that were rigged.

"How did they not go off?" Michael asked.

"You're thinking like a vamp," Claire noted.

"Huh?' Michael asked confused.

"What would you do in a panic?" Claire asked.

"Not panic, take my time, think out a plan that would get me away from trouble," Michael said simply.

"Because you've had decades to figure things out," Trent replied. "Mortals. Most don't go slow in situation like these, we run, we will skip stairs, hell we'll slide down the banister if we have too."

"So our guy is thinking like a vampire," Dani theorized. "He isn't going to think about running feet or jumping over a few steps. While he knows that mortals are frail he has forgotten how to move like one, how to think like one. We've been taught to walk quickly, to follow the exit signs. To follow the herd."

Dani stood up as she ran a hand along the wall. "Which is why he probably alternated between floors on what was rigged," Dani went on with her thought. "The first floor emergency door was rigged, then an elevator, another door, and then the stairs."

"He knows enough about humans that some will try to take the elevator even though they're supposed to take the stairs," Claire replied. "Or they're disabled and have the emergency key to the elevator."

"So what do we do?" Michael asked.

"Simple, the next door we walk through then take the elevator down," Dani replied.

They all looked at her but she was already moving down the stairs. Sighing, Claire followed after her. When they reached the next door they saw it was blown out. Trey with some help from Claire was able to move the door enough so that they could all get through it. Smoke filled the hallway as they made their way through it. Michael took the lead again as he could see a bit through the smoke. When they got to the elevator door, Dani touched it trying to see if she could see anything.

Michael went to the press the button but she stopped him. "Not that way," Dani replied.

Treny caught on. He joined her as they got their fingers between the doors. Michael and Claire soon joined as they slowly pried open the door. Red emergency lights flashed in the shaft. They could see smoke from where the one explosion went off.

"I'll go first," Michael replied. "If I see an obstacles I can call them out."

"It should be Claire or me," Trent argued.

"He's right," Claire told Michael. "You're injured."

"Neither of you have my vision," Michael pointed out.

It was Dani that spoke. "I do if I have blood."

They all stared at her. "It will heighten my vampire senses, between the blood and walking parallel in the astral plane I will be able to pick out our path and see the dangers."

"If you take blood from me it will be tainted," Michael

warned her. "But it will also partly bind you to my house."

Dani looked at him and saw understanding in his eyes. "If I take from a witch?"

"That's always risky, no offense Claire," Michael replied.

"Worst case scenario," Dani said.

"You'll be high as a kite and think you're flying on a broomstick," Michael answered.

"Is that where that came from?" Trent asked.

"Best case?" Claire asked ignoring Trent.

"You'll heighten her abilities even more than the blood alone," Michael replied.

"What about me?" Trent suggested.

"Your mortal," Michael said. "And none of us want to go through that kind of paperwork even if it is an emergency."

"Then I drink from Claire," Dani said simply.

"And if you think you're flying on a broomstick?" Michael asked as Claire got out her knife.

"Catch me," Dani said. She then looked at Claire. "You sure?"

"I am," Claire assured her. Dani didn't have her fangs

yet so Claire would have to make a cut for Dani to drink from.

Claire cut from her wrist knowing that would be the easiest for Dani to drink from. "You are going to feel a pang at first," Michael warned Dani. "It's your body accepting the blood. Then there is going to be a rush. When you begin to feel the world shift that is when you know to pull pack."

"Ok," Dani said then recited an ancient prayer that all vampires said before they fed from someone for the first time. "With this blood freely given, I thank thee for this gift. May peace fall upon you with this gift you have bestowed."

Taking Claire's wrist Dani put her mouth on it and felt her fangs grow. They pierced the wound, in the background she heard Claire hiss. She also heard Michael talking to her, guiding her along the way. The first pull of blood brought a burning sensation through her veins, she almost pulled back but heard both Claire and Michael tell her not too. Pushing through the pain she continued, soon the rush came as if for the first time she was seeing the world with new eyes. When the colors began to become so vibrant she slowly began to pull back from drinking.

When she was done she collapsed next to the wall panting. Michael was already looking over Claire's wrist. He licked it so that the healing properties in his saliva would help close it while Trey got the medical kit out.

"Shit, that was like better than sex," Claire stated as they wrapped her wrist.

"Well you have been in a dry spell lately," Dani laughed. Claire flipped her off.

Michael stood up then looked at Dani. She was glowing. "How do you feel?"

"Like I could take on the world," Dani replied. Her mind was so much clearer, her senses were heightened to such a degree she could feel Claire's and Trent's heart beat. Knowing she could get distracted she turned her focus onto the shaft. "Let's do this."

Claire watched as Dani went over the ledge. "She's going to be scary as a vampire," Claire said to Michael.

"I feel bad for Lucas," Michael stated as he helped Claire up. "He's going to have to keep up with her."

"Um, hello people!" Dani called from the shaft. "I'm waiting!"

"Definitely not high as a kite," Michael replied.

"More like running a marathon on speed," Trent com-mented.

Chapter 26

Dani laid on the hospital bed, her head was pounding, fluids were being pumped into her, while the heart machine monitored her heart rate and pulse. Lucas sat in the chair next to the bed holding the hand that wasn't attached to wires. They were all being monitored for smoke inhalation, blood had been taken to look for airborne pathogens. Because three of the four were supernaturals, the ambulance brought them to Price Memorial in midtown. It specialized in supernatural medicine and care, it also worked with the Jensen clinic. When they had arrived Alistair was there with his middle son Todd and Lucas was also there. With Dom stuck at the building handling search and rescue, it had been agreed that Dani needed new protection. Todd volunteered.

Lucas rubbed his thumb over the vein in her wrist. "Your pulse is returning to normal," he noted.

"I hate hospitals," Dani commented as she tried to get comfortable. "I feel like I ran four marathons in one day."

"You pushed your abilities harder and farther than you have before," Lucas replied.

"How's Michael?"

"He was being wheeled out of surgery when you were asleep," Lucas told her. "They had to flush him due to the holy water mixed with liquid silver in the bullets. Whatever they were able to get out is being sent to one of Alistair's labs to have tests run on it."

Dani nodded. There was a knock on the door, Helena walked in with a doctor. "You're awake," Helena said as she walked over and kissed her on the cheek.

"She's been lucid for thirty minutes," Lucas told the

doctor.

"Good," the doctor replied. "Danika, I am Doctor Olsen, I just want to check you over."

She nodded. He went through some tests, checking her pupils, tracked her eye movement. He heard her breath as he listened to her lungs before listening to her heart.

"Alright," Dr .Olsen said when he was done. "You are good. Everything sounds strong, your pupils are reacting properly. How's the head?"

"Hurts."

"It will," he replied. "You inhaled a bit of smoke and pushed your psychic abilities quite a bit today. Those two things are going to leave a headache."

"Nothing to do with drinking Claire's blood?" Dani asked.

"Nope," Dr. Olsen said. "That was your first time, correct?"

"Yes, Michael guided us through it," Dani replied.

"You don't have your permanent fangs yet," he noted as he studied her mouth. "Did they detract when you took blood?"

"The moment I brought the cut to my mouth they came out," Dani answered.

"That is very good," Dr. Olsen told her. "And Michael sealed the wound for her with his saliva?"

Dani nodded. "How is Claire doing?"

"Fine," Dr. Olsen assured her. "The wound you drank from was near closed when she arrived. So we just put some ointment on it then wrapped it. She will probably be released in the morning. Not because of the wounds, but because of the smoke. While she is a witch, they still have mortal bodies and organs. So her lungs have not fully healed from the smoke."

"And what about Danika?" Helena asked the doctor.

"I will be signing her papers in a few moments," Dr. Olsen replied. "I would like you somewhere you can be ob- served just in case the headache worsens or your start having problems breathing."

"She's going to be coming home with me," Lucas told the doctor. Helena and he had already discussed it with Alistair and Dom.

"Good," Dr. Olsen agreed. "Then I will sign your papers, a nurse will come in with instructions and warning signs. Right now, drink plenty of liquids that will help the headache. Meditation and yoga might not be a bad idea either to help with the strain on the third eye."

With that the doctor left. Helena looked at Dani and let out a long sigh. "You need to stop ending up in hospitals or clinics," Helena told her. "This case is going to give me more grays."

"Yeah, well it's not like we planned on entering a building rigged up to explode at random points," Dani replied.

"You want to talk about it?" Lucas asked.

She shook her head. Now was not the time nor the place to talk about all she saw. There were too many ears, too many people who might hear something. Later, when it was just her and Lucas at his place, she would tell him what she saw, what she heard.

Alistair walked in. "Nick has Grunt, he'll keep him for the night," Alistair informed them. "Todd is going to head over to your place, Lucas. He'll talk to building security as well as meet with some of the guards that Nick is sending over. And before you ask, these are men that Nick and Sayad both trust and vouch for."

"Thank you," Lucas said.

"I have an unmarked car waiting at one of the basement exits," Alistair continued. "They'll take you to your place. Helena, I had your car swept for any devices and it's clear. I'm going to have one of my guys follow you back to your home, they will break away the block before your house."

"Al, you don't have too," Helena told him.

"I would not sleep if anything happened to any of you," Alistair told her. "You, Dani, Nick, and Sayad are family. And we've all lost enough family at this point."

"Then I appreciate it," Helena told him.

Alistair then handed her a phone as he closed the door. "I want you to have this on you at all time's," Alistair instructed Helena in a tone barely above a whisper. "My number, my wife's, Dom's, and Todd's are programmed in there. It can only be traced by our phones so don't worry about Marcus finding it. There's a chip in there that will distort scans and other things."

"Alistair," Helena began again.

"No, Dani is right. Shit is going to happen fast," Alistair told her. "This is centered around your family for some reason. We can keep Dani safe but you are stuck in the cross hairs. Nick and I talked about this with Lucas and a few members of the council. This phone is the only way we can guarantee your safety."

"Mom, I'll sleep easier knowing you can get away," Dani said.

"That is supposed to be my line," Helena stated. She sighed though when Dani narrowed her eyes at her. "Very well. I will keep it on me at all times. How do I activate the trace?"

"The moment you turn it on, send a message, try to make a call, our phones will be alerted," Alistair told her.

A nurse came into the room and counted the number of people that were in the room. Before she could speak, Alistair and Helena both said goodbye to Dani then left the room. The nurse watched them leave then looked at Dani then smiled broadly at Lucas.

"You'll be seeing her home?" The nurse said to Lucas.

"Yes, she'll be living with me," Lucas informed the nurse not letting go of Dani's hand.

"I just have a paper for you to sign then a few sheets of instructions," the nurse said. She handed him the clipboard. "I wrote some numbers down in case there is a problem, or even if you have a question."

Dani watched as Lucas was oblivious to nurse flirting with him. Part of her wanted to strangle the nurse, another part though was still hanging on 'she's living with me'.

"Thank you very much," Lucas told the nurse as he signed his name on the paper.

The nurse went to say something but then noted what he wrote on the form by relationship to patient. "I will make copies of the paper then you are all set," the nurse replied.

She left the room and Dani looked at Lucas. "What did you write?"

"I had to write what my relationship to you was, none of the boxes applied to us so I crossed them out and wrote significant other," Lucas replied.

"It seems she didn't like that," Dani noted.

"That is not my problem if she doesn't like that I am yours," Lucas stated. "You are all I care about."

Dani couldn't help but smile at that. The door opened again, a different nurse came in. "How about we start disconnecting you," she said to Dani. "Then you are good to go."

"Sounds good," Dani agreed.

It took a little bit to get her disconnected from the machines. She refused the wheelchair which was better because it would be easier for them to sneak out if she's wasn't in a wheelchair. Dressed in yoga pants and a t-shirt, Dani slipped on sneakers as Lucas put her things in his bag. He took the instructions and put them in the side pocket. Alistair came in.

"Ready?" Alistair asked.

Dani nodded. "We're going to go slow," Lucas told her. He wasn't thrilled she vetoed the wheelchair but he also agreed that without the chair they could move easier throughout the hospital.

Putting his arm around her waist they headed out of the hospital room as Alistair led the way. Instead of radioing to the car that they were headed out, Alistair sent a text as they headed to the elevators. Dr. Olsen stood there waiting for them, swiping his key the employee only elevator opened and he let them enter first.

"Never actually helped a patient sneak out before," he noted.

"First time for everything," Alistair replied.

"Mr. Talon, any problems call me," Dr. Olsen told him. "I can always go to your place if that is safer than bringing Danika here."

"Thank you," Lucas said as Dani leaned against him.

"I checked in with Michael and he is doing better, there are signs of healing," Dr. Olsen went on. "He should be out tomorrow."

"We'll keep guards on both his and Claire's room until discharged," Alistair told the doctor.

The elevator doors opened and they all stepped out. "My excuse for taking the elevator if asked is to check on the witch's blood levels," Dr. Olsen stated. "So I will head off to the labs."

He turned and headed in the direction of the labs.

"He's a good one," Alistair commented.

"And he'll make house calls," Lucas added. He looked at Dani. "How you doing?"

"Tired," she admitted.

Alistair took the lead. They went down the hallway to where the morgue was. Passing the double doors, Alistair guided them down the delivery hallway. Grant was waiting for them at one of the exit dmicheloors.

"I got a cranky text from Cooper," Grant told them. "So he must be on the mends."

"I take it you are our personal guard," Lucas commented.

"Yep," Grant replied.

Alistair took Dani into his arms. "Lucas will explain everything," he promised her. He kissed her forehead like a father would. "You know you are the daughter I never had. So promise me you will be safe. I don't ever want to call Grey to tell him bad news about you."

"I'll be safe," Dani promised. "Now go be with your family."

"I am with my family," Alistair corrected her. He let go then looked at Lucas. "Hurt her and I sick my pack after you."

"You won't be the only ones going after me if I hurt her," Lucas commented.

Taking Dani's hand, Lucas followed Todd out the door and into the awaiting car. Dani waited until they were in traffic before she said anything. "What the hell is going on?" Dani asked.

"While you were dodging explosions four supernatural properties were set on fire," Grant explained. "House Impundulu in Harlem reported a gas smell just before their propane tank exploded. Thankfully they had started evacuating staff due to the smell. One of the shifter's safe houses went up in flames thirty minutes later. Someone caught a vandal at Brianna's tree, they were caught before any damage could be done."

"And the fourth?" Dani asked.

"Your apartment building," Lucas said gently.

"Grunt?' Dani asked grabbing Lucas' hand in hers.

"Was on a walk with your neighbors and their dog

when it happened," Lucas assured her. "Nick called Helena when we were enroute to the hospital. He has Grunt with him, he also is putting up the rest of your neighbors in various properties throughout the city so that Tabby and the coven can focus on the attack."

"Four attacks, one for each branch," Dani noted.

"Starting within minutes of Trent saying active shooter," Grant added.

"What the hell is going on," Dani said to no one in particular.

"I think you pissed Bartram off when you showed up at Savannah's apartment," Grant theorized. "He didn't plan on you being there so soon."

"Vynessa told Trent to call us in," Dani recalled. "She had already removed the body by the time we got there. I thought it was odd, because she usually waits until I see it. But maybe she picked up on something."

"Is she clairvoyant?" Grant asked Dani.

"Not enough to activate the witch blood in her ancestry," Dani replied. "It's been dormant for a few generations. Nessa can pick up on things from time to time, thoughts, impressions, feelings."

"Probably why she goes the extra mile as medical examiner," Grant realized. "She'll dig until she knows she has done all she can.

"How bad is my place?" Dani asked Lucas.

"Honestly, I don't know," Lucas told her. "Nick is going to meet Tabby and Vern in the morning and go through it with the Fire Marshall and Arson investigator. Since you had some people from your house living there the council thought Nick would be a good liaison. He'll let me know as soon as he knows information."

Dani thought she couldn't feel any more exhausted that she did but she was wrong. Resting her head against the back of the seat she couldn't believe everything that was happening. Grant drove in silence giving Dani time to process everything. He pulled into the underground parking garage, Grant pulled into the spot reserved for Lucas.

Lucas helped Dani out of the car as Grant secured the area. They headed to one of the doors, Lucas swiped a card through the card reader. The door opened letting them in. Instead of heading to the lobby area they took one of the private elevators to Lucas's floor. Security guards were waiting for them.

"Anything?" Grant asked the two men.

"Patrols have been quiet but we are being observant," the guard assured him.

"Good," Grant said.

Lucas headed to his door, paused than handed Grant his key. Grant took it, unlocking the door he was the first one to enter. He did a quick look around the apartment before letting Lucas and Dani. Dani looked exhausted as she went right to the leather chair and curled up in it.

Lucas motioned to his kitchen. "What are the plans?" Lucas asked.

"I'm meeting Dom at the apartment, Todd is going to take over your security from here on out," Grant explained. "He is working with the security team here and is going to go over ways of making you both more secure. Grey is working with Alana on figuring out how to keep everyone safe."

"Thanks, for everything," Lucas told Grant. He looked in

the living room where Dani was already asleep. "Tell Todd to text me, I'm going to put her to bed."

"If you need anything, don't hesitate," Grant offered. "A lot of people care about Dani."

"If keeping her safe means asking for help I'll do it," Lucas promised.

Grant nodded. Lucas watched him head out the front door. Going over to it Lucas locked it then punched in the security code. His phone vibrated, it was from Todd letting him know that all was good. Lucas walked into the living room and carefully picked up Dani.

Dani opened her eyes as Lucas picked her up. "Can I sleep in your bed?" she asked in a weary voice.

"Yes," Lucas told her. In truth, he didn't want her out of his sight and had planned on bunking in the chair in the guest room.

He walked toward the back of the apartment, the door to his bedroom was already open so he slid inside then gently laid Dani down on the right side of the bed. He pulled the covers over her then kissed her gently.

"I need to do somethings first but I'll be here in this room," Lucas promised her.

She nodded as her eyes closed again. Lucas watched her for a few moments. The bed was one of the few pieces of furniture that he had purchased. It was a large four poster bed that had come from an estate in England. Dragons were carved into the head and foot boards. If he had wanted he could hang panels from it but when he tried it in this apartment it had closed the room off too much. Now he was glad because he could see Dani from his small sitting area.

Heading there he sat down in one of the modern leather chairs. Opening his tablet he saw all the emails and messages that had occurred in the few hours that he had been at the hospital. Many were concern over how Dani and Claire were faring as well as Michael's surgery. Lucas sent off a large group email to update everyone on the medical status of the three. He then sent off private emails to his governors giving them a bit more detail then had been in the larger email.

His phone buzzed and he saw it was a message from Nick. **I'm at their apartment. The smoke damage is bad.**

**Packing up some things of her's and Grunt's that aren't too
bad.**

Thanks, Lucas sent back. **She's sleeping.**

**Good. Council wants a meeting, trying to set one up
as we speak.**

They sent a few more texts before he signed off for the
night. While he would usually work for most of the night until
about four in the morning, he was feeling drained. Heading to
the small fridge he kept in the closet, he grabbed a bottle of synthetic blood then headed into the large bathroom. He didn't like
all the modern touches but it wasn't his place. Stripping out his
clothes he kept the door open to the bedroom so he could hear
Dani if she needed anything. Bringing the bottle in with him he
let the the shower help ease the tension in his muscles.

In the mirrors above the sink Lucas looked at his body.
He was lean but with solid muscles. Yet, what most didn't see
were the scars that came from living through several wars, as
well as, the large dragon tattoo he had done on his back. It
would need to be updated, adding his parent's initials to the
scales of the dragon. He let the water wash away his stress while

he drank the blood. When the bottle was finished he turned off the shower and stepped out. Drying off he pulled on a pair of basketball shorts. Being here felt more intimate in away, perhaps because he never brought someone back to this apartment. He only used it when he was in the states. The bed was one of the few personal belongings he had in it.

Turning off the lights he set the security code for the bedroom. If anything happened during the night, the security would be triggered making the master bedroom a safe room. Placing his electronics on their chargers on the nightstand next to the bed, Lucas finally slid in under the covers. Rolling on his side he smiled as he watched Dani sleep. She was at peace in sleep. For a moment he thought he woke her when she rolled over, but then he realized that she was snuggling into him. Wrapping an arm around her he pulled her close so her head nestled under his chin.

Chapter 25

Alexius knocked on the door to his father's private office.
He had gotten a message on his cell that there was a family meeting. When he had arrived at the family home it was eerily quiet,
his mother was no where to be found. When Marcus barked his
command for Alexius to open the door and stepped in. He was
surprised when he saw Bartram was lounging in a leather chair
while his father paced. Alexius had figured the meeting would
be with Nick to review everything that was going on.

"You are late," Marcus informed his oldest son.

"Are we waiting for Nick?" Alexius asked knowing it was pointless to give a reason for being tardy.

"No," Marcus replied.

Unease filled Alexius, as he took a seat across from his brother. Marcus joined them. For a moment there was silence as Marcus studied the two of them.

"What happened in Istanbul?" Marcus inquired. Alexius went to speak. "I don't want eloquent speeches or finger pointing. I want the facts."

Bartram laughed as he watched Alexius look nervous all of a sudden. "Tsk tsk. And all this time you hoped that dear old dad wouldn't find out," Bartram sighed as he stretched his legs out. "I bet he's known all a long."

"Shut up Bartram," Alexius growled. Turning, he looked at his father. "We can clean it up."

"And what is 'it' and why does it need to be cleaned up?"

Marcus inquired, his patience running thin.

"There were problems with the witches," Alexius began. "They were unhappy with some of the policies that have been passed there."

"And why would this effect us?" Marcus asked.

"Don't look at me," Bartram stated. "This was all you, well mostly all you."

Alexius ran his hands over his face before he spoke. "With the political climate currently in the Middle East I formed a committee to oversee supernatural refugees," Alexius began. His father raised an eyebrow. "I worked the pantheon in Greece as well as the smaller shifter packs. The idea was to ensure placement of our people in safe locations."

"A charity," Marcus sneered.

"On the surface," Alexius agreed. "But under the surface it allowed me to map out all the territories and learn where ever a witch and a shifter lived. From there I purchased buildings they lived and worked in."

"Which explains why you went on a buying frenzy over there," Marcus noted. "Did you at least raise their rent?"

Bartram laughed so hard at that he almost fell out of his chair. "Dear father, he raised it so high they couldn't afford to live in their own filth," Bartram stated. "They were then forced to go to him begging him for aide. Why, he was his own king, with indentured servants!"

The fury that flashed through Marcus' eyes had Alexius standing up in order to leave. Marcus was too fast though and caught him by the throat.

"I watched my parents and sibling starve to death because of a greedy land owner," Marcus hissed as he slammed Alexius into the wall. "We lived in a hovel that not even pigs would live in."

Alexius all but chuckled at that. "You? All of a sudden you have morals?" Alexius challenged. "What did I do that was so different than what you have done?"

"You forced them to come to you, you made the situation one that would have them running to you for help," Marcus stated. "I now have the Council of the Pantheons calling for an investigation into our Middle East and Mediterranean holdings. Those holding have secrets, secrets that could topple this very family."

"Father you are..." Alexius began but his father's grip on his neck silenced his words.

"Bartram take him to your place," Marcus instructed. "Don't kill him, just keep him there while I figure out what to do with this mess."

"Of course father," Bartram agreed as a sinister smile grew on his face.

Chapter 26

With the exception of Michael, they met at Nicholi's apartment. Grunt was beside himself when he saw Dani and Lucas step off the elevator. He slipped and slid across the tile floor getting to them as fast as he could. Dani got down on her knees to pet him and let him lick her and sniff her. Once Grunt was done with his inspection of Dani he moved to Lucas, letting Helena hug Dani.

"I'm fine," Dani assured her mother.

"I'm your mother, I'm allowed to worry," Helena reminded her.

"Mom, let them at least come into the living room," Nicholi replied. "Clara has out done herself with the food. She has it set up in the library so we can spread out in the living room and talk."

"I'm going to go ask her if she could make some Blood Orange tea," Helena said. "Since we are still waiting on Claire, Grant, and Dom."

Walking though Nicholi's modern styled living room, they stepped through the open french doors into his large den. It was more of a library with floor to ceiling shelves lining the entire interior walls. A table had been set up with covered food dishes, and the dry bar was open with various drinks.

The elevator dinged letting them know the rest had shown up. Grunt who had just calmed down, danced in circles at the sight of Claire and went through the same ritual with her as he did with Dani and Lucas.

"You would think it's been years since he saw the three of you," Nicholi pointed out.

"In dog years, it has been, " a beautiful voice said.

Dani turned and saw Clara had entered with a tray of tea. Clara was an elf, they were extremely rare and the result of having a supernatural and a fae as parents. A pregnancy that did not result in a changing or miscarriage. Clara had been sent to the human realm for her protection. Her mother's family were fae, and they were vicious people who refused to accept her. As the oldest female she was set to inherit her mother's title. Until her mother's death, she was forced to stay in the human world. Nicholi and Brianna would make arrangements for the two to meet in safe locations, otherwise there was no communication between the mother and daughter.

"Good 'morrow, Mistress Danika and Lord Lucas," Clara said as she curtsied while carrying the tea tray. Her cover in the human world was that she was Nicholi's ward. He took her in and now she lived with him helping to take care of his affairs.

"Hello, Clara," Dani said. "Do you need help?"

"No, I have it all balanced perfectly," Clara promised as she set the tray down on the marble coffee table. "Nicholi, stop pacing."

He looked at Clara. "Could you handle things for a while?"

"Of course," Clara answered.

Once everyone had food and took places to sit around the living room. Dom finally began to talk. "Just to be clear," Dom began. "Shit is going to get real pretty fast."

"It hasn't already?" Claire inquired.

"The judges of the accords met this morning going over everything we have, including the signed statements from the Elders of House Talon," Dom explained. "They are writing out a warrant for Marcus as we speak which, once it is ready, I will be serving it. I'll be bringing Michael with me as he is House Joseph and we need a representative from that house to be there."

"He will not go quietly," Helena warned.

"I know," Dom assured her. He then looked at Nicholi, he reached into his jacket pocket and took out a sealed envelope. "You have been named Interim Head of House Centurion-Joseph until Markus and Alexius are either proven innocent and you know the rest."

"Well shit," Nicholi said as he reluctantly took the envelope.

"Sucks doesn't it," Lucas commented. "You at least are the second."

Nicholi looked to his mother. "You could object and claim your line?"

"No darling, I think we will flourish under you," Helena said with a smile.

Nicholi grumbled in Arabic as he placed the envelope on

his desk in his office. "What else?"

"There is strong evidence from Tony that someone tipped off Bartram, letting him know that Savannah had been found, and that you were in the apartment," Dom continued. "Alistair is currently scaring the crap out of the building manager for paperwork because Tony found a link to Berger and Son as being primary holders in the building."

They all heard the elevator alarm go off. Clara was there to meet whoever was on them. The fact the person didn't get announced meant they knew the passcode. Nicholi stood immediately when he saw who Clara was helping. Her hand was resting on the woman's back almost as if she was supporting her.

Nicholi went to his sister-in-law and took her from Clara. "More tea," Nicholi said to her. "Peppermint this time."

He guided Antonia to the chair he had vacated. Helena took one of Antonia's hands in hers and was shocked to find them ice cold.

"Your chilled," Helena stated."Sayad grab the throw and place it over her."

"Clara!" Claire yelled almost startling the woman. "No tea."

Claire moved Helena's hand away as she took in Antonia. The one was freezing and shaking. While vampires tended to be cooler in temperature, it could be deadly for them if they were too cold.

"A blanket, but not the fur one," Claire instructed. "Lucas can you light the fire, but don't make it too hot."

"What's wrong with her?" Nicholi asked Claire as Sayad looked for a blanket.

"She's freezing, her body temperature is too low, even for a vampire," Claire explained. "But if we warm her up too fast she could go into shock."

"What do you need Mistress Jenson?" Clara asked.

"Warm compresses," Claire replied.

Sayad draped the heavy throw over Antonia's shoulders while Helena let the woman's hair down from the tight bun she wore.

"Antonia," Claire said gently.

"I'm warming," Antonia said.

"Can you answer some questions?" Claire asked. Antonia nodded. Claire looked at the room. "Just go gentle, any sign of distress and I'll stop the questions."

"What happened?" Nicholi asked crouching down in front of the frightened vampire. He rubbed her hands in his.

"Alexius has not returned home since the other night," Antonia began. She tried to take a deep breath but couldn't. Clara returned with compresses and helped Claire place them on specific spots. "That feels amazing, thank you."

"Clare you can make tea but..." Claire began.

"Not too hot," Clara finished for Claire.

"What happened?" Helena asked.

"I don't know," Antonia admitted. "Alexius had a meeting with Marcus. Then he never came home."

"Did you check his schedule?" Nicholi asked. He knew of no meeting with their father.

"It was the first thing I did when I was called yesterday morning about him missing an appointment."

"That is not like Alexius," Sayad noted. Alexius was very much a creature of habit. He would never blow off a meeting.

"I went to the police about but was told I had to wait forty-eight hours," Antonia replied.

"Why didn't you call me?" Dani asked.

"At first I didn't want to add to your burden," Antonia replied as she took another sip of tea. "But when I returned home I decided I was going to call you. Then I don't know what happened. I woke up an hour ago in the cellar of our home. Everyone was gone and the house felt like an icebox."

"This meeting with Marcus, do you know what it was

about?" Nicholi asked her.

She looked at him oddly. "You mean you weren't there?"

"I knew nothing about a meeting," Nicholi answered.

"Marcus had told him that he needed to meet with you and Alexius to go over estate issues," Antonia replied. "Alexius believed he was going to be in trouble for what happened in Greece."

"Antonia," Dom said gently. "Has Alexius been acting strange at all lately?"

"Since we left for Istanbul and Greece," she answered.

"Antonia, do you know what happened in Greece?"

"I don't know," Antonia answered with a shake of her head. "When we go overseas, I try and spend very little time with Alexius. He is different over there, colder if you can be-lieve that. While he deals with his business I tend to our people. I travel mostly, checking in on those he sired. On my own peo-ple."

"Tell me you also go to his grave and spit on it?" Sayad asked. He was referring to the man that had owned Antonia for a century. Alexius had bought her freedom through marriage.

"That is usually my first and last stop," Antonia said with a faint smile.

"Good," Sayad replied.

"Was there anything odd from this trip," Dom suggested. "Even if it seems trivial."

Antonia nodded. Clara entered with a tray of tea, she poured a cup for Antonia then handed it to her, helping her hold on to her.

"The first odd thing is that Bartram came with us," Antonia replied. "Usually he never comes with us. Alexius figured that Marcus had forced him to come. It made me want to leave even stronger."

"I don't blame you," Dani admitted.

"Marcus usually talks business in front of me, but with

Bartram it was all behind closed doors. There was a lot of raised voices. Talks of a company I had never heard of."

"Do you remember the company's name?" Dani inquired.

Antonia thought for a moment. "Berger and Sons, or something like that."

Nicholi looked at Dani in alarm. "Well that confirms one of our theories," Dom sighed.

"You've heard of it?" Antonia realized.

"Yea, it's come up in the case," Dani replied.

"I hate my husband, he is a cold man, but he is not behind these deaths," Antonia stated.

"We don't think he is either," Dani assured her.

Antonia went to speak then stopped. "Bartram."

"What about him?" Nick asked as he sat down across from Antonia.

"He kept coming and going," Antonia recalled. The tea was helping her warm up, even though it was warm it felt hot to her. "One night he was in my bedchambers. I woke up and found him staring at me oddly. He asked me if I would be his empress. I thought he had drunk from a drug addict again. I told him he needed to drink from a pack in the fridge, then rest. He got angry. Said that one day I would see just how powerful he was. That we will all kneel before him."

"He isn't really making this easy to defend him," Nicholi replied, running a hand through his hair.

"Antonia, did you tell anyone that you were coming here?" Dani asked.

"No, I took a car that belonged to our cook, she lent it to me," Antonia answered. "I then drove to Penn Station. Left it there, then bought a train ticket. I then left with a group of commuters through a different door. Took the subway to get here."

"Good," Dani replied.

"What are you thinking?" Nicholi asked his sister.

"That Bartram is coming unglued," Dani replied.

"And he's taking care of any loose ends," Dom added.

"Antonia, you will stay here," Nicholi told her. He brushed a tendril of her hair back behind her ear.

Claire was thoughtful for a moment. "Actually I might know a place where Helena and Antonia can go to be safe from Marcus, I just have to call my aunt," Claire said.

"The farm?" Grant asked. Claire nodded and headed into another room. They all looked at him. "It's in Up-state. It's about the size of Alistair's place. We use it for training and ceremonies. Tabby owns it, it's been in her family since the 1800's, it was the family farm. It's where Tabby wants to move to when she retires."

"Is it safe?" Nick asked.

"It's completely warded and Tony did the security system, the local pack in the town over is Were-wolves and they patrol the grounds for us," Grant replied. "So Bartram would have to get past the wolves and then all the wards and traps that are laid out."

"But he has managed to do that," Dom pointed out.

"But never at the same time," Dani realized. "He didn't bypass security to get to Parker. He made himself invisible in away. He subdued Parker with the poison. But we're talking about an entire pack that he would have to encounter on top of dealing with Tony's wards and securities. And when he bypassed those at the archives it drained him."

Grant felt his phone vibrate. It was a message from Tony, telling him to put him on speaker when he called. When the phone rang, Grant set it on the coffee table on speaker.

"The gang is here plus Dani's two brother's, sister-in-law, and mother," Grant informed.

"Awesome, that actually means one less phone call if Nicholi is there," Tony said. "Okay so I've digging into Berger and Son because there is no way that there isn't a trail."

"I take it you found one," Dom said.

"Oh, did I," Tony answered. "I used the dates from those cold cases that Alistair had where they were solved but he thought there was more to it, and I also used Dani's parent's death."

"What did you find?" Nick asked.

"Large payouts to families of the drug addict that was used as the scapegoat," Tony replied. "All payouts come from Berger and Son. There is one exception and that is in the case of Dani."

"How is mine different?"

"Because a deed for the house you lived in was transferred from the bank to Berger and Sons."

"Marcus told me the bank would not do that!" Helena roared. She began to curse in a mix of Arabic and Greek.

Everyone looked at Dani for translation. "She wanted to have the property put in a trust for me, so that I could have a place of my own or I could sell it use the money for school or whatever else I wanted. It is what my parent's wanted if any-thing happened to them."

"Marcus probably figured if you ever set foot in it, it would trigger your memory," Claire stated.

"Guys," Tony said from the phone. "That isn't the inter-esting part. A representative posing as a life insurance agent for the supernatural went to both Talon house and the Clarence pack to offer them a large payout."

"Who did he contact in House Talon, because I never met with one?" Lucas inquired.

"It doesn't say, just that a representative for the House re-fused any interaction stating that the deceased did not have life insurance through said company," Tony read off from the notes. "They did get a hold of Alistair's sister and she told them very rudely, it says, to leave her and the pack alone or she would in-vestigate who this company was."

"I take it that Berger and Son owns them?" Dom asked.

"Yes," Tony confirmed.

Dom got up, taking his phone from his pocket. He walked out of the room as he asked whoever it was on the other end how the warrant was going.

"Have you sent this to Alistair?" Claire asked Tony as she entered the room.

"And to the Accords," Tony assured them all. "Also, I found Bartram's name on the apartment that Savannah lived in and it get's a bit crazier."

"How crazy?" Dani asked.

"So it took a lot of digging, and yes all through legal means so it can be used in court," Tony said. "The apartment is owned by Berger and Son, but Bartram's name is listed to be con-tacted in case of an emergency issues with the apartment. Ac-cording to the paperwork, Savannah was listed as occupant back in December."

"You said it get's crazier?" Grant replied.

"Yes, because the top five floors are owned by shell companies not individuals," Tony replied. "In tracing them, they all belong to the creeps of our community. The ones we know are shady but haven't been able to prove they are creepy."

"And it just keeps getting bigger and bigger," Claire groaned.

"Let's focus on the murders," Dani said. "Then we can focus on the other things."

"Anything else?" Grant asked Tony.

"That's it," Tony answered.

Grant took it off speaker to say goodbye. He looked at Claire. "What did you Aunt say?"

"The place will be ready for them by this evening, just let her know any blood preference to be stocked in the fridge," Claire told them. "She said that Nick and Sayad can go as well."

"It will look strange if we all leave," Sayad said.

"He's right," Nicholi sighed. He looked at Antonia, hating to see her like this. He had never approved of the treatment she received from his older brother. "Sayad, go with them. Once Marcus is arrested, I will be officially head of house so I should be here."

"Come," Helena said to Antonia. "I have clothes here, we can go through them to see what fits you for you are a bit taller than me. This way you don't have to return to that place."

Antonia wrapped the blanket around her tighter as Nicholi helped her stand up. He watched as Antonia let Helena help her head to the stairs that led to the second floor.

"I will protect them both with my life," Sayad told Nicholi.

"She has always deserved better than how Alexi treated her," Nicholi growled.

"Mistress Jensen," Clara began. "They both prefer O, it can be negative or positive. Also Helena likes orange blood tea and Antonia likes any tea there is."

"Thanks, I will text my aunt," Claire said.

Dom entered the room. "Are we getting them out of here?"

"Yes," Nicholi said. "Why?"

"How long to the farm?" Dom asked Claire.

"About a two hour drive," Claire replied. "And no, that is not me driving."

Dom nodded. "We need somewhere safe for Claire and Dani as well, and Grant."

"The warrant went through," Lucas realized.

"Yeah."

There was silence for a few moments. "They can stay here," Nick replied. "Your Aunt can as well, and so can Vern."

"Tabby said she was going to be at the clinic over night," Tabby replied. "Have Vern go there. That place is Fort Knox."

"What about Tony?" Dani asked.

"No one is getting into his apartment," Grant replied.

"Trust me. If we could fit in his place I would say let's go there."

Dom looked at his watch, it was after 1:00 p.m. "Let's eat, then I'll call Michael and have him meet me at the precinct for five. We can head to New Rochelle. By then everyone should be where they need to be."

"Nick, are you sure?" Lucas asked.

"The only entrance into this place is the elevator, and emergency stairs that are in a safe room hidden in my closet," Nick replied. "That door is locked, and coded. To access the elevator without me being told, you need the code or a finger print. Marcus and Bartram had neither. And Alexius has an older code."

"Antonia got up here though?" Grant pointed out.

They all watched as a vampire blushed a bit. "Yes, well, that's because she has both," Nick said clearing his throat. "Dom is right, let's eat and then we can figure out what to do next because we know arresting Marcus isn't the end of this."

"Do we have enough for a warrant for Bartram?" Dani asked.

"The Accords are working on that as we speak, the memory is proof for Dani's parent's," Dom explained. "Getting him for the current case is trickier, my hope is the Berger and Son connection might be enough for them let us arrest him for them as a person of interest."

Sayad looked at his brother as a smile formed on his lips. "I'm taking your car."

"Which one?" Nick asked slowly. Sayad just smiled. "A scratch, a ding, a dead bug on the windshield, and I will hurt you."

"Agreed," Sayad answered. "I need to call someone to let them know I will be out of town."

They watched Sayad leave. Claire smiled at Dani. "Ten bucks its Gregoir he's calling."

"Do we even need to bet on that?" Dani asked.

"This might be a stupid question," Nicholi began. "But why didn't Michael come?"

"He had to do something with a family member, I think a cousin," Grant replied.

"Michael doesn't have a family besides the bloodline," Helena said as she joined them. "Claire, Antonia is laying down. She was tired and I made sure it was a light blanket."

"I'll check on her in a little bit, resting will help regulate her temperature," Claire told them.

"What do you mean Michael doesn't have family?" Dom asked Helena.

"He was an orphan," Helena told them. "He was turned by one of the members of our line, but his sire died just before we came out to the public."

Helena looked at the shocked faces around her. "You did not know this?"

"No, I mean he doesn't bring it up much," Grant admitted.

"But he's talked about cousins and family before."

"Odd," Helena answered. "Sayad, when Antonia is awake we can leave."

Sayad nodded. "Also, the rest are staying here at Nicks."

"And Dom, you will be careful?" Helena asked.

"I always am," Dom promised ignoring the snorts from Claire, Dani, and Grant.

* * * *

Marcus sat across from the fireplace in his home office. All the staff had been dismissed, the lights were turned low. The house was as quiet as a tomb. Everything he had built, everything he schemed for, it was all falling apart. Marcus didn't even flinch when the door to his office opened.

"She made an Oath to another house," Marcus stated as Micheal and Dom stepped into his home. "She betrayed her own blood."

"I'm sure you are real broken up about it," Dom said. "You know why we are here."

"Who saw it?" Marcus asked as he stared at the flames.

The day he dreaded had finally arrived. He had always hoped she was a witch like her father was. But when it became apparent she was a vampire like her mother, he began to fear this day.

"One hundred elders and ten ancients," Michael replied. "Including Absjorn."

Marcus laughed at the last name. "The old hermit showed up I see," Marcus replied.

"We know what happened that night," Dom told Marcus.

"What you think happened you saw through the eyes of a five year old who had no comprehension of what was going on," Marcus argued as he stood up. "You come here with nothing but heresy."

"We come here with a warrant to search your property and bring you in for questioning," Dom corrected him.

"On what grounds?" Marcus demanded, caught off guard for a second. Danika being in a coma would not give them permission to search his grounds, not even a walk through her memory could do that.

"The disappearance of Alexius Jospeh," Dom said handing Marcus the formal summons.

"What do you mean?" Marcus asked refusing to take the paper.

"Your oldest child has been reported missing by his wife," Dom explained. "His last known whereabouts are here."

"And so that gives you cause to come barging into my house?" Marcus demanded.

"Actually, it does," Dom replied.

"The human laws are very specific..." Marcus began, he stopped when he saw Dom smile.

"Good thing than that the human laws don't apply here," Dom said. Marcus went to protest so Dom reminded him of the laws. "I'm sure you remember that human laws only apply to us when a human is involved otherwise the STF help police our own people. The council is allowed to issue warrants and judgement. And our laws are not as lenient as the humans."

This time Marcus looked at the paper in his hands. For the first time in centuries he felt fear creep into his bones when he recognized the insignia on the search warrant. He had expected to see the STF logo on the paper instead it was the insignia for the High Court of the Accords. Dom was an enforcer of the High

Court.

"There was no meeting," Marcus argued as he tried to come up with someway out of this. "I was not informed."

"You wouldn't be since you are being questioned for a series of crimes against our kind," Dom informed him. "It is stated clearly in the accords that when a member of the High Court is involved in a case they are not to be involved in any sessions that involve the discussion of the case outside of courtroom appearances."

"If I recall you were the one that made sure that rule was in there," Michael recalled as he finally spoke. "I believe you wanted to ensure that the corruption that tended to be in governments was easily handled."

"So you use my own words against me?" Marcus asked.

"Michael, can you get the search started," Dom inquired. Michael nodded, another enforcer stepped in to take his place. The laws were strict, more than one person had to be in a room at all times with the accused.

"You're taking the word of a slave over the word of a Head?" Marcus argued as he studied the new member who was covered head to toe.

"You mean former slave," Dom corrected as he sat down in one of the chairs.

"The marriage contract might have allowed her to live as a free person but she was still very much a slave," Marcus stated as he folded his arms across his chest.

"Oh then Alexius didn't tell you?" Dom asked with a hint of fang. Marcus raised an eyebrow in question. "It seems your oldest grew a heart and released her as of three days ago. Funny timing, since he vanished two days ago."

"And you jump to the conclusion that I had something to do with it?" Marcus countered. "Perhaps he got tired of the charade and decided to leave his marriage?"

"Under any other circumstance I could see that," Dom agreed. He stretched out his arms, cracking his knuckles as he did. "But you see along with the statement of release, we found a copy of the the marriage contract."

"Is that so?"

"Apparently, if anything was to have happened to Alexius, the ownership of his wife would go to Bartram than to you," Dom answered.

"Back then it was common for the wife of a brother to be married to his brother or closest male relative," Marcus replied.

"Don't do the "back in the day" thing," Dom warned. "You got fifty years on me or did you forget that? I might lurk in the shadows, Marcus, but I am just as powerful as you. I just don't see the need to broadcast it for the world to see."

"Well when you act like an insufferable child it is hard to remember you are an elder," Marcus chided.

"Where is Alexius?" Dom asked growing tired of the word games.

"I honestly don't know," Marcus replied, which was true. He didn't know where Alexius was. It was better that way so that for moments like these he could tell the truth.

"Where's Bartram?" Dom asked. Marcus looked at him confused for a moment. "The guest house that he lives in is empty, has been for a few days."

"I don't know."

Dom looked at Marcus as he leaned back against the couch. "Really?"

"I don't keep tabs on my children."

Dom laughed hysterically at that. "Who are you trying to fool, Marcus?" Dom asked him. "Do you forget that I work with Dani. That I know you keep a GPS tracking on her phone, that if she disables it you know in a moment. That you do the same for your wife and other children as well. So don't tell me that you don't keep tabs on your children. The minute any of your vampires step out of line you are on them."

"I want to see my daughter," Marcus said.

"You can't," Dom informed him knowing the master vampire was trying to change topics to throw him off.

"You can not deny me the right to see my child."

"You are right, I can't. But a restraining order can," Dom replied. "And an emergency one was placed not allowing you anywhere near her."

"Lucas should not have done that."

"It was Helena and Nicholi who did that," Dom said referring to Nick by his full name. "This might also be the time to tell you that Nick has been named emergency Head of your line."

The anger flashed in Marcus' eyes. Dom's old training

paid off for he was off the couch before Marcus reached it. He dodged a blow to the head grabbing Marcus by the wrist and yanking it behind the man's back. He didn't move his head fast enough so he caught Marcus' head slamming back into his nose. But Dom didn't release his grip, instead he rammed a knee into the back of Marcus bringing the older vampire to his knees.

The enforcer tossed Dom a pair of silver handcuffs. Ignoring the blood coming from his nose, Dom read Marcus his rights as he cuffed him. Once he was done the enforcer took over, Dom followed them out of the room.

"Dom, I'm really sorry," Michael said as they watched Marcus being driven away.

"For what?" Dom asked turning to face Michael.

"For this," Michael said.

All Dom saw was black.

Chapter 27

It was close to midnight when Nicholi got a phone call from the front desk that an Anthony Vizzinni was requesting permission to come up. Grant was in the room with Nick and nodded to let the witch up. The others had gone upstairs to settle in for the night, Lucas was going to work from the room that Nicholi had given them. What neither expected was Alistair to be with him when the elevator opened.

"We need Lucas," Alistair said immediately.

"Somethings wrong," Lucas said as he came running down the stairs with Dani behind him. He slid to a stop when he saw Alistair there. "Dom?"

"We have lost communication with him since he served the warrant," Alistair replied. "Marcus arrived at the Accords building but the car with Dom and Michael has never shown up."

"Bartram," Dani whispered.

"And it get's a bit complicated," Tony warned.

They heard footsteps coming down the stairs and saw Claire and Grant coming down them. "Good, we're all here," Alistair noted.

"What's going on?" Claire asked.

"Dom is missing," Lucas replied. "So is Michael."

Alistair looked at Nicholi. "Would you be able to pick up on distress?"

"No," Nicholi answered. "He took and Oath to mom. I'll

call her."

Alistair nodded as Nicholi went to his office. "Tony, how come you're here?" Grant asked.

"Tony contacted me and made me see that Dom is not missing by his own will," Alistair replied.

Tony motioned everyone to follow him into the living room. He set his messenger bag down, leaning the cane against the couch as he sat down. Tony took his sleek laptop out of the bag and opened it.

"In everything that I have been going over, I found phone numbers that kept showing up on the Berger and Son information," Tony began. He opened up the screen to pull up what he had shown Alistair. "Now most led to burner phones except for three numbers. One was the phone in Marcus' office at the house in New Rochelle. The second is to the guy who approached Lucas' representative and Alistair's sister. The third took some digging."

Grant looked at the number that Tony had highlighted. "No way in hell," Grant said.

"What?" Claire asked him.

"The number belongs to Michael," Alistair replied.

"Absolutely not," Claire said. "He's been STF since the start."

"He sent a text message to Bartram's number a few minutes before the gunmen opened fired at the apartment," Tony replied. "And yes I know he got hit."

"There has to be more," Dani said. "This can't be the only thing."

"Every meeting we had that Micheal was at is a phone call or text to the number," Alistair said, worried they would start yelling at Tony. "A phone call was received on Michael's end three days before we found Evelyn's body, shortly before Vynessa has placed her time of death. And then another phone call to Bartram's number several hours later. "

"SHIT!" Grant yelled as he began to pace.

Claire went to go to him but Tony shook his head. Lucas returned giving them a distraction from Grant.

"Mom said that she has felt no sign of distress from Michael," Lucas told them knowing it was not good news by the look on all their faces. "He is also in a way trying to block out the link."

Grant rested his hands behind his head as he began to pace. Tony got up without his cane, steadying himself with the arm of the couch. He walked over toward Grant, and placed a gentle hand on his shoulder. Grant stopped, in low tones Tony talked to him.

"Okay," Claire said. "Where would they be?"

"No where in New Rochelle or the city," Dani replied. "Bartram wouldn't want to risk us finding him yet."

Grant joined them again. "Tony, you said that Berger and Son have the deed to the place that Dani lived?"

"Uh yeah," Tony said as he sat down on the couch again. He brought up the list of property holdings.

"How many holdings do they have by Mount Hope?" Dani asked. Grant nodded at her, glad she understood his line of questioning.

"None," Tony said.

"Any others in Orange County?"

He shook his head as he scanned the list. "The only properties that are not in Manhattan are on Long Island," Tony stated.

Grant and Dani looked at each other. "Your house," Grant said.

She nodded in agreement. "It has to be."

"Okay, Dani," Alistair said. "You are going to tell us everything you remember about your house. Nick, can I bring in my head SWAT guy?"

"Yes, give me his name and I'll let the front desk know he's coming," Nick replied.

Dani sat down next to Tony with Lucas watching her closely. She ran a hand over her face as it all began to sink in.

Alistair joined them after he made the call. "Dani, I hate asking you this," he confessed.

"No, it's fine," Dani replied. "Claire, you're the better drawer. If I talk it out can you draw?"

"If not I'll do that trick Gloria taught me," Claire said. She looked at Nicholi. "Plan paper and a pen?"

Nicholi nodded as he rushed to his office grabbing printer paper and a bunch of pencils. Tony moved his laptop off the coffee table as they cleared it.

"It's a red brick cottage," Dani began. "It had a second floor but that was dad's office and the attic. There was the front door and a back door. Those were the only two ways to enter the house. Dining room opened into living room. He can't have Dom there. The house was too small."

"Okay, any other buildings?" Alistair asked.

Dani had to think. "There's a detached garage," she recalled. It had been years since she even thought about her old
home. "Wait. There was the old Barn at the edge of the
property, it backed up to the woods. My parent's never wanted
me near it, there was an old root cellar, and if I remember, a tun-
nel or something with hiding slaves. It was falling apart and the
floor boards were unstable so I wasn't allowed in there."

"How big was it?" Alistair asked.

"Bigger than the house," Dani recalled. "Or it seemed
like it to me, I was five."

"Tony you think you could bring it up?" Alistair asked.

He nodded already typing in the information he needed to
know. The elevator dinged and Allan Morrison stepped off the
elevator. He was a large were-wolf that Alistair's pack had
adopted when his parents abandoned him at thirteen.

"What do we have?" Allan asked as he entered the room.

"Tony Vizzini is bringing up an image of the farm that

Dani grew up on," Alistair caught him up. "There's an old barn that she thinks is the best place for Bartram to be hiding."

"Not the house?" Allan asked Dani in his deep voice.

She shook her head. "The house is maybe twelve hundred square feet, it was built in the 1800's, it's all small rooms that have been opened up to make bigger living spaces."

"And the barn?" Allan asked her. He understood why she would think the house would be out.

"Is almost double the size of the house and has a second floor," Tony stated. "Or it did when pictures were taken for Google Earth two years ago."

He turned the screen so they could all see it. Claire sketched it out, where it fell on the property and the trees that surrounded it.

"The woods will give us coverage," Allan noted. "Is that a service road?"

"It used to connect one of the main roads to an old wood

trail," Tony said from what he could see from the information he got. "That's where we could park and set up. I can set up from there and let you know what type of security Bartram has on the place."

"You're coming?" Allan asked the computer guy.

"You know any other hackers that can bring down pretty much anything he finds?" Tony challenged. He knew with the cane most people saw him as weak, that he wasn't able to take care of himself or others.

"Alright," Allan agreed. "He can ride in the van."

"Which means he can hook up to our communications," Alistair agreed. Alistair turned to look at Lucas.

"I'm coming," Lucas informed him.

Alistair saw the look on Lucas' face. "Give me a legal reason so that we don't get killed in the court room because you were there."

"Dom is part of my bloodline and is danger, therefore as

his Head I am there so that if blood is needed he can take it from me," Lucas answered.

"That works," Alistair replied.

"I'll get my guys ready," Allan said. "Nerd-dude, you want to ride with me so you can start doing your computer thing en-route?"

"That would be perfect," Tony said. He shoved his lap top in his bag and used the arm of the couch to get up. Tony liked that the new guy didn't try to take control or offer to help. He saw that Tony knew what he was doing. Grabbing his cane, Tony followed Allan.

"I'll send updates as I get them," Tony promised them.

Alistair nodded. "That is the weirdest pair I have ever seen, Allan has like a foot on Tony and is twice his width," Alistair noted.

"And the scarier thing is that Tony could take him down in under a minute," Grant added. "Don't let the cane fool you into thinking he's not dangerous."

"So true," Claire replied. She had sparred with Tony before and he had her on her ass in under a few minutes.

"Alright, everyone get your stuff," Alistair said. "Lucas you will get in the van with Tony when we arrive. That's as close as you are getting."

Chapter 28

As Dom slowly became aware of where he was, he realized by the pain in his head and throughout his body that he was alive. Wherever he was, it was cold and damp. He could smell the mustiness of being underground. When he went to sit up, strong hands held him back.

"Take it slow," a familiar voice said. "Your ribs might be broken."

Dom groaned as he sat up confirming the broken rib theory. When he opened his eyes he saw he was in a stone root cellar of some-kind. A lightbulb dangled from the ceiling, giving off minimal light. Then he noticed his companion.

"Alexius," Dom said almost growling.

"Surprise," Alexius said weakly as he sat down next to Dom on the cot. "Welcome to Bartram's master plan."

"And do we know what it is?" Dom asked as he took in everything around them. Alexius, he noted, did not look good.

"To take over the universe, to be the ultimate asshole, to be worshipped as a god," Alexius rattled off. "You realize that your buddy Michael is in on this?"

"Figured that out when he bashed me in the head," Dom admitted. "Did he get you too?"

"Nope that was my amazing father, he turned me over to Bartram because I was asking too many questions."

Dom looked at Alexius. "Alexius..."

"Don't," Alexius replied. "I'm an asshole, I know that. I

knew something was going on for years, but I didn't want the family name to be tarnished so I pretended to know nothing."

"You, um, don't look so good."

"I'm getting a mild dose of the poison in the blood that Bartram is giving me," Alexius informed him. "And no, I will not take your blood. Because I don't know if the poison will transfer when I bite into you."

"Look, what do you know?"

Alexius let his head rest against the damp stone wall. "We are on the property that once belonged to Danika's parents," Alexius began. "We are in the old root cellar which is part of the basement of the barn that is above us. There is a hive of tunnels and rooms down here. Apparently it was used to hide slaves on their way to freedom."

"And upstairs?"

"Is not dilapidated like the outside," Alexius answered. "Computer monitors, security system, constant guards and a torture room. Everyone is armed and you know they are packing silver bullets and holy water."

"Way's out?"

Alexius snorted at him. "We're dying here, Dom."

"I don't know about you, but I haven't been alive for almost five hundred years just to die by the hands of your crazy brother," Dom informed him.

"And how do you plan on doing this?"

"You've been here longer than me. Tell me about this cell."

Alexius sighed wearily. "The bars are made with a high level of silver," Alexius replied. "Every twelve hours he sends someone down here to wipe them down with holy water. There is one key to this door."

"And who has it?" Dom asked.

"The head guard for that shift," Alexius asked. "Look, Dom this is...it's not going to work."

"He is going to lure your sister here are some point," Dom told him. "You might not care about her but if she died it will destroy Lucas, Claire, your mother, and two of your brother's. He already went after Antonia."

Alexius had been leaning against the wall with his eyes closed but at Antonia's name they flew open. "Is she...?"

"She went to Nick," Dom said. He wasn't sure how Alexius would react to that. He saw relief wash over the vampire at his words.

"Nicholi, he is a good man, better than I could ever be," Alexius commented. "She is safe now."

Dom nodded, not wanting to say how exactly. As Dom watched Alexius, he began to understand just how ill the vampire was. His movement's were slow and precise, as if he was trying to spend the least amount of energy doing something. He was pale with a gray undertone that was not normal. His eyes were bloodshot, a dangerous sign for vampires.

"I told you that I'm dying," Alexius said. "And no, I haven't started to cough up blood yet. He's giving me just enough to slowly kill me."

"I... shit," Dom stumbled at what to say.

They heard a door open followed by footsteps coming down cement steps. Dom almost growled when he saw who appeared before their cell.

"We trusted you!" Dom yelled. He wanted to grip the bars so bad but recalled what Alexius had told him about the bars.

Micheal on the other hand, leaned against the stone wall watching Dom. "I know, and I'm sorry about that," Michael stated.

"How long?" Dom asked him.

Micheal debated on how to answer. He knew the plans that Bartram had laid out for the evening. "Longer than you expect," Michael answered.

"Who else from our precinct?"

"Shockingly, just me," Michael informed him. "I know I would be surprised too. The terrible twosome seem like much better candidates for murder and betrayal. Though, Holtzen isn't too clean but does he know the extent of all of it? No."

"Why are you here?" Alexius asked.

"To inform you both that Bartram is going to wish to speak with both of you in a little bit," Michael answered. "He's just finalizing a few things so that he can focus all his attention on the both of you."

"And he sent you down here why?" Dom inquired.

"To see how well you two were getting along," Michael admitted. "He was hoping for something a bit more dramatic than idle chit chat."

With that, Micheal turned to walk away. "Oh, Dom," Michael stopped. "While you are here being entertained, what Bartram has planned for your partners is quite horrible. I wonder how they will feel when the great Dominykas doesn't come to save the day. But then this wouldn't be the first time you failed a female that was important to you."

Alexius caught Dom before he could grab the bars. Holding Dom back was taking up a lot of the reserves he had try to store. Dom realized this when Alexius began to tremble.

"Shit," Dom said as he helped Alexius sit on the cot. "I'm sorry."

"Don't be," Alexius told him. "I have been an utter asshole to you for the time we have known each other."

"Doesn't mean I want to see you die painfully," Dom replied. "Bartram, yes. But you, no."

"And that is how we have always been different," Alexius noted. "I see black and white and you see the gray area."

* * * *

Claire was reading through the notes of Abe. She had Tony scan the note's when she first got the book so she didn't have to fear ruining it. Now she was glad, because as they headed toward Dani's childhood home, she could read everything they needed to know. Vynessa had confirmed that Evelyn was killed by the poison, however, so far Savannah had no trace of it in her system.

"Anything?" Alistair asked from the car.

Claire flipped him off as she read through the notes. "Shit, shit, shit."

"Three shit's is never good," Dani commented.

"I need the radio," Claire said. Dani handed it to her. "Everyone this is Claire Jensen. Report in if you hear me."

Once everyone had called in she continued. "The poison that Bartram is using, at the dosage that he's been making it in, it corrupts the blood of the victim," Claire explained. "Touching any blood that comes from a victim or the poison within seconds of it leaving the body could in fact poison you through the skin."

"Everyone, leather gloves," Allan said through the radio. "Treat every person we find with suspicion of being poisoned.

Jensen, can you radio the EMTs that are meeting us there. Tell them this as well."

"I can," Claire replied.

Dani was the one that actually radioed it for Claire had gotten absorbed by another passage.

"How's Lucas holding up?" Alistair asked Dani.

"Stressing," Dani answered. She could feel it through their link. "He has notified the House that Dom is in danger, so those closest to here who Lucas trusted with that information, will meet us when he gives the signal in case Dom needs blood."

"And if he's been poisoned?" Alistair asked.

"Claire will figure it out," Dani answered. She wasn't thinking about the what if's, that would drive them all crazy.

"And are you ready to go back?" Alistair asked. He was worried about Dani, about how she would react when they showed up at her childhood home.

"Is anyone ready when they are about to face their

demons?" Dani asked him.

There was one piece of the plan that Alistair and Dani had failed to mention to the rest of the team. Even Claire in the back seat had not been informed of it. Alistair thought it was crazy, but it would buy them time to set up and get the teams in with little detection. It's why he suggested that they all come in from different directions, so that no one would be suspicious of a line of vehicles all coming from the same direction.

"Lucas have any idea?" Alistair asked.

She shook her head. Gloria had been teaching both of them how to shield thoughts from the other so that they could close their link down. There were memories that Lucas didn't want Dani to see, and when Dani was working a case there would be information that need to be confidential.

"How long can you hold it?"

"We are going to find out," Dani admitted. "Hopefully long enough."

Alistair nodded as they kept driving. They had all left at different times, with ten minutes in between each group that left. This allowed for the van to get set up so that when everyone showed up, communications would be up and running.

"In my glove compartment is an ear piece that is already paired with mine and Tony's," Alistair told her. They were getting close.

Dani opened it and found a small plastic container with a transparent ear bud. No one would see it in her ear. Taking it out, she placed it in her ear. She turned it on. Claire was still distracted in the back. It wasn't until Tony slowly pulled to a stop that Claire realized what was going on.

"Don't even think about it," Claire said as she realized that Dani was unbuckling her seat belt. "You are not offering yourself up for slaughter."

"You're right, I'm not," Dani agreed. "I'm just buying you guys time to get here. So you and Tony are going to go the rest of the way on foot, and I am going to go visit my childhood home."

"Dani," Claire whispered as her door opened and Alistair stood there.

"It's going to be fine," Dani assured her. "I have no intentions of dying."

"And if he poisons you?" Claire asked.

"You'll figure out the cure and save us all," Dani answered as she slid into the driver's seat.

Alistair nodded to Dani as he got their bags from the car. Quietly he closed the doors. Dani waited until they vanished into the woods before she started the car up again. They were two blocks from her childhood home. This was going to be hell.

Chapter 29

The driveway was still gravel but was now overgrown with weeds and nature. Dani pulled the SUV up to the garage and just sat there as she looked at what had once been her home. Shingles were missing from the roof, vines covered much of the brick. A few windows had been boarded over. Climbing out of the car, she shut the drive's door and took a deep breath. She could do this.

She took the key that she had found in Marcus' drawer

when they stopped at New Rochelle out of her pocket and stared at it. Walking to the front door was numbing in a way. Dani had no clue what memories would awaken as she stepped over the threshold. The key slid in with little issue, the door took a few tries before it opened. The house smelled musty as she stepped into what had been the living room. The furniture was still there, the television was so out of date she had to laugh as she looked at it.

Dani closed her eyes as she remembered snuggles on the couch, Saturday morning cartoons, blanket forts, and just a home that had been filled with laughter and love. Her toy box still stood in the corner of the archway that led into the small dining room. It had rarely been used as a dining room, she remembered her dad working there as her mom made dinner. Dani would be in the living playing or watching television. Running her fingers over the furniture that was covered with decades of dust, Dani fought back the tears that she had never really shed over her parent's deaths.

She stopped at the doorway to the small kitchen. The table had been removed, the floor had been removed so that the sub-flooring was exposed. Cabinet doors hung at odd angles from hinges. The fridge was gone but the stove was there. An image of her mom cooking flashed before her eyes. Her mom turned to where Dani stood and smiled at her.

Dani couldn't bring herself to walk into that room, it was where they had died. Instead, she turned down the short narrow hallway. The bathroom door was closed, but the door across from it was missing. Dani stepped into the room that had been her bedroom. The purple paint on the walls had long since faded. Her white furniture, now a faded yellow color. Moth's had eaten holes in the canopy and sheets. Dani opened the closet doors and looked at the place she had hidden that night.

"Whatever you hear, you do not come out," Ava told her. "You do not come out until I or your father come. Or Auntie He-

lena. Do you understand?"

Danika nodded clutching her favorite stuffed animal. A unicorn that her father had surprised her with. "I love you so much, my sunshine."

"I love you too, mommy," Danika said.

"Now you pretend to be a brave princess hiding from an evil monster," Ava instructed her daughter.

Danika nodded again and the closet doors closed on her.

Dani now stood with the doors open and stared at the empty hangers. Someone had cleaned out the closet at some point. Most likely Helena had come to get her things that she would know. They had never found Princess, her unicorn. Crouching down, Dani looked for into the back, where the slope of the front stairs made it hard for adults to reach. She smiled when her hand brushed against something soft. Dani reached further and pulled out a very dusty and well-loved unicorn. It was purple with a silver main that had rainbow streaks in it. It's horn was silver and white, though the white was more a cream color. Taking the unicorn she walked to the bed and sat on it. This is where she made her stand.

It took him thirty minutes to find her. When his men said they heard a vehicle pull up to the house, he figured someone got lost or needed to make a u-turn. But when he watched the SUV stop in the driveway and saw who got out, fear and excitement ran through him. He had not planned this, he had not planned for her to come to him. She made no indication that she heard him enter the bedroom. It was only when he sat down on the bed that she acknowledge him.

"Do the other's know you are here?" Bartram asked Dani.

"I left a note," Dani told him. "If I had told them, they would have stopped me. They would have tried to talk me out of it."

"How did you figure it out?" Bartram asked.

"A guess really," Dani said shrugging her shoulders.

"When I began to realize that it was you, that it had always been you, I realized that this place would be special to you. When I couldn't find any real estate sales on it, I figured that it was abandoned."

"And your purpose on coming?"

Dani turned to look at him. "I'm not sure, I hadn't really thought about that part."

"I had different plans for you," Bartram admitted. "Though, I must say, I do like how this turned out. Its poetic in a way."

Dani just nodded. Bartram stood up and took her arm, pulling her up off the bed. "Why don't you meet my two other guests?"

His grip tightened, letting her know that she wouldn't be able to break away. Dani set the unicorn down on the bed. Bartram pulled her through the room and into the hallway. He took especial joy as he shoved her into the kitchen. Dani stumbled and fell, her hands touching the floor. The visions slammed into her, there was screaming, laughter, and chaos.

Bartram dragged her to her feet and through the back door. Her mind still back in the kitchen as he pushed her toward the barn. He gave a whistle to inform his men that it was him. They lowered their weapons as he approached.

"No one lays a finger on her," Bartram informed them all. "Danika is my special guest tonight."

They all gave a nod, letting him know that they under-stood his orders. He spotted Michael and smiled as Dani seemed to pull herself from her memories and saw Michael standing there.

"Tell me he's one of your guest?" Dani asked. Her voice filled with bitterness and betrayal as she stared at the shocked look on Michael's face.

"No," Bartram told her as he pulled her right up against him. He brushed a strand of hair out of her face. "No, you see, that was what was brilliant. Mikey, here, he's been mine this whole time."

"What do you mean?" Dani asked.

"Since even before you became an orphan, since before I dined upon your parents," Bartram whispered in her ear.

Dani screamed and launched herself at Bartram. He laughed as he flung her off of him. "Tie her up, I want her facing where the main event will be," Bartram instructed Michael. "Are the video feeds ready?"

"Everything is set," Michael told him as he grabbed Dani who was struggling to get up. "You give the signal and they will be all be dialed at the same time."

"Excellent," Bartram replied. "You get her comfy while I get our other two guests."

Michael nodded as he all but dragged Dani to a chair one of the guards had placed there for him. She was bleeding from the hairline, her lip was busted, and he figured she had a few bruised ribs. As he tied Dani to the chair she spit at him.

"And to think you would be ruling along with Lucas and here you are spitting blood at people," Michael tsked. "How unbecoming of a female of your stature."

"At least I don't betray the people I consider friends," Dani answered.

Michael smiled at her as he crouched in front of her. "See that's the thing," Micheal said. "None of you were my friends. You were means to an end. A way to keep an eye on things without being noticed. A friendly face that no one would ever consider as being the 'bad guy'. Nah, everyone looked to Hinderman and his stupid partner. It was great."

"And Grant?" Dani asked.

"Would meet the same fate as some of my partners if he started asking too many questions," Michael sighed. "Though I have to admit, him being Vern's heir, that kind of makes things even more amazing."

There was a commotion on the other side of the room, Michael watched as Bartram came through the doorway with two hooded figures being shoved at him by guards with guns.

"And it's show time," Michael told Dani. "So sit tight, and enjoy!"

He then gagged her so that she could not say anything or scream. Michael stood up and headed to where all the monitors were. He motioned for guards to take up their positions. Pulling a lever, two chains were lowered from the rafters, where the guards attached the chains to the bound hands of the two prisoners. He pulled it again so that their feet barely brushed the ground. Both groaned in discomfort.

"It's time," Bartram informed Michael.

"Time to go live," Michael said to one of the men who stood next to him. "Let me know when we are green across the board."

The man nodded as he began to punch in the commands.

Micheal wanted to laugh, the paranormal community was never going to recover from tonight. It was going to be glorious to watch.

* * * *

It took five of Allan's toughest members to hold Lucas back from Alistair. Not that he could blame the Head of the Talon line, he just learned that his bond mate had pretty much offered herself up as a distraction. To be fair, he was a little pissed at Alistair for not clueing them into that plan. Allan watched as Alistair took the verbal abuse that Lucas was screaming at him.

He felt a tap on his arm and saw it was the witch called Tony. "Yes nerd-dude," Allan asked.

Tony smiled at the nickname. "I'm getting a weird signal from the barn," Tony told him.

That got everyone's attention, Lucas stopped yelling as everyone turned to look at Tony. The guy might act like he enjoyed being the center of attention but when three dozen pairs of eyes were focused on you, Allan watched Tony squirm for a moment. He noticed that Tony was trying to grab onto something. Reaching behind him, Allan grabbed Tony's cane and handed it to him.

"What kind of signal?" Allan asked.

"It's a few different signals," Tony answered feeling better with his cane in his hands. "Similar to telemarketers when they robo-call a whole bunch of numbers at one time. Only these are very specific numbers and not random."

"How specific?" Alistair asked.

The answer came from Lucas' cell going off. "That specific," Tony replied. "I need your phone, Lucas."

Lucas nodded and handed the tech wizard his phone. Tony hopped up into the van and plugged the phone into ports. "I need everyone silent while I copy his phone so we can hear and see everything but we won't be heard or seen."

By the third ring, Tony handed the phone back to Lucas

and nodded. Lucas took a deep breath and answered the video call.

"Welcome, welcome, Lord Talon," Bartram said with a huge smile on his face. "I don't know if you can see. But many other big people like you are joining us on this call."

"What do you want, Bartram?" Lucas asked.

"There is so much that I want," Bartram answered. "But I can think of at least one thing you want."

The video panned to Dani, blindfolded and bound to a chair. "You know, Lucas, I have some concerns with how lady like she is going to be as your Queen," Bartram stated in a fake concerned tone. "I mean she spat at one of my trusted men. She has been cursing me out from under her gag. Really, that mouth on her is quite extraordinary. But then I'm sure you know just how talented she is with her mouth, don't you?"

Bartram paused and then beamed. "Lovely, my dearest brother Nicholi has joined us as well," Bartram clapped his hands. "I think that is everyone on our list. So welcome all! Now Danika here was not planned, but think of her as a consolation prize."

The camera panned to two figures hanging from chains with hoods over their faces. "These are the real prizes."

The hoods were pulled off to reveal Alexius and Dom.

Chapter 30

His plan was going perfectly. Everyone was on the line
that should be, Lucas and Nicholi were ready to kill through the
phone. While Sonya and Jin were trying to told to him with reason. And Alexius looked like he was almost dead. Dom was
fighting against his restraints despite the pain that was causing
him. Yet the most brilliant thing of all, was that for this moment
they all had to listen to him. For he held something important to
each person on the phone and they had to listen to him.

"How humbling must it be," Bartram began. "To know that one of your own has orchestrated this whole endeavor?"

Bartram walked around the area. "To know that I hold in my hands a weapon that can destroy you? It must be so ... human to learn we are fragile after all."

"Bartram," Nicholi said. "Why?"

"That is such an important question, brother," Bartram agreed. "It's simple. Because I can. Because I have always understood that we, vampires, should be above all others. They should serve us, bow to us, we should be above their laws."

He muted all their phones so that he couldn't hear their protests. "And since I have been the only one to realize this, then I am going to take it and show all you fools how to truly be in charge."

He motioned for the video to get in close to Alexius. "As you all can see, this is my dear, dear, oldest brother," Bartram replied as he walked around where Alexius hung. "For the past few days I have been slowly poisoning him with my little weapon. I've only ever used the more lethal amounts so it has been fun to slowly watch him die. It appears to a very painful process. One that I will not hesitate to use on anyone that opposes me."

"Then I hope you have a lot of it," Dani commented from her chair.

Bartram turned to stare at her, he had made sure she was gagged. She had worked the gagged down off her mouth so that it was now hanging around her neck.

"What's really your, game?" Dani asked him. "Because making us kneel to you, you being all 'I will be your supreme ruler', that isn't your thing."

Bartram had to laugh. "You know me so well," Bartram said as he walked toward her. "Tell me darling sister, what do you think is my thing?'

"You like to manipulate and torture people, that you like

to kill," she answered.

Bartram was silent as he stared at her. She knew that Tony was probably ready to kill her but she needed to stall him while SWAT made their way to the barn. Alexius and Dom dangling from chains had changed their plan of attack, as did her being tied to a chair.

The silence was broken when Bartram started to laugh. None of his men knew what to do by their boss laughing at what his sister said. "I'm impressed," Bartram admitted. "I thought you were going to say that I wanted to show that I was better than Alexius and our father. But, bloody hell, you went right to the heart of it, didn't you?'

"Why prove you're better when you could prove you're deadlier," Dani commented.

"You are so right," Bartram replied as he studied his sister as if he was seeing her for the first time. "I will let you into a little secret, one that our father would kill me for divulging. You see, dear old dad likes to hide the fact that I was born with blood lust."

Alexius squirmed in his chains when Bartram said this. One of the guards smacked him to stay still.

"He had me put it to good use as a soldier, then when I became a vampire, he thoroughly enjoyed my abomination as he called it," Bartram explained as if it was just Dani and he in the room. " I became his silent executioner. Anyone who opposed him, who risked unveiling all his secrets, he sent me to quiet them."

Bartram walked to where the two vampires dangled from chains. "He didn't care how they died, just as longs as they were out of his way," Bartram went on. "And by the gods, it was glorious. To kill with a purpose, to do what I wanted with them, to take my time if I wanted. It was beautiful. And then we came out to the world, and the Sacred Accords was made public so that the mortals could sleep at night that there was no monsters under their bed. That we were controlled."

"So you couldn't be his executioner anymore?" Dom croaked out from his spot. "And this is what, your temper tantrum?"

"I've always been his executioner," Bartram corrected him. "I have just learned to hide how I kill. At first I worried that it would take the pleasure out of killing, but there is a secret thrill in knowing what I have been able to get away with."

"And all of this?" Dani asked.

Bartram just smiled. He walked to a surgical table and picked up a syringe that was already filled with a substance. Once Dom saw what Bartram was doing he began to try to break the chains that bound them. He ignored as the silver burned through his skin.

"Do you want to see what happens when you inject some-one with the poison?' Bartram asked. "Alexius has been drinking it mixed with his blood that I have been giving him. But injecting it into a person, the results are amazing to watch."

"Bartram," Dani said. "You don't have to show us any-thing."

"Oh I think I do," Bartram replied, his voice taking on a sinister tone as he said the words. "I think for you to fully under-stand it all, I need to show you it."

As Bartram checked the dosage, Dani tried to get out of her restraints as she watched Dom struggle against his restraints. A sound of a gun going off had Bartram almost dropping the needle to the ground. He growled as he realized what the gun shot meant.

Dani choked for a moment as she watched red mist swirl around Bartram. Alexius sagged in his restraints as Bartram yelled orders to his men. Throwing the needle back on the table, Bartram grabbed a gun from Michael as they both readied for the invasion that was going to happen.

"How?" Bartram yelled.

"I don't know," Michael answered. "Nothing came onto any of our feeds, we didn't see anyone approach."

"Did you know that there is a service road behind the woods?" Dani stated in a calm almost bored voice. "You can access it by taking two of the main roads in the neighborhood, never having to drive by the house to get to it."

Michael whirled around to stare at Dani. "You came alone."

"I pulled into the driveway alone," Dani clarified as the sound of bodies hitting the floor echoed. "I did not drive all the way here on my own, though."

"You bitch!" Michael yelled as he went to lunge for her.

Bartram caught him though, holdng him still. "We can deal with her later," Bartram promised.

He went to yell out orders but there was sounds of gun shots and bodies hitting the floor.

"I don't think you realize how screwed you are, Bartram,"

Alistair stated as he appeared from behind the monitors.

"How?" Bartram asked as he stared at the team that swarmed in.

"We have this guy, he can pretty much do anything with technology, so the feeds you've been watching, their fake," Alistair explained. "Allowing us to approach the barn and quietly take out your men as we moved our way through the grounds."

Bartram raised the gun at Alistair. "You are surrounded, we have several warrants, surrender peacefully," Alistair suggested.

Behind Bartram, SWAT members were getting Alexius and Dom out of the chains. Claire was there to check on Alexius, but with the state of Dom's wrists Alexius brushed her off so she could tend to Dom.

"What makes you think that I will go peacefully?" Bartram asked.

"He doesn't," Michael answered. "He is trying to buy

time like Dani did."

"Possibly," Alistair stated. He watched as Dom was attended to. "Look around you, it's falling apart."

Bartram had heard the chains fall, he knew that his prisoners had been freed. He cold smell all the people that were in
the barn and those surrounding the barn. This was not in his
plan. He had hoped to be back in Greece, reveling in all the mistakes that Alexius had seemed to make on the last trip. Bartram
saw all the guns in the room, all the other supernatural creatures
in the room.

Dani saw the red mist swirling again, she pulled at
Claire's link. The red head looked up from Dom and went to say
something but froze as she saw what Dani was seeing. With
hand signals, Claire began to instruct those with her to get Dom
out of there while she helped with Alexius. He had already been
freed from his chains, a team member had given him a small vial
of blood for Claire feared if they gave him too much it might put

him in shock. Her aunt was already brewing an antidote that Claire had figured out from the notes.

Alistiar noted what was going on around Claire and made a signal behind his back to inform Allan things were going to hit the fan.

Michael took it all in. "'Shit! They have the order to shoot to kill."

"Then she's coming with me," Bartram yelled pointing his gun at Dani as she was being freed from the restraints.

There was movement all around as Bartram fired his gun, Dani braced for impact as the SWAT member tried to get her off the chair. The force that collided with her sent her and the chair flying backwards. Her head hit the ground causing everything to go black for a moment. And then chaos happened.

Chapter 31

Murmuring buzzed all around Dani, as did an annoying

beeping noise. Her right arm felt like it was being held into a

roaring fire, while something was clinging to her left hand as if it

was the only thing keeping her grounded. Her body ached and

she was pretty sure she was running a really high fever. Cau-

tiously, she opened her eyes slowly and groaned when she saw

she was in a hospital room. Again. The glass wall and door that

led out to the hall indicated she was in the ICU floor at Price

Memorial Hospital. Three iv's were being pumped into her right arm and Lucas was asleep holding onto her left hand. She gave it a squeeze and he jerked awake.

"You're awake," he whispered in disbelief.

Dani nodded. She watched Lucas reach over the side of the bed and hit the call button for the nurse's station. Within seconds a team of people, including Claire, came rushing into the room.

"She's awake," the lead doctor said.

Claire almost collapsed when he said those words, a nurse caught her. Congratulating Claire that the antidote worked.

"What happened?' Dani asked.

"You were shot and some of the poison got into your system," the doctor explained. "Ms. Jensen can give you more detail. Her antidote is what saved the day."

Dani knew there were questions to ask but her brain was fuzzy. She looked at Claire who had sunk into a chair and was crying. Lucas looked exhausted as he gripped her hands in his. She watched as Helena appeared in the door way with Nick and Sayad behind her. But she was so tired so she let sleep overtake her.

****

It was a several days later when Dani could finally sit up in her hospital bed and carry a conversation. Lucas had barely left the hospital room, when he did half of his guard stayed behind. Dani thought Dom had come into her room a few times but she wasn't sure what was hallucination and what was real.

But now with Lucas, Claire, Dom, and Alistair in her room she knew it was all real. That her nightmares were real.

"When I gave Bartram the ultimatum, he summoned the power he had absorbed by the blood ritual," Alistair explained form his chair. "The red mist you described in your dreams, we all saw it."

"He fired his gun," Dani recalled.

"Him and Michael fired theirs at almost the same time," Claire answered.

"Bartram shot first," Alistair corrected. "By a few seconds. He didn't count on Alexius protecting you. But Michael did. Batram's bullet killed Alexius and Michael's hit your knee."

"Did Alexius suffer?" Dani asked.

Claire shook her head. "No," Claire whispered. "If anything it ended his suffering. I gave him the antidote, I mean I knew it wouldn't help, but it would ease his pain."

"He was an asshole," Dani said torn between laughter and tears. "What happened?"

"Bartram was killed," Alistair continued. "He wanted it. He knew it was over, knew what was waiting for him."

"Vynessa did note that the blood magick, it took its toll on him, and most likely he would not have lived long enough to stand trial," Claire added. "It poisoned him almost worst then what he was doing to his victims. His life force was corrupted, dependent on the blood magick. She figured if he went a month without it he would have ended up dead from organ failure."

"And Micheal?" Dani asked. She noted that both Dom and Lucas had been silent so far.

"Is in a highly secure cell within the Accords building," Dom spoke. "Surprisingly, he is talking."

"Where's Grant?" Dani wondered.

"At the coven farm in upstate," Claire replied. "He is taking it hard. He feels like he should have known that Michael was corrupt. We've all talked to him, including Nick and your mother. Micheal, he fooled all of us. No one suspected him."

"I gave him a month's leave," Alistair added. "Give him time to clear his head, get back on his feet."

"What about Holtzen?"

Alistair and Dom both groaned which had Dani raising an eyebrow. "He is being investigated for his part in covering up the murders that Bartram committed," Claire said with a hint of smile. "Alistair has been named acting Commissioner of STF and Dom is now our acting Chief and Captain. Something they both are pissed off about."

"Added to that, Abe has decided to move in with Dom to help him recover from his wounds," Lucas said finally speaking up. He had a smile on his face as he spoke. "I can manage," Dom grumbled from his chair.

"Right, with two bandaged wrists and intensive physical therapy," Claire replied. "Yes, you can absolutely handle your-self."

"I'm flipping you off in my mind," Dom informed her.

"I'm trembling," Claire commented.

"Anyway," Alistair said ending their argument. "We are going to be creating a task force to go over everything we uncovered in this case. There will be members from STF, NYPD, and the Accords."

"We did learn a lot," Dani admitted.

"You will also be on the task force," Alistair told her.

"Once we get the all clear from your doctors."

"Yeah, well I think it's going to be a while before I am able to move around crime scenes," Dani admitted.

The bullet from Michael had shattered her left knee cap. The surgeons had repaired what they could but she had a long road of therapy and more surgeries ahead of her. Even then they weren't sure if her knee would ever be the same. One doctor theorized that when she finally became a full vampire it might repair the damage they couldn't fix.

"Just think you and Dom can do physical therapy together," Claire noted.

"I really hate all of you," Dom commented.

"No you don't," Lucas replied.

Alistair looked at his watch. "We should get going," he replied. "Claire and I have to get Dom back to his room before we head to the station. And I know your mom and brothers want to spend some time with you."

Dani nodded. They each hugged her before heading out of the room. Once they were out of view, she slumped into her pile of pillows.

"Tired?" Lucas asked as he kissed her hands.

Dani just smiled before yawning. Lucas leaned over and kissed her forehead. "Sleep, your safe now," he promised her.

www.ingramcontent.com/pod-product-compliance
Lightning Source LLC
Chambersburg PA
CBHW050839030726
47503CB00007BA/2247